ASSIGNM

by

JENNIFER JANE POPE

CHIMERA

Assignment for Alison published by
Chimera Publishing Ltd
PO Box 152
Waterlooville
Hants
PO8 9FS

Printed and bound in Great Britain by
Omnia Books Ltd, Glasgow

ASSIGNMENT FOR ALISON

Jennifer Jane Pope

She felt a hand on her buttocks, the fingers forcing their way between the taut rubber of her thong, pulling it down and to one side, and then another pressure against her bottom hole, cold and slippery. For a second her muscles tensed, resisting, but Alison realised it was a futile gesture. She forced herself to relax and grunted into the gag as the oiled dildo was pushed up inside her and the crotch of the panties snapped back into place over it.

'We'll leave your cunt,' Kristin said, turning her around to face her again. 'The Master will want to attend to that himself.' She reached out and tweaked Alison's nipples and Alison felt them hardening once again. Kristin laughed her reedy laugh. 'Oh yes, you really are a dirty little whore, aren't you?' she taunted. 'I wonder how randy you'll be when Master Ralph's through with you.'

Chapter One

Learning the Ropes

Alison Katt stared at the newspaper cutting in total disbelief, her mouth hanging open, as she read through the fuzzy type for the fifth time. Across the desk, Mike Hallet's face remained as impassive as ever as he studied her reaction. Placing the paper down carefully, holding it by one corner as if it might bite her, Alison shook her head.

'You've gotta be joking,' she said, her voice scarcely more than a whisper. 'I joined this paper as a journalist, not as some kinky whore.'

'And I was the one who gave you the job,' Mike reminded her. 'And I also remember telling you that we often have to do things we don't particularly like, in order to get a story. This is potential dynamite, girl. My information is that this club draws its membership from among the richest and most powerful people in the country.'

'And you want me to get photos of them playing their little games and expose them all over our front page?'

'Only if the other part of my information is true.' Mike reached down, opened a drawer in his desk and took out his pipe. 'If the people behind this place really are using their position to exert undue influence on politicians, judges and the like, that's pretty serious stuff. This is supposed to be a democracy we live in, after all.'

'Which gives me the right to turn this job down,' Alison said, sourly. 'This is nineteen sixty-nine, you know – equal rights for women. We got the vote nearly fifty years ago.'

'Not in this firm you didn't,' Mike snapped back. 'As long as I'm editor of the *National Enquiry*, democracy of that kind stops at the front door. Now, are you going to do it, or do I get the wages department to make out your P45?'

'That's blackmail!' Alison screeched, standing up and leaning across the desk. Mike remained unmoved.

'No,' he said, quietly, 'what they're doing is blackmail. What I'm doing is my job, same as I'm telling you to do.'

'But why me?'

'Because none of the blokes could possibly do it, and the only other females on the editorial staff are nearer fifty than forty. You happen to be twenty-four and, if I'm allowed to be a bit chauvinistic, bloody good looking into the bargain. You're exactly what that advert there says they're looking for.'

'Except I'm not into latex and I'm not looking for a so-called "strong hand" to keep me under control.' She stabbed her finger at the discarded cutting. 'This sounds like someone needs to see a shrink, and you're asking me to walk straight into their hands like a lamb to the slaughter.'

'You won't be on your own,' Mike promised. 'I'll arrange for Johnny McCoy to keep a constant watch on the place. Any trouble, you can signal him and he'll get onto Old Bill straight away.'

'But he'll still be on the outside.'

'There's not a lot I can do about that, I'm afraid,' Mike replied. 'But one thing I will promise – if you pull this off, I'll pay you a nice bonus. How much do you earn a year at the moment?'

'Fifteen hundred, give or take.'

'Then I'll see to it that you get an extra five hundred, tax free, and a raise of another two hundred a year.' He watched Alison's face as she took in the figures, but she was getting good at concealing her emotions nowadays. She simply pursed her lips, stroked the side of her jaw with one elegant finger, and turned her eyes to the ceiling.

'Seven fifty and a raise of three hundred,' she said, evenly. Mike gave a little snort.

'You're pushing your luck,' he said. She was, but she knew she could and, although he tried to haggle, she refused to budge. Finally, Mike conceded. From his desk drawer, he took out a small card and passed it across. Alison peered at it, eyebrows arching.

'What's this?' she asked. He grinned.

'That, my girl, is the business address of an old college friend of mine. She studied philosophy at Oxford, but she now teaches contemplation of a different kind. Before you jump in at the deep end, I thought it would be an idea if you got yourself a bit of tuition from an expert. I rang her earlier and she's expecting you at three this afternoon. I'll meet you at her place tomorrow morning.'

'You seem to have been pretty sure of me,' Alison said, tartly. Mike shrugged.

'I know a good reporter when I see one,' he replied. 'And don't slam the door on the way out.'

The address on the card was a three storeyed Georgian house in a terrace facing the river. Alison's tentative knock was answered by a girl of about her own age, dressed in the uniform of a Victorian housemaid, long black skirts rustling as she moved, her dark eyes darting furtively up and down the street outside as she stepped aside to let Alison pass. As the maid closed the door behind her, Alison opened her mouth to speak, but the girl simply smiled and held a finger to her lips. With a gesture of that same finger, she indicated that Alison should follow her.

Shrugging her shoulders, Alison fell in behind, studying her rear view with a mixture of intrigue and astonishment, for one thing she could see as the long skirt swayed to and fro, was that the girl was wearing incredibly high heels, the sort of footwear that had gone out of fashion a decade or more since. Her dark hair, which was tied back and topped with a lacy white cap, also seemed to be a wig and, from her pierced ears, hung a pair of heavy gold pendants that Alison would not normally have associated with a domestic servant.

The maid stopped at a heavy panelled door, knocked once, and turned the massive brass handle. As she stepped into the room ahead of Alison, a tall woman, dressed impeccably in a black two piece suit, rose from a massive Chesterfield and stepped towards them. One word summed up Marcia Davenport, Alison decided – imposing. The woman, who, like Mike Hallett, was in her mid-forties, stood nearly six feet tall, even without the high stiletto heels and, although she was fashionably slim, the leather jacket did little to conceal the power of her shoulders and hips. She had raven black hair, green eyes, and a face that was both beautiful and yet uncompromising. Marcia Davenport, Alison further decided, was not a woman to trifle with, though her voice, when she spoke, was like liquid silk.

'You must be Michael's Alley Cat,' she said, extending a perfectly manicured right hand. 'He's told me all about you.'

'I'll bet,' Alison said, accepting the handshake and wondering how many of her fingers would survive it. She made a mental note to kick Mike in the shins when she saw him again, and also cursed the sense of humour that had persuaded her father to give her a first name to go with a surname that could be so easily turned into such a disparaging epithet. Behind her, she heard the door softly closing behind the departing maid.

'Nothing but good, I assure you,' Marcia said. 'I doubt

he'd have chosen you for this assignment if he had any doubts about your ability.'

Alison sighed. 'Miss Davenport,' she said, 'I got this assignment only because I'm young, blonde, have a decent figure, and am passably good looking. And because there's nobody else,' she added.

'I'm sure you are underrating yourself,' Marcia said. She stood back, appraising Alison critically, noting the miniskirt and Alison's long, tanned legs. 'Apart from your journalistic qualities, you are indeed very beautiful. And please, call me Marcia, at least until we get downstairs.'

'Downstairs?' Alison echoed. 'What happens downstairs?'

'Downstairs,' Marcia told her, 'is my own special domain. It's where I entertain certain, uh, guests, you might call them. Downstairs I am always addressed as Mistress.'

'Hold on a minute,' Alison said, raising one hand like a traffic policeman trying to halt an oncoming stream of cars, 'no one said anything about that. I came here for you to give me a few tips and pointers, nothing more.'

Marcia smiled. 'My dear girl,' she said, 'that's exactly what I intend to do; broaden your education, so to speak. If you just turn up for an interview with these people, they'll know straight away that something's wrong. You're supposed to be a confirmed submissive, but, with your present bearing and attitude, I'm afraid they'd be more likely to believe that the Pope is a Hindu!'

Alison relaxed a little, smiling at Marcia's joke. 'Okay,' she said, 'so what's involved in all this?'

Marcia motioned her towards a huge armchair opposite the Chesterfield. 'I'm going to assume,' she said, when they were both settled, 'that you know absolutely nothing about this scene.'

'Fair assumption,' Alison confirmed, nodding.

'Well, suffice it to say, there are plenty of people whose attitude to sex and to relationships with the opposite sex are not what the world at large would recognise as normal. There are leather fetishists, rubber devotees, dominants, submissives, bondage enthusiasts, and many many more. The "Outer Fringe of Sex" one writer has termed it, but it's a far wider fringe than most people would imagine.

'Now, this place you are investigating is a sort of private club, set up to cater for the varying tastes of a lot of people with more money than they know what to do with, generally. For a price, they will supply willing slaves to the dominants, strict mistresses to the submissives, and facilities for both to enjoy their particular penchants to the full.'

'Excuse me for being pedantic,' Alison cut in, 'but isn't that what you do? I mean, why should you be interested in helping me – us – to bring down something like that?'

'Not from a jealousy standpoint,' Marcia assured her. 'If that were all it amounted to, I'd simply say good luck to them. However, as Michael has probably intimated, it goes further than that. The people behind this place are using it for blackmail and extortion. They are unscrupulous in the extreme, and should be stopped as quickly as possible.'

'Which they will be, if I can get the goods on them,' Alison finished for her. 'So, why don't I just pose as some rich bitch who fancies having her own slave for a day or two?'

'Because their clients are very thoroughly vetted and, if they don't measure up, they don't get in. Unless your father is a millionaire, or a lord, or maybe an archbishop, you wouldn't stand a chance. On the other hand, posing as a potential new staff recruit is a lot more straightforward. They'll still ask questions, of course, but different ones. You can use my name, which will lend an air of authenticity to your story. You tell them that you came to me to act out your fantasies and then saw the chance to do the same, but getting paid for it instead of the other way around.'

'You know these people then?' Alison asked, somewhat taken aback.

'Oh yes,' Marcia replied. 'I know them all right. One of them is my ex-husband.'

The bottom floor of the house was a demi-basement. From the street, it had looked innocuous enough, but viewed from the inside, the rooms were a different prospect altogether. The windows were all blacked out with heavy velvet curtains, beyond which, Marcia assured Alison, the windowpanes were triple glazed.

'Some of my guests get a bit noisy,' she explained. 'All five rooms down here are fully soundproofed. It cost me a fortune, but it's been well worth it.'

The whole setup must have cost a fortune, Alison thought, for no expense had been spared in creating an atmosphere which would have been worthy of a medieval dungeon. The colour scheme was predominantly black, including the corridor off which the individual rooms ran. The lighting was provided by a series of naked red bulbs, which lent an eerie glow to everything. Marcia opened the second door and ushered Alison inside.

As her eyes grew accustomed to the gloom, Alison saw that one wall of the chamber was lined with doors and drawers. The only furnishings were two high, padded stools, both of which appeared to have been bolted to the floor, and a plain rustic-looking timber table, about five feet by two.

'Put your things on the table,' Marcia said, walking across to open one of the cupboards. Alison stared at her, bemused.

'What things?' she asked. Marcia looked back over her shoulder.

'Your clothes, silly,' she said. 'You have to strip off… everything.'

'But why?' Alison protested. 'I never agreed to—'

'Listen,' Marcia said, turning around, 'I promised Michael I would give you a proper induction course that would ensure you know enough to carry this thing off. Now, that means getting used to the sort of costumes and accessories you're likely to have to wear. They'll be mostly latex, but there's bound to be some leather, as well as the usual satins and laces and so on.'

In the back of her mind Alison had realised this already, but until now it had been something to worry about in the future. Now, face-to-face with the actuality, it suddenly seemed even less of a good idea than it had originally, when she had argued with Mike in his office. Marcia sensed her reluctance.

'Listen to me,' she said, walking back to Alison and laying a hand on her shoulder, 'it'll be a lot easier for you if I prepare you properly. I wouldn't like to be in your shoes if you lose your nerve once you're there. These people are not very nice, believe me. Now, I know you're nervous, but no one's going to hurt you under this roof, okay? And if you decide you don't want to go through with it after all, that's okay, too.

'It's your decision, little Alley Katt, and it's a big one. But I can't help you with it, other than to suggest that you try it first and then make up your mind.'

As she spoke, Alison's nose detected the first faint aroma of rubber, and she stared past Marcia to the open cupboard door. Inside, everything seemed one black shadow, but she had little doubt that this was where the smell was coming from. It was heavy, sweet and cloying, but not unpleasant.

She took a deep breath.

'Okay,' she said, trying to keep her voice steady. 'I'll give it a go.'

She kept her back to Marcia as she slowly began removing her street clothes, folding them into a neat pile, her white patent shoes next to them. As she peeled away her brassiere she stared down at her breasts, evenly tanned as was the rest of her body, thanks to the privacy of the roof garden above her flat. Even the removal of her white cotton panties betrayed no trace of white. She turned slowly back to face Marcia at last, her hands clasped to cover her sex and the little triangle of almost white pubic hair. Marcia, who was holding something black in her hands, looked her up and down, appraisingly.

'Place your hands by your sides, please,' she instructed. Reluctantly, Alison let her arms drop, revealing her most intimate secrets. Marcia nodded.

'You are a natural blonde, then,' she commented, nodding again. 'Excellent. A good body, nice firm breasts and very good legs. Turn to one side.' Despite her annoyance at being summed up like a prize mare, Alison did as she was told. Again, Marcia nodded. 'Very prominent buttocks,' she said, almost to herself. 'Yes, very sweet. Now, turn back to face me and place your hands on the top of your head.' There was something about her tone of voice that brooked no argument and, to her surprise, Alison found herself obeying the older woman without a second thought. Marcia stepped closer, holding out the black garment.

'What's that?' Alison demanded, feeling more and more uneasy with each passing second. Marcia regarded her, her face expressionless.

'Slaves are not permitted to ask questions,' she said. Alison bridled at that.

'I'm not your slave,' she retorted. 'This is just a dress

13

rehearsal, remember?'

'Maybe so, but in a dress rehearsal, the cast do everything exactly as they would on the first night,' Marcia snapped. 'If you're supposed to be experienced, you'd know exactly how to behave at all times, so we go through this as though it were for real, okay?'

Somewhat chastened, Alison nodded. 'I guess so,' she mumbled.

'Good,' Marcia said. 'And, for your information, this is a corset, or, to be more accurate, a waist-cincher, as there are no cups for the breasts. As you can see, it's made from rubber – very thick, strong rubber.' She wrapped the garment about Alison's waist and began securing the front fastenings, pulling in her stomach dramatically.

'God, that's tight,' Alison gasped, when she had finished. 'I can hardly breathe.'

'You'll get used to it,' Marcia assured her, moving around behind her. 'And, as for tight, you haven't seen anything yet.'

Alison very soon did, however, for at the back of the corset were laces to tighten it even further, reducing her waist by still another two inches. The top of the corset was cut so that it sat beneath each breast, rising to an inverted V-shape where the two halves joined in her cleavage. At the bottom another tapering point stopped just short of her pubic hair, but at the back the leather was cut higher, leaving her buttocks exposed and looking more prominent than ever in comparison to her newly reduced waist. As Marcia knotted off the cords, Alison began to feel lightheaded.

'I can't breathe properly,' she said. Marcia patted her buttocks.

'Don't try to breathe so deeply,' she said. 'Just take it easy and don't fight against the pressure. Here, come over and sit on this stool.' She took Alison's arm and guided her towards the nearer seat, helping her to perch up on the cool leather padding. Alison, for her part, tried to breathe as per instruction and, to her relief, found that it worked. Marcia left her there and went to another cupboard, drawing out an outrageously long pair of black boots, with even more outrageously long, tapering heels.

'Feeling better?' she asked. Alison nodded. 'Good. Usually I introduce my slaves to corsets by degrees, working down an inch or so at each session, but unfortunately, in your case, we don't have the luxury of sufficient time.' She stooped and began fitting the first boot, which was something of a struggle, even though the laces which ran up the back were still slack. Alison felt her instep being arched incredibly and her toes bent upwards to their absolute limit.

It took Marcia a good ten minutes to get both boots on and laced, drawing them so tightly about Alison's legs that it became difficult for her to bend her knees. At Marcia's instruction, she swayed unsteadily to her feet, convinced she would overbalance if she tried walking. The dominatrix held out a steadying hand and made her take a few experimental paces. To Alison's surprise, the tight rubber braced her legs and ankles in such a rigid fashion that walking was much easier than she had dared anticipate, though she was forced to take much smaller steps than normal.

'That's very good,' Marcia complimented her. 'Now, turn around and go back to the stool on your own.' Carefully, Alison turned, using her arms to balance her poise. 'Put your arms down and try again,' Marcia ordered. 'You won't always have the use of them.'

She made Alison parade back and forth for several minutes in this fashion, but at last seemed satisfied that her protégé was beginning to master the heels and allowed her to sit again.

From the cupboard, again, Marcia took out two long tube-like lengths of rubber. Alison saw that there was lacing along the length of each, to allow for the tubes to be made tighter, but initially, she had no idea as to their purpose. She soon understood, though, as Marcia guided her right arm into the first one, drawing it up to her shoulder and working the laces tight from wrist to shoulder. As she turned her attention to the other arm, Alison saw they were a type of glove, though they terminated, not in fingers, but in a kind of elongated mitten, at the end of which was attached a thick steel ring. Once in place, the wearer's hands were rendered all but useless, for the mitten was tight and compressed the fingers hard together and the thumb firmly against the palm of the hand.

'May I ask something?' Alison ventured, as Marcia finished tying off the second glove. The older woman smiled, encouragingly.

'You should say: "May I ask something, *Mistress*,' she said, gently but firmly. 'It is essential to address your masters and mistresses correctly.' Alison sighed and repeated the question as directed.

'Better,' Marcia said. 'Yes, you may.'

'Do people actually pay to be dressed and trussed up like this?' Alison asked. 'I mean, what do they get out of it?'

'Very good questions,' Marcia replied, crossing the room and opening one of the drawers. 'Yes, they do and, well who can say? Sexual satisfaction, certainly. Stimulation, certainly. It varies with the individual.'

'And these "slaves", what do they actually do?'

'Exactly what they're told,' Marcia said, firmly. She had returned, carrying two short, broad, leather straps, which

16

she proceeded to buckle around Alison's wrists. Alison saw there was a heavy steel spring-clip on the inside of each and, as soon as Marcia had secured the second strap, she seized the ring on the end of each mitten in turn, forced Alison's fingers over into a fist and snapped the clip to the ring, preventing her from straightening her hand. Then, from the pocket of her jacket, she drew out a businesslike padlock.

Stepping behind Alison, she drew her arms behind her back and slipped the padlock through the two rings. It was done before Alison realised what was happening and only the dull click of the lock being closed alerted her to the fact that she was now completely helpless. She tugged at her bondage, but the gloves and the metalwork had been designed to withstand far greater force than she would ever be able to exert. As Marcia stepped back in front of her, Alison looked up at her, dubiously.

'I'm not sure I like this,' she said, plaintively. Marcia patted her cheek.

'Give it time, kitten,' she said. 'I haven't finished with you yet... not by a long way.'

Another trip to the cupboards produced a length of chain with more thick straps at each end. Working with assured fingers, Marcia fastened one strap about Alison's arm, just above the elbow and then, using one arm to pull her elbows together until they were nearly touching, secured the other end similarly to the other arm. The effect was to force Alison's shoulders back and thrust out her bare breasts in a manner that was totally brazen.

'This isn't very comfortable,' she complained.

'It isn't supposed to be,' Marcia said. 'Remember, you're a slave now, and slaves have to suffer.' There was something about the change of tone in her voice that made Alison shudder

17

'I don't think I want to go through with this,' she said, quietly. 'I think, if you'll just undo all this, I'll get dressed and get out of here.'

Marcia stared at her, a mocking expression on her face. 'I'm most dreadfully sorry,' she said, 'but you don't seem to understand the situation. You don't have any say in matters now. You will do exactly as I tell you, until I decide it's time to release you. You were sent here to learn what it means to be a slave and, by George, that's exactly what you're going to do. Michael would never forgive me if I failed you both.'

'Leave Michael to me,' Alison snarled. 'Just get these things off me. This has gone far enough... Yeoww!' The slap across her face was so swift and unexpected that Alison nearly toppled from the stool. Tears filled her eyes and her head rang from the blow, her cheek burning fiercely.

'This has not gone anywhere near far enough yet,' Marcia said, calmly, though her voice was as cold as ice. 'Any more insubordination from you and I'll whip that delightful bottom of yours until you won't be able to sit on it for a week.'

Alison stared up at her, blinking furiously to clear her vision. 'You wouldn't!' she gasped, but she knew that Marcia would. She cursed Mike under her breath, and herself, too, for being stupid enough to get into this mess.

Marcia was opening another drawer, and Alison heard the clink-chink of metal as she searched through it. A few moments later she was back at Alison's side, buckling a wide collar, from which hung a chain leash, about her neck, forcing her chin up in an even more uncomfortable position. She stepped back, taking the loose end of the chain, to which was fixed a leather loop, in her hand and slipping it over her wrist.

'Much better,' she said, and tugged the chain, hauling

Alison up onto her feet. Marcia drew her closer, her free hand moving to Alison's right breast, thumb and forefinger seizing her unprotected nipple and squeezing it. Alison let out a little squeal and tried to back away, but Marcia kept the leash taut, preventing any chance of a retreat.

'You have big nipples,' Marcia told her, rolling the teat between the two digits. 'They'll look even better when I have Melanie ring them. Melanie, in case you were wondering, is my maid, the girl who let you in earlier.'

'What do you mean, ring them?' Alison wailed, really scared now.

Marcia pulled a wry smile. 'You'll find out soon enough,' she said. 'Now, time for a little walkies.'

She led the way out into the corridor, with Alison stumbling and tottering behind her, but, fortunately, their journey was not a lengthy one. Marcia stopped two doors further along and produced a key, which she inserted in the sturdy and ancient-looking lock.

'I like to keep the punishment cells locked,' she said, casually. 'Even when they're empty.'

'Punishment cells?' Alison echoed, her whole body trembling violently. 'You can't be serious?'

'Oh yes,' Marcia said, nodding. 'It's all part of the ritual, you see. A good slave learns to accept that punishment is not only their due, it is also part of their need.' The door swung open to reveal another black-walled room, slightly larger than the first, but with a lot more furniture, if furniture was the correct term to describe its contents. Alison looked about her in disbelief and desperation, her gaze taking in the heavy wooden pillory, the plain steel-framed bed with its lattice of bedspring fully exposed, the timber seat that looked like it had come straight out of the execution chamber in an American film, and a final structure that resembled a vaulting horse, but from which dangled several leather restraints to indicate it was intended to serve a totally different purpose.

A barred cage, the narrow door of which hung open, separated one corner of the room from the main area. Inside there was no seat, but a thick round pole jutted out about two feet from the wall. Above it, set into the masonry, a wide strap hung open and below it, near to ground level, two shorter straps hung about three feet apart.

'No!' Alison whispered, as Marcia dragged her towards the cage. 'I won't! You can't!' But the relentless pull on her leash offered her no option. On the floor beneath the pole stood a low dais, about eighteen inches square and, propelled by Marcia, Alison was forced to step up onto it and turn with her back to the wall. The powerful Marcia, still slightly taller than Alison despite the extra inches of the platform, pushed her back, forcing her legs apart so that she straddled the projecting pole, her naked quim only an inch or so above it.

The upper belt was drawn about her, just below her breasts, and buckled tightly, before Marcia turned her attention to Alison's legs. Seizing one foot, she drew it out wide until the ankle was level with the lower strap on that side, and deftly fastened the leather restraint around it. When the remaining leg was treated similarly, Alison slumped down, some of her weight initially supported by the strap about her upper body, but most of it and eventually all of it, settling onto the stubby pole beneath her crotch. To her relief, although the position was far from comfortable, she realised that the pole was actually padded and not, as she had assumed at first, solid timber.

Marcia straightened up and stepped back, admiring the effect of her work. 'Yes, that's suitable to begin with,' she said. 'A couple of hours in here should warm you up nicely. And I'll send Melanie down to see to your nipple rings.'

'You're not going to leave me here, are you?' Alison wailed, panicking. She tried to struggle against the straps, but it was an impossible battle. All she succeeded in doing was setting up a friction against the gaping lips of her unprotected sex and against her clitoris, which was also just in contact with the padded surface. Marcia smiled.

'That's the spirit,' she said. 'I like to see a girl stimulate herself like that. Keep it up and you'll probably make yourself come before too long.' Alison froze, staring wildly at her.

'You bitch!' she hissed. 'You perverted bitch! You think everyone's the same, don't you? And yes, go on, hit me again if you want. I can't even defend myself, let alone fight back. People like you make me sick. You're a bully, a cow – umpphhh!' Her tirade was cut short as Marcia stuffed the rubber ball between her lips and quickly secured the strap behind her neck, preventing her from expelling it. Where the woman had got the gag from, Alison did not know, but the operation was performed so skilfully and so swiftly that she had no chance to resist.

Silent now and breathing heavily through her nose, Alison hung in her bonds and let the tears flow down her cheeks, from where they dripped onto her naked breasts, running over the silky flesh like twin rivers.

Marcia patted her cheek. 'I'm not going to hit you, sweetie,' she said, softly, 'but neither can a slave be permitted to abuse her mistress. A few hours gagged is usually a salutary enough lesson, and there's something about a slave wearing a ball gag which is so appealing. It lends the face – and especially the eyes – a delightfully surprised expression. I shall instruct Melanie to take some photos of you to take away as souvenirs when you finally leave.'

She stepped outside the cage and swung the door shut. It

closed with a hollow clang and the key, which she turned in the lock, clicked with a dull sound of total finality. Never had Alison felt so helpless, or so scared. She made a soft, whimpering noise through the gag, but Marcia was unmoved. She pocketed the key and turned towards the outer door.

'Melanie will be down later,' she called back, cheerfully. 'Don't you go away now, will you?' The sound of her mocking laughter seemed to echo around the cell for a long time after she had left it.

By the time the outer door reopened and the strange maid, Melanie, entered, Alison had largely succeeded in conquering her original feelings of panic. The gag was uncomfortable and, at first, had caused her to dribble, until she finally mastered the art of swallowing whilst it was in her mouth. Furthermore, she was astonished to discover, although her position could scarcely be described as comfortable, that it was nowhere near as bad as she had at first dreaded it would become. In fact, to her chagrin, the constant pressure between her splayed legs was beginning to have a marked effect on her, and not in a way she would ever have thought possible.

The maid, still wearing her uniform complete with pinafore style white apron, was carrying a small silver tray, upon which were several small objects covered by a black cloth. On top of the cloth lay the key to the cage door, which she quickly employed and stepped inside, placing the tray on the floor in the corner. She straightened up and stared at Alison for several seconds, her brown eyes unblinking, before reaching out with her right hand to caress the nipple on Alison's left breast. Instantly, to Alison's horror, the teat began to harden and the soft touch sent little ripples of electricity running up and down her spine. The maid smiled.

'Mistress was right,' she said, her voice husky. 'It's quite often the spirited ones who respond the best.' Her other hand sought and found the right nipple, rolling and squeezing, tugging and tweaking. Behind her gag, Alison groaned, though not from pain. She felt her sex becoming unbearably hot and knew she was growing very wet. She closed her eyes in shame, not wanting to look at the girl when she discovered the truth and instantly, one hand was removed from her breast and she felt a single finger probing, pushing its way beneath the padded crotch pole and her most tender, intimate flesh.

'Aah, yes,' she heard the husky voice croon. 'Sopping wet already, I see.' The finger pushed against Alison's stiffening bud, forcing another groan past the ball, and her eyes flew open. The maid's face was impassive, but her dark eyes glinted with undisguised amusement. She leaned forward, pressing against Alison's breasts and gently sucked Alison's bottom lip between her own, their noses brushing gently together. Alison wanted to cry out, to push her away, for this should not be happening; not with another female. But the burning well of passion deep inside her was already beginning to approach boiling point, and she knew she was helpless to resist in any way. She closed her eyes again, surrendering her mind to join her captive body, but suddenly the intimate contacts were broken.

'Not yet,' she heard Melanie whisper. 'Not until those gorgeous teats have been properly taken care of.'

Through flickering eyelids, Alison watched as the girl stooped and drew something out from beneath the cloth on the tray. When she held up her hands, Alison saw she was holding two gold rings, each little more than a half inch in diameter, the inner circumference of each slightly serrated. With a sly grin the girl placed one of them into her mouth, holding it between her teeth and then, leaning forward and cupping Alison's right breast in her hands, she began to suck gently on the nipple, moistening it and stimulating it all at the same time. The teat began to respond immediately, as did the rest of Alison's body, swelling and elongating under the constant suction until, quite suddenly, it began to slide through the ring, the pressure of the metal adding to the stimulation.

Melanie continued for a full minute and, when she finally drew back, Alison stared down at her chest in amazement, for the swollen nipple now seemed to be a separate part of the breast, sticking out from the tiny gilded collar like a misshapen pear. Two minutes later the other nipple looked identical and, as Melanie traced both outlines with her feather-like fingers, Alison began to groan anew, for the sensation was unbelievable.

'That's much prettier,' Melanie said. 'Mistress will be very pleased, but I must hurry. I have to take some photographs of you, so I'm told.' From beneath the black cloth she drew one of the new fangled Polaroid cameras, on top of which was mounted a flash cube. Stepping back outside the cage she focused on the helpless Alison, moving back a little further to take in everything. The flash was blinding and Alison blinked furiously, just screwing her eyes tightly closed before the flash fired again.

'That's it,' she heard the maid say, and opened her eyes to see the girl standing with one rectangular print under each armpit. 'Sorry about this,' Melanie said, 'but apparently it helps them develop quicker. Pretty clever stuff, don't you agree?'

In reply Alison could only groan, for the truth was that Melanie's attentions to her nipples had started a fire that could only be quenched in one way. She wanted to cry out to her to finish what she'd started and release her from the torment that was threatening to engulf her, but Melanie seemed in no hurry. Eventually, after a few minutes had passed, the maid removed the two pictures from their warm incubation and studied them in turn. She nodded, apparently satisfied, and stepped back inside the cage, placing them under the cloth on the tray.

'Time enough for you to admire yourself later,' she said, straightening up and moving closer to Alison. Her hands moved like two cool snakes, one to the left nipple, the other seeking Alison's clitoris. 'I think, if we don't do something a bit quick, you're likely to explode,' she whispered.

Slowly Alison began to surface from the depths of a mist of exhaustion and total, abandoned release. Whether Melanie had brought her to several successive orgasms, or whether the shattering climaxes were simply individual parts of one sustained orgasm, she neither knew, nor cared, finally slumping, comatose, in her bonds, as the violent tide eventually receded. She was dimly aware of hands supporting her as she was unstrapped from the wall and taken down from the pole, and she retained just sufficient cognizance to know that Marcia was present again, but at what stage the dominatrix had re-entered the cell, she had no idea.

She felt her arms being unfastened as she was laid out on a horizontal surface, but the heavy rubber bondage sleeves were not removed. Instead, her arms were drawn up and outwards, the steel rings at her wrists locked to what she could feel was the metal bedsprings. Heavy bands were used to secure her ankles similarly, spreadeagling her helplessly, before sufficient strength returned to enable her to struggle. Fingers reached behind her neck, fumbling with the gag strap, and then the rubber ball was removed from her mouth and a soft cloth wiped away the spittle from around her lips and chin.

'I think perhaps you understand a little better now,' Marcia said softly, very close to her ear. Alison opened her eyes and turned her head in the direction of the voice. The woman was crouching alongside the bed, an enigmatic smile playing on her lips. 'That really was quite a performance,' Marcia continued. 'Melanie is very expert, of course, but it's a while since I've seen a slave come as you did. Are you feeling a little better now?'

'I think I need the loo,' Alison managed to gasp between ragged breaths. 'Please, let me up; I really can't hold it for much longer.'

'No problem,' Marcia said, stroking her shoulder. 'There's a large enamel bowl immediately beneath your bottom. You just pee away. We provide our slaves with all the mod cons.'

'I – I can't!' Alison protested. 'It's not – it's not decent!'

Marcia's only reaction was to laugh. She turned to Melanie, who was standing at the foot of the bed.

'Did you hear that, Melanie?' she snorted. 'Our little Alley Cat thinks it's disgusting to pee in a bucket with us watching, yet she comes in torrents like the base slut and makes more noise than a herd of elephants on heat.'

'She is very new to everything, Madame,' Melanie replied, quietly. 'Perhaps I should assist her?'

Marcia nodded. 'Yes, you go ahead and do that, my girl.' She remained crouching as Melanie came around to that side of the bed. 'Melanie is very good with those fingers,' she said, 'as you already know.' As she finished speaking, Melanie reached over and began pressing those very fingers into the soft flesh around Alison's groin, working upwards until they suddenly began exerting pressure on Alison's already painful bladder. It took only a few seconds and a brusque massaging action to destroy the last remnants of

26

her self-control. With a gasp of anguish, Alison surrendered to the inevitable, shutting her eyes in shame and humiliation as the hot stream cascaded noisily into the bowl beneath her.

'Now, isn't that a lot better?' Marcia asked, as Melanie wiped her clean between her legs. It was, but Alison wasn't going to admit it.

'When are you going to untie me?' she demanded. 'You've made your point by now, surely?'

'My dear girl, we've hardly begun,' Marcia said. 'This induction package lasts two days.'

'Two days?!' Alison shrieked. 'You're mad. Mike said he'd see me tomorrow, or had you forgotten?'

'I hadn't forgotten,' Marcia said, easily. 'And he will see you tomorrow. He'll see you exactly as you are – well, maybe not exactly as you are now, but he will see you in the role you're being trained to play.'

'You can't!' Alison protested. 'He can't possibly see me like this. I won't have it, I tell you! It's not decent!'

'I'm afraid, as I told you earlier, you have no say in the matter while you're in my charge. And, if you're worried about him seeing your pretty little pussy and your lovely teats with their rings, then don't. I think Michael should see what he's asking you to let yourself in for. It would be all too easy for him to fool himself into imagining something far different from the truth.

'Michael is no innocent, of course, but as far as I'm aware, his ventures into this side of life have been no more than little dabbles. You, on the other hand, have been thrown in at the deep end and already know what it's like to have your raw sexuality dragged to the surface while you're helpless to prevent it. Perhaps now you can begin to understand and answer for yourself the question you posed me earlier.

'You lie there protesting, but you must know you're not going to be released yet, and I suspect there's already a part of you that's quite glad of that. I suspect that little alter ego is quite excited at the thought of experiencing more of what you just experienced. And believe me, you will relive that experience.'

'You mean you intend to make me – make me go through that more than once?'

'Oh yes. That's what a slave is for; that and bringing pleasure to others. The "others" bit will come later, of course, once we've finished exploring your inner self. It is quite possible, of course, that when your two days are up you will not want to take up your assignment, but at least you'll find out your limits, whatever they may be, while still on safe ground.'

'If my so-called assignment means anything like this,' Alison snapped, 'then there's no way I'll be accepting it. Bloody Mike can have my resignation right now!'

'I don't think you're in the best position to use a pen,' Marcia grinned.

'And I don't think I need to stay here for two days to make a decision!' Alison shouted. 'I've already made up my mind. I'm not going through with it, so you can let me up now and save us all a lot of time.'

'I have never failed to honour a contract to the letter,' Marcia said. 'Two days was the agreement, and two days it shall be.'

'But it's not necessary, I tell you! It's not – aaahhh!' Alison's tirade disintegrated as Melanie's mouth closed on her sex, her tongue curling over her still swollen love bud. 'Noooo!' she squealed, but the upward thrust of her hips belied her noisy protestations...

Chapter Two

Demonstrable Progress

Alison opened her eyes slowly and, for several seconds, she was completely disoriented. Only when she tried to move her outstretched arms did everything come flooding back to her and, as she stared along the length of her horizontal form, taking in the tight rubber corset, the long black boots and the leather straps holding her legs widespread, she groaned. The bare steel mesh on which she lay squeaked as she tried to move and she wondered how she had ever managed to sleep on the hard metal. She turned her head and looked up at her right arm, like the left, still laced tightly inside the bondage sleeve, its tapering end locked over to her wrist, forcing her fingers into a tight, useless fist and the end ring, in turn, fastened securely to the mesh.

At least, she thought grimly, they took the gag out again before leaving her for the night – if it had been all night, for here in this little soundproofed demi-basement cell, its windows completely blacked out and boarded over, there was no way of telling if it were yet morning. By the dim red glow of the ceiling light, Alison looked about her, her eyes resting on the dully gleaming steel bars of the cage in which she had originally been imprisoned at the mercy of the maid. She let out a long sigh as she thought of herself strapped, spreadeagled to the wall, firmly gagged, yet still moaning and squealing as she had risen inexorably to the shattering climaxes that had all rushed into one long, agony-ecstasy orgasm.

She shuddered at the memory of how she had abandoned herself so easily to the pleasure waves, how she had wanted to beg Melanie not to stop, only the hard rubber ball gag preventing her from voicing her shame. A slave, Marcia had called her, and how right she had been, for Alison had been a slave to her own desires, succumbing swiftly in her bonds a second time, when, strapped spreadeagled as she was now, sex gaping helplessly, the touch of the cunning maid's mouth and tongue on her love tunnel and bud had rapidly induced a second surrender.

How could she have done that, she asked herself? It was degrading, sluttish behaviour, not worthy even of the cheapest whore. Was that what she really was, deep inside, a cheap whore? No, she knew that wasn't true, but from deep inside her had come something dark, some monstrous, lustful desire, released from its bonds of normal decency by the bonds which had rendered her own will a superfluous spectator. Vaguely, she recalled something Marcia said, just before the two women had left her, something about animal instincts.

'A true slave takes to her chains as an excuse to free the animal inside her,' Marcia had whispered. 'A free woman can use guilt and propriety as shields against accepting her real needs, her true desires. The chains and the straps lock up the guilt, not the spirit.' Alison felt again the cool touch of the dominatrix's fingers on her hot, wet entrance, stroking gently as she spoke, and the fire had threatened to rise up again. Only the sudden breaking of that intimate contact had prevented yet another explosion, and Alison's face reddened at the thought. It was as well there had been no one she knew there to witness—

'Oh God, no!' she gasped out loud. 'Mike! No, he can't...' For a few seconds she struggled vainly against her bondage,

30

but, as she had discovered before, the leather and chains had been designed to hold against any human force. She slumped limply, tears welling up in her eyes at the thought of her editor, Mike Hallet, seeing her as she was now. She had been reluctant enough to even come to Marcia Davenport's strange house, agreeing only because of the huge pay rise and bonus he had dangled before her, for even she knew enough to admit that she would have no chance of succeeding in the undercover assignment unless she did some research into the curious world of bondage, submission and domination, and its accompanying mysteries of rubber, leather and chains.

Never in her wildest imaginings had Alison realised that she would discover so much in such a few short hours! Neither had she expected to still be here, lying chained, exposed and helpless, apparently to remain a slave for two full days, rather than to receive just the cursory instruction and background lecture she had originally visualised. She knew now that she should have walked out the moment Marcia had asked her to strip and to accept the strictures of the fierce rubber corset and the long rubber boots with their impossibly high heels. And when those long sleeves had been laced up her arms, even then she had some chance of pulling out. However, the moment had been lost, when her hands had been forced into those helpless fists and no amount of pleading or protestation had moved Marcia.

'I have never failed to honour a contract to the letter,' had been Marcia's reply and now, to make matters even worse, if that were possible, Mike was due here today, at some time, to see her "progress" for himself. She groaned again, vowing that she would tear the devious bastard's eyes out at the first opportunity!

However, it did not appear that that opportunity would present itself for some time yet, for, when the door opened

31

and Marcia and Melanie appeared some minutes later, they took no chances with their captive. The collar to which her leash had been attached was removed and, in its place, a substitute, fashioned from chrome plated steel and hinged at the back, was locked about Alison's neck. Her right wrist was then freed, but immediately forced up and locked to a steel staple on the side of the collar. The left wrist was treated similarly and then, finally, Alison's ankles were released, but, in place of the leather bands that had secured them apart, steel fetters were locked over the tight rubber of her boots, connected together with a chain that was no more than six inches long. The leash chain was then clipped to a third staple at the front of the collar and she was hauled to her feet.

The entire proceedings were carried out in total silence, broken only by the clink-clink of metal on metal, neither of her captors speaking and Alison herself, not wanting to suffer the humiliation of being gagged again, following their example. Her caution, however, proved in vain, for no sooner was she standing, than Marcia produced the dreaded rubber ball with its attendant restraining strap and lifted it to Alison's mouth.

'Oh, please,' Alison wailed, 'not that. Haven't you done enough to me?' Marcia smiled, not unkindly.

'Slaves must become accustomed to taking the gag and wearing it for hours at a time,' she said. 'Where you're going, you won't get a lot of choice.'

'I've already tried to tell you, you stupid bitch, I'm not going ooommphhhughh!' As Marcia forced the ball home and drew the strap tightly about her head, Alison's eyes filled up yet again. It was all so unfair and all so unnecessary. She had already told them that if this was what she could expect then there was no way she was going through with her assignment. She would resign, get another job; even six months on the dole was preferable to this!

Or was it?

To her horrified amazement, the familiar stabs of fire began clutching at her belly again, the moment Marcia tugged on her leash. No, it wasn't possible! Just being rendered helpless was turning her on! She stood, slightly swaying on her tapering heels, bracing herself against the pull of the chain, determined to make some show of resistance.

Marcia met her eyes and grinned. 'If you'd rather go back on the bed and pee into the bowl, that can be arranged,' she said. 'And I expect you're hungry, too, not to mention thirsty. So don't be obstinate, there's a good girl, or I might have to give you a sound whipping. I've got a beautiful riding crop which is guaranteed to bring recalcitrant slave girls to heel.'

Alison's eyes went saucer shaped at the prospect. The bitch really meant it, she could see. Whatever else she might call herself, Alison was convinced that Marcia Davenport was completely mad!

The hobble chain meant that climbing the stairs back up to the ground floor was out of the question, but Alison soon realised that Marcia had no intention of taking her out of the gloomy, forbidding demi-basement atmosphere just yet. At the end of the passageway was a small bathroom and toilet, again with everything, including the black hardware, lit by the same red bulbs. Alison squirmed with embarrassment at being made to squat over the cold porcelain bowl and perform her ablutions whilst the two women looked on. Even worse, when she had finished, the maid wiped her like a helpless baby and patted talcum powder over her sex and bottom.

The gag was finally removed when she was returned to her cell. Melanie offered her a bottle of iced water, which was welcome, apart from the indignity of Alison having to suck it through a large teat. The maid then left the room, returning after a few minutes with a plate, on which were several small pieces of ham, a portion of cold baked beans, and some scrambled egg. Alison stared at the plate and snorted.

'I won't need to worry about losing my figure here, will I?' she sneered. Melanie laughed.

'There's enough here to keep you going for a few hours,' she said. 'Believe me, you wouldn't want big helpings while you're wearing that corset. You'll be fed something five or six times a day, so don't worry.'

Marcia, who had been fiddling with something black and soft on the far side of the cell, turned and added her agreement. 'We don't starve anybody here,' she assured Alison. 'There's no mileage in a slave who's too faint from hunger. We want you fit and full of energy.'

Very briefly, Alison considered refusing the food, but her stomach was already beginning to make little grumbling protestations and she sat meekly, while Melanie fed her with a fork. It was very undignified, sitting there with her arms drawn up alongside her chin like two stubby wings, trying not to dribble the sauce in which the beans were served, and chewing on the pieces of ham one at a time. When she had finally finished, Melanie wiped her mouth with a tissue and offered her the water bottle again. Alison sucked gratefully, but the bottle was removed before she had swallowed more than a few mouthfuls.

'You can have some more later,' the maid promised. 'Too much at one go can give you stomach cramps.'

'And then you'd have to take off this damned corset,' Alison said, but Melanie shook her head.

'The corset stays on, whatever,' she informed her. 'Now, I believe Mistress has something for you.'

The "something" turned out to be a hood, which covered Melanie's head entirely. Made of black rubber and lacing tightly at the back, it pressed in on her features like a second elasticated skin, leaving only her eyes and mouth visible. There were also two small apertures below her nostrils, but the rest of her head was now one black, featureless oval, the neck of the hood tucking in beneath the steel collar. When Marcia had finished fitting the garment, Melanie produced a small mirror and held it up for Alison.

She gasped at the transformation, for beneath the black rubber it could have been anyone. The sight of her head, totally encased, should have been sinister, threatening, but there was something else quite opposite about her new appearance. The hood, she realised, was a symbol of her subservience, of her complete anonymity, the lack of importance that her captors placed on her individuality, of her very personality.

'You are now slave Mitzi,' Marcia informed her, as if to confirm this. 'In your hood, your mask, you are nothing but a pleasure zone, nothing but a beautiful body, breasts, buttocks and a hot little tunnel into which any red-blooded male would wish to thrust his manhood. As you are now, is how Michael will see you, plus your gag, of course.'

'Of course,' Alison muttered, sourly. Marcia ignored her sarcasm and continued.

'I have also decided that we'll make your meeting a little more interesting. Rather than just present you to your erstwhile editor as a single slave, you will be part of a group.' Alison was totally taken aback by this announcement.

'What are you talking about?' she demanded.

'You will have three companions, all about your height and build and all similarly attired and chained, though all much more experienced than you. They are waiting in the

35

large cell at the end of the passageway.'

'You mean you keep girls down here all the time?' Alison said, aghast, but Marcia shook her head.

'Not usually,' she said. 'No, these are slaves I've trained myself, who I can summon when the occasion demands. And this occasion, I think, justifies their attendance. Come along, slave Mitzi, I think it's time for you to meet slaves Suzi, Poppy and Honey. I can assure you, they are eager to meet you.' She held up the ball gag and, with a resigned sigh, Alison dutifully opened her mouth.

The room to which Marcia led Alison was large, some thirty feet by twenty, blacked out in the same way as all the others, but with more red light bulbs so that the illumination was much brighter. There were various frames and benches set about the space, but the first thing that Alison noticed was the row of silent females standing with their backs to the farthest wall.

As Marcia had said, there were three of them and all were attired in various bondage outfits, as different from each other as they were from what Alison was wearing. The girl on the left was clad in a bright red straitjacket made from shimmering PVC, with matching thigh length boots and full hood, through which only her eyes and the outline of her lips, stretched around a large ball gag, were visible. The jacket was buckled very tightly, holding her arms firmly against her ribcage, just below her breasts, which were left exposed by two strategically placed cutouts. Below the hem of the jacket a little tuft of pale coloured hair did nothing to conceal her sex, the prominent lips thrust outwards enticingly.

Next to her, the motionless figure looked as though she had been poured into a one-piece bodysuit of thin white latex, which was only just winning the battle to control her impressive breasts. Her nipples were clearly visible through the barely opaque fabric. She stood perched on white sandals, the ankle straps of which had been secured with tiny padlocks and were connected to each other by a short thin chain. A steel bar had been passed behind her back, around which her arms had been hooked and her wrists then manacled by a chain passing across her stomach. The effect of having her elbows crooked around the bar in such a cruel fashion was to pull her shoulders back drastically, which thrust her breasts out even more. The suit incorporated an oval crotch opening, through which the pink of her already open sex pouted lewdly. A helmet of white leather completed her bondage, white tinted lenses obscuring her eyes and a zip closing the fabric over her mouth.

The last slave was dressed in an electric-blue leotard with attached helmet, covering her completely from the thighs upwards, though with openings to display her crotch, nipples and eyes. She wore matching knee length boots and ankle chains and her arms were pulled back behind her and, as Alison saw a few minutes later when she had her first view of her from the rear, connected to the thick neck collar by short lengths of chain.

'As you can see,' Marcia said, turning to Alison, 'we have selected different colours today. Usually I prefer my slaves to wear black, like you, but I thought it would make identification easier. Poppy is in the red there, Honey is in the white, and Suzi the blue, but of course, that is no help to anybody. Michael will have no idea which of the names refers to you, so it will be interesting to see his reactions. Now, come over here and stand between Honey and Suzi.'

As Alison followed Marcia towards the trio, she saw that a square section in the middle of the floor was made of what seemed to be thick rubber and was careful to copy Marcia's example in avoiding it. As she approached the line, Suzi obligingly shuffled to her left, leaving a space for her. Marcia positioned her carefully, detached the leash and went back across the room to rejoin Melanie.

'Our guest will be arriving in just a few minutes,' she told the silent line. 'Three of you already know what is expected of you, but Mitzi is a newcomer, so you'll have to lead by example and she will follow.'

Alison looked discreetly to either side of her, trying to see past the obstruction of her elbows, but not one of the other slaves stirred so much as a muscle. Only the gentle rise and fall of three pairs of breasts betrayed the fact that they were living beings and not just a set of erotic statues. She also noticed that all the visible nipples were ringed like her own, and even the girl whose breasts were not exposed, the white rubber suited Honey, had probably been treated likewise, judging by the strangely elongated shapes beneath the stretched latex.

Marcia turned back towards the door and moved through it into the corridor, leaving her bizarre harem under the watchful eye of Melanie. The room was eerily silent, the atmosphere tense and laden with the combined odours of rubber, leather and another, warm, musky scent, that of unmistakable female arousal. Alison could hear her heart thundering against her ribcage and the sound of her own breathing echoing inside her skull. She could also feel herself growing damp between her legs, and cursed herself under her breath.

What was the matter with her? She was a liberated woman, a professional, a journalist with a university degree, for God's sake, not someone's docile little sex toy! But then why was she trembling like a bitch in heat? Why was she standing here, chained and exposed, humiliated beyond anything she had ever dreamed was possible, and growing more and more aroused with every passing second? What secret switch had they touched last night? Alison stood as motionless as her companions, her eyes fixed immovably on the door, wondering what her boss's reaction would be when he saw what was waiting for him. Surely he would be shocked, for Alison could not really believe he had fully understood what he was asking of her.

At last the door opened again and Marcia strode in. Behind her came Mike Hallet, but a different Mike Hallet from the suave, suited boss whom Alison was used to seeing sitting behind his editor's desk every morning. Now the suit was gone, replaced by a black T-shirt and gleaming, black leather trousers, which he wore tucked into Cuban heeled boots, the outfit topped off by a black leather zip fronted jacket, which he wore open. He stopped two paces into the room and, as his gaze travelled from one end of the line to the other, he let out a low whistle.

'Very impressive, Marcia,' he said. 'Very sexy. Which one is she?'

'Ah, that's our little secret,' Marcia grinned. 'As far as you're concerned these are Mitzi, Suzi, Poppy and Honey.' Her finger stabbed out, indicating each girl in turn as her name was mentioned. 'As you can see, their outfits provide an excellent disguise, as well as adding an air of suitable submissiveness. I doubt if you could tell me the colour of your Alley Cat's eyes – most men are very unobservant – but even if you could it wouldn't help you. As you will see if you examine them closer, they all have blue eyes.'

Except for Honey, Alison guessed, which was why her eyes were hidden behind those tinted lenses.

Mike turned to Marcia and said something which didn't carry to the slave line. Alison saw the dominatrix nod and gesture with an open hand, palm upwards, an unmistakable invitation.

'Go ahead,' she said. 'Have as close a look as you want.

They're all slaves at the moment, and you're in the position of master.'

Mike stepped forward, careful to move around the perimeter of the rubber floor insert, and walked up to stand in front of the blue clad Suzi. Peering sideways, Alison saw that the slave girl returned his stare unblinkingly, and seemed to thrust her breasts slightly further forward. Unable to resist, Mike reached out and gently stroked her left nipple. He half turned, looking back to where Marcia remained standing next to Melanie.

'Is this all right?' he asked. 'Touching her, I mean?'

'Of course,' Marcia said. 'As I said, you can be their master for the moment. Touch her anywhere you like.'

Alison had expected a reaction of a different kind from this and she was certainly not prepared for what her usually reserved boss did next. He delved between Suzi's thighs, cupping her sex. Suzi let out a tiny moan and pressed herself deeper onto his palm.

'My God!' Mike exclaimed. 'She's wringing wet!'

'Of course she is,' Marcia agreed, walking slowly up behind him. 'She's been well trained and she's now just a horny little pleasure slut. She wants what you've got in your trousers just as much as you evidently want her. I suggest, however, that you examine the others before you choose which one you want the most.'

Mike's eyes widened with disbelief. 'You're not suggesting—?'

'And why not?' Marcia said. 'You wouldn't be doing anything they wouldn't expect, or like.'

'But what about Alison?'

'There is no one here today called Alison. Alison is from a different world,' Marcia said, quietly. 'Here we have simply four slave girls, all of whom you may pleasure, or have pleasure you, if you wish and if you are up to it.'

'But I couldn't,' Mike protested. 'I mean, yes I could, but not with – well, you know what I mean.'

'Yes, indeed I do. You could quite easily have your fill of any of these delightful specimens of female subservience, as long as none of them was your little Alley Cat. Well, Michael, you were the one who wanted her to undertake all this. Did you think she wouldn't have to go through the same sort of thing when she finally gets to Dennison Hall? Did you think she could just dress up, pretend to be one of the slaves, and just snoop around?

'You've not thought this out too well, have you? I mean, if you can't bring yourself to think of your girl jiggling on the end of your cock, then how could you expect her to agree to undertake the assignment?'

'But if I do – well, you know – with Alison, how could I ever look her in the face again?'

'I doubt you'll be able to look her in the face again anyway,' Marcia said. 'And certainly not if you get all squeamish now.' She paused, looking along the line of girls. 'I have an idea, which I think would solve all our problems and maybe, just maybe, save a whole day's uncertainty.' She stepped back a pace and clapped her hands.

'Girls,' she said, in a voice like a headmistress addressing a school assembly. 'Master Michael is obviously quite taken with what he sees, but as you heard, he has certain, uh, doubts. Now, to save a lot of trouble, those of you who would like to feel his stiff rod in your hot little pussy, take one step forward.'

There was an immediate clatter of stiletto heels on the hard floor and the line moved forward as one. Before she could stop herself, Alison had moved too and she was not sure who was the most astonished, herself or Mike!

'You're having me on, Marcia,' he said. 'None of these is Alison. You were just getting me at it. I mean, she wouldn't—'

'Apparently she would,' Marcia broke in. 'And I assure you, she is definitely in this line up.'

'Then tell me which one,' he persisted. Marcia shook her head.

'Not a chance,' she said. 'You can just play a little game of Russian Roulette with that great big cock I seem to remember from a few years ago.'

What on earth had Alison done? The shock reverberated around her head as Mike Hallett finally moved from Suzi to take up a stance in front of her. The man was supposed to be her boss. She could have stayed where she was and he would have known which one was her immediately. Now she'd as good as told him that she was offering herself to him along with the other rampant bitches!

She stared at him through the narrow eye slits, studying his face for any sign of recognition, but all she saw was a mixture of perplexity, apprehension and... lust. There was no doubt about it, Mike Hallett was growing rapidly excited at the prospect of being able to take his fill of whichever of them he decided. He reached up, gently fingering her beringed right nipple and, as he had done with Suzy, he used his other hand to cup her sex, his middle finger gently sliding between the moist lips. Alison managed to suppress an audible groan, but his touch triggered off a surge of desire deep in her belly. She couldn't believe it, but she wanted him, wanted him to want her, to take her, to fill her and screw her until she exploded!

'This one's wet as well,' Mike said, trying to keep his voice calm. Marcia nodded.

'They all should be,' she said. 'All my slaves are eager little sluts.'

'But not Alison, surely?'

'Maybe not Alison,' Marcia agreed. 'But the person she's become for today is probably completely different.'

That was it! She wasn't really Alison any more. Not like this; dressed in her boots and corset, hidden away inside the anonymity of her mask and gag. She was Mitzi, slave girl in training, available for the pleasure of any man, or woman, her mistress decreed. Mitzi let out a little moan and thrust her damp sex harder against the firm hand, moving so the invading finger brushed against her swollen clitoris.

'This is quite incredible,' Mike said, withdrawing his hand and moving along to Honey. His eyes went up and down her body, which appeared almost naked through the thin latex. 'I wonder which one you are,' he said softly, almost to himself. 'You're certainly a Honey all right, but are you an Alley Cat?'

So, Alison thought, he'd memorised the four slave names all right. She studied him out of the corner of her eye, looking down at the massive bulge forming at the front of his tight leather jeans. Would he really go through with it? Why not, she thought. After all, she had...

But then she was now Mitzi and she had no real choice, locked securely in her bondage, her breasts and sex exposed and vulnerable. She watched as Mike repeated the performance with his hands and fingers, before finally moving to do it all over again with the red shrouded Poppy at the far end of the line.

'I can't believe all this,' he said, at last. 'I haven't got a clue which one she is. Are you saying she really is prepared to give herself to me?'

'They all stepped forward, didn't they?' Marcia reminded him. 'If you want, we'll give her a second chance. Any of you slave sluts doesn't want Master Michael, one step back.'

Last chance! Step back! But Alison's feet refused to move, her body overruling her brain, the surging hormones and the cramping fire demanding release in the only way possible.

'Well, there you are,' Marcia said. 'Four slaves at your disposal. But first, perhaps a little entertainment to get you in the mood, Michael.' She clapped her hands. Melanie moved to where a small trunk stood against the wall, opened the lid and took out a tangle of leather and rubber.

Alison immediately realised what it was intended for and felt a tightening of her vaginal muscles at the prospect. The device consisted of two huge rubber penises, joined at their base, from where projected a massive pair of black rubber testicles. The leather straps were a harness, designed to strap it onto the wearer. Melanie brought the double dildo over to Marcia, who looked thoughtfully from one slave to another.

'Poppy, I think, Melanie,' she said, and the maid walked to the end of the line. As Mike stepped back, the maid stooped, proffering one of the huge phalluses to Poppy's lower lips. The red slave obligingly opened her legs wider, but she could not restrain a muffled grunt as Melanie inserted the bulbous tip into her and then rammed its ten inches home in one thrust. As she drew the straps around Poppy's hips and waist and tightened the buckles, Marcia turned to Mike.

'Would you like to choose,' she asked, 'or shall I?'

'Er, I think you'd better,' Mike stammered. 'After all, they're your girls.'

'Yes, they are,' Marcia agreed. She appeared to consider her choice, but Marcia was certain she already knew. Sure enough, one elegantly manicured finger was pointed straight at her. 'Mitzi, I think,' Marcia said, as Alison's heart began to thunder even harder. 'And I think we'll use a spreader bar.'

Without waiting to be told, Melanie was off across the room again, rummaging in the trunk. She returned with a length of tubular steel, about eighteen inches long, on each end of which was a leather ankle cuff. In fact, Alison noticed when the maid came up to her, it was really two lengths of steel telescoped one inside the other, and there were small holes at intervals, through which she guessed some sort of locking pin could be inserted to determine different lengths.

The first cuff was quickly buckled into place. There was no lock but, Alison reflected, there was no need of one, not while her hands were so uselessly confined and shackled. She felt a pressure on her free ankle as Melanie moved her feet wider apart and the second cuff was quickly secured like its fellow. Now Alison felt even more exposed than ever, her sex wide open, but Melanie was not finished yet. The bar was slowly opened out, straddling Alison wider and wider and threatening to throw her completely off balance in the towering heels.

'Back against the wall,' Marcia instructed, when the bar had finally been locked off. With Melanie steadying her, Alison shuffled slowly backwards until her shoulders came up against the cool brickwork. Gratefully, she leaned her weight back, bracing herself, as the straitjacketed Poppy began to move towards her, the massive cock bobbing obscenely in front of her at every step.

'I think you'll find this interesting, Michael,' Marcia said. 'It's a little like a ritual sacrifice, don't you think? The poor little slave, bound and straddled, helpless to resist the cock whether she wants it or not. See, she's already wide open and her juices are flowing wonderfully.'

Indeed they were, Alison knew only too well, as she stared, transfixed, at the approaching rubber dildo. It looked huge, much larger than any real cock she had ever seen, larger even than the one which had earned Greg Sturgess his reputation at university. And Greg's organ had not boasted the raised triple-ridge near its base that Alison could now clearly see. She couldn't imagine taking it, not just because of its length, but also because of its unbelievable girth.

Poppy was right in front of her now and Alison could see her eyes glinting behind the mask as she bent her legs a little, bringing the tip of the false organ in line with its target. She moved forward and Alison let out a tiny cry as she felt the cold rubber probing at her labia, searching for the opening. Without the use of her hands, it was quite a challenge for Poppy, but she had evidently practised the art before, for the smooth knob quickly settled into the right place and began pushing its way inexorably into Alison's vagina.

Mitzi! Alison screamed to herself. She was Mitzi and she was being fucked by a woman she'd never met and wouldn't recognise if she saw her again!

But Alison's vaginal entrance stretched to accept the invader and, so well lubricated was her tunnel, the entire length slid smoothly home. Alison gasped and grunted as she was completely filled, a feeling she had never experienced before, and as the ridges made contact with her clitoris she knew her orgasm would not be long in coming. From somewhere beyond Poppy she heard Mike saying something to Marcia, but that was now in a different world and the words meant nothing to her. All that was important was there, inside her and in front of her, as the red masked and straitjacketed Poppy began pistoning the colossus in and out of her, leaning closer so that their bare breasts were pressed together, Poppy's trapped arms pressing into Alison's corseted waist.

With a screeching gargled cry, Alison came, her knees

46

buckling, the strength draining from her. But Poppy was relentless, thrusting hard and holding her upright, impaled on the dildo, crushing her groin with her own and grinding her hips remorselessly. As the first wave finished its crashing impact a second came immediately in its wake, flooding Alison's senses until the last vestiges of reality were washed away. From somewhere she heard a high-pitched animal wail, only dimly aware that it was torn from her own throat by the violence of her passion.

'Multiple orgasms,' Marcia explained to a wide-eyed Mike in a matter-of-fact voice. 'Surprisingly few women are able to achieve them, though most slaves seem to do much better. Mitzi, it would appear, is a natural, though it does leave her somewhat drained afterwards.'

As a testimony to the accuracy of her appraisal, Alison lay slumped in one corner, where Melanie had lowered her when Poppy had finally withdrawn the glistening dildo. The maid had released her wrists from the collar, but her hands remained in their enforced clenched fist position, as useless as she was.

Through misted eyes she watched as preparations were made for the insatiable Poppy to service the latex clad Honey, who, at a command from Marcia, stepped onto the rubber cushioned area of the floor and dropped to her knees, bending at the waist until her head touched the floor, projecting her firm buttocks upwards, knees spread, sex blatantly spread and clearly eager. However, before Poppy was unleashed upon her, Marcia had another refinement to add.

She nodded to Melanie, who, from the pocket in her voluminous black skirt, produced another black phallus. This one was much shorter and slimmer than the monster that still glistened and swayed at Poppy's groin, and appeared to taper at its base. Bending down behind the kneeling figure, Melanie inserted it easily into her wet quim, rotated it back and forth and withdrew it again, now coated liberally with Honey's juices. It was then presented to the tiny puckered opening of Honey's bottom, which although looked far too small to accommodate it, opened easily at Melanie's insistent pressure, stretching as the shaft was pressed home and closing about the narrower base.

'Honey likes to be plugged like that,' Marcia explained. 'She actually prefers to take a cock there to taking it in her quim, but, as I always say, slaves have to do what they are told, and the small butt dildo is simply a concession on my part.'

'What about the rings on their nipples?' Mike asked hoarsely, his voice close to cracking. 'What are they for?'

'Apart from their purely decorative function,' Marcia said, 'they also serve to remind the slaves of their status. The blood that rushes to them when they are stimulated is kept there for longer, because of the pressure of the rings. This, in turn, makes their teats even more sensitive and, in Honey's case, with her shoulders pulled back by the posture bar and her breasts thrust out even more than they would normally be, the external counter-pressure of the latex multiplies the effect. I've seen a slave come, just by being treated and dressed as you see her now.'

'Good grief,' Mike said, 'this is all unbelievable. I never really imagined any of this, not when I first heard about the supposed goings on at Dennison Hall. I'm not so sure it was such a good idea, now.'

'Well, you can allow the Alley Cat to be the best judge of that… later. For the moment, we shall continue. Unless you don't want to watch any more, that is?'

Mike hesitated, but only for a moment. 'Uh – no, you carry on,' he croaked.

'And how about a little audience participation?' Marcia suggested. The editor looked bemused and then embarrassed.

'Wh-what do you mean?' he stammered.

She reached out and patted his bulging groin. 'By the looks of this, you could do with a little relief yourself,' she said. 'Get your trousers off and kneel in front of Honey and she'll suck you off while Poppy screws her.'

'I couldn't!' Mike blustered. 'No, no way. I mean, for all I know she could be—'

'The Alley Cat?' Marcia said, with an amused expression. 'Well, if she does decide to go through with the assignment after all this, she's going to have to get used to the taste of male cock in her mouth, believe me. But that's not it, is it? Some sort of warped professional etiquette, I suppose. Well, I'll put your mind at ease, Michael. Honey isn't Alison. I won't tell you which of the other three she is, but it won't be Alison's mouth you're putting your cock into.'

While this exchange had been taking place, Melanie had moved around in front of the kneeling Honey. Now, at a signal from her mistress, the maid unzipped the mouth on Honey's leather mask and removed the rubber ball gag it had been securing. At another signal from Marcia, the slave girl turned her head to Mike and spoke, her voice steady, but quiet.

'Please, Master Michael,' she said, 'let this slave suck on your magnificent manhood, while her unworthy cunt is punished.'

Mike stared at her, jaw slack. 'Now I've heard everything,' he gasped.

Marcia placed a hand on his shoulder. 'You haven't heard anything yet,' she said, quietly. 'Honey is an experienced slave, one of the best, a natural submissive who's been trained to perfection. Get out of those things and let her pleasure you.'

From her position in the corner, Alison watched, mesmerised, as her boss, as though in a trance himself, began to strip. When he was finally naked, his impressive erection jutting out like the bowsprit of an old sailing ship, Alison had to admit that he was a fine specimen of his sex, his body as trim and well muscled as that of any man half his age.

Wordlessly, he allowed Melanie to take him by the hand and lead him over to kneel before Honey's hooded face. The slave girl shuffled forward, stretching out her neck, and Melanie drew Mike's hands away and guided them to her shoulders. With slow deliberation, Honey drew the head of his cock through the opening in her mask and into her mouth, drawing also as she did so, a long quiet sigh from him.

Meanwhile, Poppy had dropped to her knees behind Honey and once more, with unerring accuracy, the monster phallus found its mark. Despite her mouth being crammed with Mike's erection, Honey let out an ecstatic groan as she was penetrated, but then instantly began to suck with great fervour as Poppy, in turn, began to ream her sodden sex.

Immediately Alison felt her own belly responding and, as the three figures writhed together in the centre of the room, she found that her right fist was rubbing furiously at her own sex. She also saw that Suzi, who had remained standing in her original position throughtout, was slowly grinding her hips in tiny circular movements, clearly as excited by the scene, though unable to touch herself as Alison now was.

Mike came very quickly, choking back a strangled cry, but either he made no attempt to withdraw or Honey's grip on him was too strong to resist, for he remained within her for a full minute, clutching her shoulders for support as Poppy thrust away at the other end. Finally, Honey too came, suddenly jerking upright with a scream that was more like a war cry, releasing Mike's cock from between her lips, but still connected to it for several seconds by a long trail of saliva and semen. Mike fell back onto his haunches, arms flailing for support and balance, staring in disbelief as the white latex and leather figure before him writhed in the throes of her release, until, with a loud groan, she slumped forward again, her forehead on his thighs. Satisfied, Poppy carefully withdrew and slowly rose to her feet.

Alison, meanwhile, not caring if anyone saw, once more fell into the abyss of her own climax, while Suzi, still frustrated, stepped back against the wall and moaned quietly through her gag.

Chapter Three

Second Thoughts?

Hanging by her wrists, her toes barely touching the floor, Alison watched as preparations were made for the next stage of Marcia's demonstration. To either side of her hung the other two slave girls who had taken part in the earlier activities: Poppy, clad in her red straightjacket and matching helmet, chains hooked into sturdy rings stitched into the shoulders of her outfit, the massive double-ended dildo still sticking out from between her thighs, and Honey, in her semi-transparent latex body suit and white leather helmet, the mouth now zipped closed again over the gagging rubber ball, chains attached to either end of the steel bar around which her elbows were crooked and tightened, so that she too had only minimal contact beneath her feet.

Only Suzi, in her electric-blue leotard with its attached hood and mask, remained in her original position next to the rear wall, poised on the six inch heels of her knee length boots, her wrists still cuffed cruelly up to the back of her collar. During the ten minutes when Poppy had been putting her artificial phallus to such good use on the crouching Honey, who in turn had been using her mouth to satisfy Mike, Suzi had been writhing and groaning in sheer frustration. But now she stood calmly once more, though her breasts, projecting through the cutouts, still rose and fell heavily.

In the centre of the subterranean cell, just away from the rubber-floored area, Melanie the maid, was setting up what looked like an old-fashioned vaulting horse, which she had wheeled in on its castors from one of the other basement rooms. Marcia Davenport stood watching, together with Mike, who now his part in the proceedings was over, at least for the present, had donned a brief rubber robe tied loosely at the waist with a sash of the same material. He still looked completely bemused, and was puffing nervously on a cigarette.

He should try it from her side of things, Alison thought grimly. At least he had a choice. But then, she knew, so had she. She had stepped forward with the other three slaves when Marcia had asked the question, and she had stayed steadfastly in the line when the dominatrix had offered her the second chance. And, squirming and gasping on the business end of that massive dildo of Poppy's, she had abandoned herself to her lust and climaxed time and time again in front of them all; including her own boss – her editor! What was it about this place and these outrageous costumes, all the leather and chains? Even Mike Hallett had been overwhelmed by it all, stripping naked and offering his rampant erection to the mouth of the helpless Honey.

Melanie was between Alison and the horse, making some final adjustments and, when she stepped away, Alison saw that another huge dildo had been mounted in the centre of the polished leather top. A small wooden box was dragged up alongside and Melanie beckoned Suzi forward. The slave girl shuffled across, her ankle chains jingling at every step, and stopped while the maid unlocked the hobble. Then, climbing onto the box, she threw one leg easily over the horse and, despite being deprived of the use of her arms, mounted it easily, sitting just behind the jutting phallus.

Now Marcia joined in, grasping Suzi's right knee and foot, while the smaller maid, taking advantage of the box on her side to compensate for her lesser stature, did the same on the left. Together, they raised the bound girl several inches, moved her forward, and lowered her again, so that she sat impaled on the malignant shaft. Marcia turned to Mike, who was still smoking furiously.

'She cannot raise herself sufficiently to escape from the rubber cock,' she explained. 'Not that I think she would want to. The randy little bitch was near to coming just watching you three earlier, so she'll be desperate for some sort of relief. The dildo is actually a vibrator; the mechanism is inside the seat, but we'll not activate it just yet. We'll let Suzi do most of the work herself. Melanie, if you please.'

The maid, who had quickly moved into the corner by the trunk, produced from it a long, slender, braided riding crop.

Alison gasped from behind her mask as the significance of Marcia's statement slammed home. She was actually going to whip Suzi! Mike, too, realised what was about to happen and started stammering something about things getting out of hand, but Marcia cut him short with a wave of the crop.

'Nonsense,' she said. 'Slave's bottoms are for whipping, among other things, and this slut hasn't had a good beating for over a week. Now, Melanie, you'd better secure her properly, just in case she gets too carried away with things.'

'Of course, madam,' the maid replied, already on the move, as though she really were able to read Marcia's thoughts. She moved alongside the hapless Suzi once more, and Alison saw that there were straps dangling down level with mid-thigh, from the "rider's" position. She quickly buckled the first one and moved around the horse to repeat the process on that side.

'That's better,' Marcia said. 'This little whore's come right off before now, ripping the vibrator clean out of its mountings. My own fault, I suppose,' she added. 'After all, the straps were there to prevent that sort of thing. Now, Melanie, I'd like her leaning a little more forward, I think.' Once more, the maid seemed to be moving before her mistress had spoken, for she was back from the trunk with a length of slim chain in her hands within seconds. Climbing back up onto the box, she reached up and clipped one end of the chain to a ring at the front of Suzi's collar, training it over the front end of the horse, where, jumping down and moving around, she fastened it to something that Alison could not see, drawing it tighter, so that Suzi was forced to lean forward. The bound girl let out a soft sigh and Alison tried to imagine the pressures inside her as her weight pressed down onto the penetrating shaft.

Marcia at last seemed satisfied with the arrangements. But no, at the last moment another idea occurred to her.

'Take the bitch's gag out,' she told Melanie. 'I think Master Michael may find it more interesting that way.'

In a trice it was done, the ever efficient Melanie a blur of black skirts, white apron and clicking high heels.

'That's better,' Marcia said, taking up a stance to Suzi's left and swishing the crop experimentally a couple of times. 'Now then, my horny little hussy,' she said, addressing her victim, 'let's see how you like this. And I want to hear you count the strokes, understand?'

The blue hood bobbed acknowledgement. 'Yes, mistress,' Suzi said, her voice betraying a slight Irish accent. Mike had now finished his cigarette and was desperately looking around for somewhere to stub out the smouldering butt. True to form, Melanie appeared at his elbow, holding out a heavy brass ashtray.

Marcia pushed the little box-stand out a few inches with her foot, and climbed onto it, so that her waist was level with the quivering buttocks on the horse.

'You are a worthless slave who keeps her brains in her

cunt, aren't you?' she said.

The hood nodded. 'Yes, mistress,' came the soft, lilting reply. 'I am worthless and I deserve to be punished.'

Crack!

Alison jumped in her bonds as the crop slashed home, leaving a vivid red mark across the centre of the pale globes. She expected Suzi to scream out, but the only sound to escape from the girl's mouth was a sharp gasp, and then:

'One, mistress,' she intoned.

Crack!

Another gasp… 'Two, mistress.'

Crack!

'Three, mistress... oooh! Please, mistress!'

'What, slut?'

'Switch me on mistress, please!'

'No, not yet.'

Crack!

'Four, mistress... pleeease! Aaah!'

Crack! *Crack*! Two strokes, one immediately after the other. The striped buttocks were glowing now and writhing about.

'F-f-five, s-s-six, mistress. Ohhh! God, I'm c-c-coming, mistress! Aaaahhhh!'

Four more times the crop rose and fell in quick succession, but Suzi was beyond keeping count now. She was more concerned with a different score as, to Alison's amazement – and to Mike's too, judging from the expression on his face – the helpless girl reached her orgasm with a piercing banshee wail.

Satisfied, Marcia reached under the horse and pressed a button. There was no visible change, but Alison guessed she had just operated the switch that activated the vibrator, for Suzi continued to wriggle, gasp and screech for several more minutes, until finally she slumped forward, completely exhausted.

The ever resourceful and prepared Melanie was immediately there, supporting her weight, as Marcia unfastened the thigh straps. The two women dismounted the gasping slave and laid her gently on the rubber covered flooring, her weight on her bound arms, her thighs wide apart, revealing the glistening mouth of her sex, which was oozing with her juices.

'A very satisfactory morning's work,' Marcia announced, turning back to Mike. His face looked pale now, although it was difficult to tell in the red glow. 'And now you and your Alley Cat both have a better idea of what's in store for her, I think it's time the two of you had a little chat.'

She nodded to Melanie, who walked across and started slackening the chain which held Alison's arms aloft, unbuckling the wrist straps when they had descended far enough for her to reach them. She made no attempt to loosen the straps which kept her fists in their tight balls, however. Nor did she touch the gag. Instead, taking Alison by the arm, she led her back across to stand in front of her boss. Mike peered hard at her and, close up, Alison could see he was actually trembling.

'It – it can't be,' he said, very quietly.

Marcia stepped behind Alison and she felt the gag strap being unbuckled. A moment later, Marcia drew the saliva soaked ball from her mouth. Feeling strangely calm, Alison licked her lips, removing the traces of spittle left by the gag. She was aware of her near nakedness, of her ringed nipples and her exposed sex, but she felt curiously in charge of the situation. It was almost as though, whilst it was she who was still helplessly restrained and she, not Mike, who should have been at a disadvantage, she was more in control of events than her editor.

'Hello, Mike,' she said softly, and then to her own

surprise, as well as to his, she dropped to her knees before him. He reached out, trying to pull her back to her feet.

'What are you doing?' he protested. 'Get up, Alison, for goodness sake.'

With some difficulty she stood up again. She fixed him with a steady gaze.

'I thought you realised that a slave is supposed to kneel before her master,' she said, coolly.

Mike looked at Marcia for help, but the dominatrix had backed away and was regarding the proceedings with an air of amused detachment.

'What may this slave girl do to please her master?' Alison persisted. 'Would my master like to suck my tits?' She took half a step towards him, but Mike held up his hands, horrified.

'Alison, stop pissing about!' he shouted. 'What's gotten into you?'

'About ten inches of rubber prick, actually,' Alison replied. 'And a whole different sort of understanding.'

Mike gaped at her. 'I don't believe this,' he said. 'Look, cover yourself up and let's get out of here.'

She held up her helpless hands. 'I can't do anything unless Mistress Marcia frees me,' she pointed out. 'Besides, it's a bit late now, isn't it Mike? You've seen everything there is to see.'

'Look,' he blustered, 'this has gone far enough. Marcia, get her loose and let me get her out of this place.'

Alison turned to Marcia, who had not moved a muscle. 'I think, mistress, if you don't mind,' she said, 'I would prefer to remain as I am, at least until I have had the opportunity to talk to Mike. Is there somewhere we can talk in private?'

Before Marcia could reply, Mike interrupted. 'Alison,' he begged her, 'will you please stop playing silly buggers and let's get out of here. The deal's off. I never realised what I was asking you to do, honestly.'

'Maybe not,' Alison agreed, 'but maybe, also, the decision isn't yours to make... not any longer. If you think I've been through everything I've been through just for you to bottle out on me, then think again. If there's a story to be had, then I'll get it.'

'You must be *insane*!' Mike snapped. 'I mean – look at you!'

'No, *you* look at me,' Alison purred. 'After all, I do look rather sexy, don't I? And I reckon, though I've got a lot to learn, that I could make a very passable slave, don't you? Now, let's go somewhere private and discuss my salary scale. I reckon we need to renegotiate the original terms.'

Alison's heart was pounding steadily as she followed Mike into her original cell room and Marcia closed the door behind them. Her editor was visibly disturbed by the turn of events and was trying to avoid looking at her. Walking past him, Alison entered the cage and looked around it.

'We should have one of these back at the office,' she said, turning and brazenly facing him, her legs apart, her sex inviting. Mike wrung his hands in a pathetic gesture.

'Look,' he implored her, 'okay, if you really want to go ahead with the assignment, that's fine by me, but please, can't you... well, you know,' he finished, helplessly.

'Try to act like a proper modest little girl?' Alison suggested, helpfully. She brought her fists together, covering her mound. 'There, how's that?' she asked, brightly. 'Afraid I can't do anything about the tits, but then, they are rather pretty in their nice rings, aren't they?' She stepped out of the cage again and walked up to him.

'Listen,' she said, 'don't start getting all moral and guilt-ridden now. If you'd said or done anything when you first walked into that room, maybe I'd feel differently. But the fact is, you didn't.'

'I was taken off guard,' Mike protested. 'I sort of got, well, you know, swept along by things. I wasn't thinking properly.'

'No, your balls were doing all the work, weren't they? Well, okay, fine. You saw me shagged nearly senseless by that Poppy, though you didn't realise it was me at the time, and then you stripped off and let Honey give you the blow job of your life, while Miss Cock of the Year fucked her too. Okay, you knew Honey wasn't me, but then you still stood there while Suzi, who could have been me, played Ride A Cock Horse – literally – with Miss Female Domination making pretty patterns on her bum with a whip.

'Then all of a sudden, when you come face to face with the real me, you go all to pieces. Tell me, if Marcia had invited you to fuck me in there, before you knew who I was, would you have done it?'

'I – er, well, what sort of a question is that?' Mike snapped.

'An honest one. And I want an honest answer. It's the least I deserve.'

'Well, okay, yes,' Mike blurted out. 'I probably would have. I'm sorry, but—'

'Don't apologise,' Alison said. She reached out with her right fist and pressed it gently against the robe, where it was just covering his manhood. 'Don't apologise,' she repeated. 'Why don't you just do it now, instead?'

'What?' He stared at her, his mouth working but no other words forming.

'You heard,' she said. 'Why don't you give me a taste of what I can expect at this Dennison Hall place? And stop looking at me like that. I know it sounds crazy, but then this whole thing is crazy. I just want to feel a real flesh and blood cock in me, and you happen to be handy.'

A sensation of pure mad power was running through Alison's veins. She was the slave, she was the one bound and wantonly displayed, but she was definitely in charge of the situation and she really did want him. In fact, she realised, she'd wanted him from the moment Honey had taken his powerful erection into her mouth. As she had lay slumped, watching the threesome, Alison had suddenly known, to both her horror and her amazement, that she was jealous of Honey and would have given anything to have changed places with her.

'Well,' she said, silkily, 'are you going to act like a real master, or should I tell Mistress Marcia I need Poppy and her cock again?'

Behind Mike the door opened, framing Marcia herself. She stood motionless for a few seconds, and then walked slowly past Mike and faced Alison.

'Slave Mitzi,' she said, quietly but firmly, 'you obviously do have a lot to learn. For one thing, slaves do not tell me what they need. I already know what every slave needs. And, if I ever hear you speaking to a master in that tone again, I'll have you on the horse and whip you every hour for a whole day. Now, on your knees, slut.'

Unhesitatingly, Alison obeyed. Marcia stepped to one side and turned to Mike.

'If this slut thinks she can wind you up she's got another thing coming,' she said. 'Pass me that ball gag on the stool behind you.'

'Why?' Mike asked. 'What are you going to do?'

'Shut her insubordinate mouth, for a start. After that, it's up to you.'

With trembling hands Mike picked up the gag and handed it over. Alison immediately opened her mouth wide to accept the ball, and felt yet another tremor of anticipation as the buckle was tightened at the back of her neck.

'I should have thought,' Marcia said, 'that you wouldn't need me to tell you the obvious, Michael. Your little Alley Cat here has discovered something about herself and now she wants you to help her prove it. Of course, if she were an experienced slave, I'd say the best punishment would be to leave her chained up and frustrated, but I think, all in all, that would be grossly unfair at this moment in time.'

'What are you talking about?' Mike demanded.

'Alison here – or should I call her Mitzi? – has realised that she enjoys sex far more when she is totally helpless and in no position to resist. It's not an uncommon fantasy, though few females ever get the chance, nor do they have the guts, to take it to this extreme. There now,' she said, tucking the end of the gag strap out of the way, 'that's better. She's all ready for you now, aren't you, Mitzi?'

Lowering her eyes, and glad that the ball gag prevented her from having to hide a smile of triumph, Alison nodded.

'I'll be upstairs in my sitting room when you're through here,' Marcia said to Mike. 'Only please, do dress yourself first. Melanie will have folded your clothes in the other room.' She began moving towards the door. 'Oh, and lock Mitzi in her cage when you've had enough of her.'

As the door closed behind her, Mike turned to the silent Alison and grasped her gently by the shoulders.

'One or both of us is going mad,' he whispered. He removed his right hand and, with his index figure, slowly stroked what he could see of the ball gag. 'I reckon I'm going to feel a complete fool afterwards, but if this is really what you want...' Alison nodded, unblinkingly. 'Well I have to admit you're a beautiful girl anyway, but like this, you're an *incredible* turn on.'

His right hand moved down, palm spreading to cup her left buttock, tenderly kneading the flesh, his left hand seeking her right breast, fingering the ringed nipple. He lowered his face and slowly sucked the engorged teat into his mouth. Alison groaned ecstatically, her bound fists massaging his back through the thin latex robe, her hips rotating slowly, encouragingly. Removing his hands, but retaining his oral hold on her nipple, Mike slipped out of the robe, tossing it away, then released her from his mouth and pulled her towards him. She felt his stiff shaft pressing against her belly and desire welled even more. Little mewling noises squirmed their way past the gag and she rubbed her rubber hooded head against his shoulder, cat-like, trying to communicate her need.

And then he was inside her, impaling her where she stood, pumping her as she writhed and wriggled like a fish caught on a hook, the muscles of her vagina spasming and sucking him deeper, her arms about his neck, her legs thrown up around him and locked together behind his back. She felt his hands under her buttocks, lifting her up and down, and she marvelled at his strength and at the prodigious size of the weapon with which he was punishing her eager tunnel.

They came, almost together, the hot surge of his seed in her belly triggering Alison over the edge. She heard his roar, penetrating the symphony of noise that was her own mind exploding in relief and gratification, a slave girl who had reached a new zenith in the service of her first master.

He lowered her onto unsteady feet, and she sighed sadly as his deflating rod slid out of her. But a sudden urge gripped her, for she knew what she had to do. Grunting to communicate her urgency, she motioned with one fist to the gag. Perplexed, but at least understanding that she wanted it removed, Mike obliged.

'Is something the matter?' he asked, pulling the ball from between her lips. Alison smiled.

'Yes, master,' she said, stepping back and indicating his

drooping shaft, still sticky and shining. 'I have soiled my master and must clean him.' Before Mike had time to take in the full significance of her statement, Alison dropped to her knees and sucked him into her mouth. Her head bobbed furiously as she used her lips and tongue, the taste of her juices and his spendings mingling together in a bitter-sweet cocktail. A minute later, when she straightened up again, his member was completely cleansed, shining only from Alison's spittle – and ramrod stiff once more!

Turning away from him, Alison spread her legs wide and bent forward, her fists resting on the floor, her gaping sex fully available and inviting. Mike needed no second bidding. He grasped her hip with one hand and with the other guided his bulbous knob unerringly to its target.

'Oh yes,' Alison groaned, as she felt the eight inch shaft slide into her. 'Ohhhyeeessss!'

'I'm not sure what I've started,' Mike said, slumping down in the armchair opposite Marcia.

The elegant dominatrix smiled across at him. 'Whatever it is,' she said, 'it's too late to stop now.'

'I'm not so certain,' he mused. 'I mean, it's one thing to play games here, but Dennison Hall is a different kettle of fish, isn't it? Your ex is a pretty nasty piece of work, by all accounts. And if you're right, the men he's in with now are just as bad, maybe even worse.'

'I think Alison is aware of that,' Marcia pointed out. 'And it has to be her decision. If you ask me, the thought of being in danger, as well as playing slave to a horde of total strangers, is a big turn on to her.'

'I'd worked that one out for myself,' Mike said, wryly. 'What I don't understand is how she can have changed so much in less than twenty-four hours.'

'It's not necessarily a case of changing, more a case of

touching a circuit that was hidden a bit deeper than others, that's all. There are a lot of people – more than you'd realise – who really get their kicks out of being tied up and "forced" to do things they wouldn't normally do. Alison's a prime case. She's not truly bisexual, not in the normal sense of the word, so she would never have dreamed of sharing any sort of sexual experience with another female.

'However, once we had her properly attired and in a secure bondage from which she could not escape, the rules changed. She didn't have to feel guilty because Melissa brought her to orgasm. It wasn't her fault, you see? And then again, when you arrived she was just one of four helpless slaves, performing as per their mistress's instructions.'

'But what about afterwards? What about me?'

'Ah well, there could be many reasons for that. You'd seen her as a slave and you'd seen her reaction to that. She's also seen your reaction to her and the others and she was determined to show you – and herself – who was really in control. She may have been bound and gagged, but she was the one in charge, out of the two of you.'

'You can say that again.' Mike wiped his brow with the back of his hand. 'It's one hell of a long time since I felt this knackered before lunchtime. Anyway, I'd better be going. I've a few items to collect before Alison goes to Dennison Hall.'

'Well, she won't be going very far until tomorrow morning. That's if you still want me to keep her for the full forty-eight hours?'

'What do you think?'

'I think so. We need to go through one or two points with her. She may be a natural, but there are certain routines – rituals, if you like – that have to be learned. If she's supposed to be a fully trained slave, then she'll need to be a fast learner. Did you lock her back in the cage, by the way?'

'Yes. I gave the key to Melanie before I came up. It felt really strange, putting that gag back on her and then pushing her inside like she was some animal.'

'We're all animals,' Marcia told him, standing up. 'And we're most of us in cages of one kind or another, even if they're not made of steel. Alley Cat is far freer in her cage than most people will ever be lucky enough to be.'

Alison, in fact, was no longer in her cage, for no sooner had the door closed behind Mike, than it reopened to admit Melanie. The maid swiftly unlocked the cage, removed Alison's gag and unbuckled the straps which held her fists closed. It took her less than a minute to slacken the laces on the first sleeve and slide it from Alison's arm.

'You can remove the other one yourself,' she said, 'but don't touch the helmet, the boots, or the corset. And don't attempt to leave this room, either. I'll be locking the outer door in any case. There's a flask of water over there in the corner and there's a bucket if you need to pee before I get back.'

The water was welcome; Alison hadn't realised just how thirsty she had become. But the bucket was superfluous, at least for the time being. She gulped down about half a pint, replaced the cap on the flask and looked about her. On a rack in the corner of the room opposite the cage, hung a sinister looking collection of straps, chains, whips and masks. Gripped by a grim curiosity, Alison walked over and began examining some of the more complex items more closely.

She took down a black mask, a full head helmet like the one she was wearing, except that it was made from soft leather, not rubber, and the rear opening closed by means of a series of small straps and buckles, not laces. There were openings for the eyes, but they could be covered by oval flaps which fastened down by means of press-studs. But there was no aperture for the mouth at all, not even a zipper, as there had been on Honey's mask. Furthermore, when her fingers explored the inside, Alison felt a thick wad of leather in line with where the mouth opening should have been, and tried to imagine how it would feel being strapped inside the cruel garment, mouth stuffed and eyes covered, leaving the wearer in total darkness.

Hurriedly, she replaced the hood and took down a curious arrangement of leather, chains and steel. She turned it over in her hands, shaking out the tangle of straps in an attempt to identify its purpose, but gave up after a few minutes. She hung it back on the rack and turned away, crossing the room to where the heavy timber chair stood, its restraining straps hanging loosely, but its air of menace no less now than it had been when Alison had first seen it. She stared down at the seat and at the two round holes near its centre, needing no instruction booklet to work out why they were there. Slowly, her heart pounding, she lowered herself into the chair and laid her arms along the timber arms, noting that there were straps to secure at wrist and elbow and, from the back upright, straps which would pinion the upper arms and the torso, as well as a stiff leather band which could be adjusted up and down to coincide with the throat of the wearer, no matter how tall he or she was. Further straps were provided for buckling about the thighs, the knees and the ankles, keeping the victim's legs wide apart. Anyone secured in the chair would be as immobile as it was possible to be, the only movement left being the head, the fingers and the toes.

Alison was so engrossed, eyes half closed trying to imagine what it would feel like, that she didn't hear the door opening, and only the tattoo of Melanie's stiletto heels on the stone floor jerked her back to the present. She jumped up guiltily, but the maid merely seemed amused.

'I'll ask Mistress to let me put you in that for a couple of hours, if you like,' she said. 'But, for the moment, we've got to get you dressed. She's expecting a couple of guests for a late lunch and she thinks it would be a good idea to have you wait table. I'm taking care of the cooking, but it's nothing complicated.'

'What sort of guests?' Alison asked, warily.

Melanie wagged a finger at her. 'Now, now,' she said. 'Haven't you learned yet that slaves don't ask questions?' She laughed and started emptying the bag she was carrying, turning its contents out onto the wire frame of the bed. 'Actually,' she went on, 'one of them is Mistress's former husband, Ralph Hancock. Although she hates him, she makes a show of keeping on friendly terms, purely for certain business advantages, though I shouldn't go into that.'

'This Ralph is the Mr Nasty I'm supposed to be exposing,' Alison said. 'Well, I reckon I'm the one who's more exposed so far.'

'And Ralph is bound to take the bait if Mistress suggests you might be looking for a – um, position,' Melanie told her. 'So, let's get you into uniform and I'll explain a few things to you.'

Alison had expected her uniform to be the same as Melanie's, but the only similarity between them was the colour; black. The dress, which was made of latex, was very tight fitting around the bodice, with a scooped neckline trimmed with white lace that revealed most of Alison's breasts, barely covering her nipples. The sleeves clung to her arms like a second skin and ended in attached gloves that required quite a lot of talcum powder, a lot more effort, and extreme patience to ease over her fingers. The skirt was brief and flared and there was a multiple layer of white latex petticoats, complete with lace edging, to make it bell out properly. It really was, Alison was forced to admit, a very sexy outfit.

But Melanie was far from finished with her. She made Alison hold up her skirt and petticoats and, after a few minutes unlacing her boots and removing them, began fastening strong rubber suspended straps, three at each side, to the lower hem of her corset. Then, opening a new packet, she drew out a pair of sheer, black nylon stockings. They were extra long, reaching right to the tops of her thighs, and had seams running up the back.

'In future,' Melanie told her, 'you will probably be expected to put on your own stockings most of the time. Slaves usually wear only latex or fishnet or seamed stockings, like these. Often the fishnets are seamed, as well. Make sure you get the seams perfectly straight. Crooked seams are a punishable offence. There now,' she said, fastening the final suspender and straightening up, 'that's much better. Shoes next, I think.'

The shoes selected were an open-toed court style with heavy, lockable ankle straps and heels equally as high as those of the boots Alison had just been wearing. Without the support of the thick rubber about her ankles and knees, Alison felt very unsteady in them, and said so to Melanie. The maid shrugged.

'You'll just have to practise out in the corridor,' she said. 'It'll be a dead giveaway if they see you tottering all over the place. But don't worry, you'll soon get used to them.' She picked up a white pinafore style apron from the bed. It was made mostly from latex, but the frilled edges were of lace. The bib fastened to the front of the dress by means of two tiny, strategically placed Velcro pads, and the sash tied at the back in an enormous bow. When Melanie had finished adjusting it to her satisfaction, she reached up and began unlacing the back of Alison's helmet. As the rubber was pulled from her head, Alison was amazed at how cool it felt without its tight embrace. However, her relief was not to last for long.

Melanie worked swiftly and expertly. She pinned Alison's blonde tresses up in a neat coil and then instructed her to sit on the edge of the bed and await her return. She was only gone a matter of seconds, and Alison gawped at what she was carrying. At first sight it appeared to be a wig, but what a wig! The hair was blonde and curly and there was so much of it, it almost looked as though Melanie was carrying an Old English Sheepdog. Alison calculated that it would fall nearly to her waist. It was not just the volume of hair that was so astonishing, however, but what it was attached to. For instead of the normal skull cap arrangement that ordinary wigs were set on, this was fixed to a full facemask, made of pale pink latex and complete with glossy red lips, arched eyebrows and the beginnings of eye-shadow on the half lids.

'Better take another drink of water,' Melanie advised her. 'Not only is the mouth sealed, but there's an internal gag. Maid slaves are not allowed to talk.'

'How come I'm not surprised to hear that?' Alison replied, teetering over to pick up the water flask. 'And am I allowed to ask how long I'll have to wear that thing?'

'At least two hours, probably four,' Melanie said. 'But if you're lucky you might get ten minutes between courses in the kitchen. If so, I'll take it off you for a minute or two and you can grab another drink.'

'And if not?'

'You suffer in silence.'

'Naturally.'

The latex mask molded itself tightly to Alison's features, the rubber ball slipping easily into her mouth. It didn't seem too large at first, and felt very soft compared with what she had endured earlier. However, she had not noticed the tiny metal valve opening between the pouting lips. As soon as the mask had been smoothed carefully over her neck and a wide rubber collar locked over it, Melanie produced a small hand pump, shaped like a melon, and attached it via a short length of rubber tube. She only had to squeeze four times and the ball inflated, completely filling Alison's mouth and puffing out her cheeks. She grunted in protest, but Melanie simply shrugged again.

'These guys will know you're wearing an inflatable,' she said, 'and if they don't see your cheeks bulging, they'll start to wonder. Now, just put these ruffles around your wrists and you're ready.'

Alison grunted and pointed down towards the hem of her dress. Melanie understood immediately.

'Oh, you want to wear something underneath?' she said. Alison nodded, fervently. 'Well, we can soon take care of that,' the maid laughed. She walked over to the corner rack and studied its contents for a few seconds. 'Ah yes, here we are,' she said, and reached up.

Alison groaned through her gag as Melanie turned and walked back to her, for she was carrying a long V-shaped strap, in the middle of which were attached two black phalluses, about two inches from each other. It was not quite what Alison had meant when she had signalled her desire for an additional piece of clothing beneath her skirts.

'Open wide,' the maid said, 'and lift your skirts. Time to put the plugs in.'

Chapter Four

Enter the Enemy

Ralph Hancock was a big man in every sense of the word. Alison guessed that he stood at least six feet six and that his broad, well muscled frame must tip the scales at sixteen or seventeen stone, not an ounce of which could have been described as surplus fat. Guessing his age was no easy matter, for the finely chiselled features, topped by the meticulously groomed fair hair, could have belonged to a man of little more than twenty-five, or to one twice that age.

Seeing him for the first time, Alison was reminded of newspaper photographs she had seen of European mercenaries involved in the various conflicts on the African continent, equally at home in camouflage battledress or smart business suit, an easy confidence oozing from his every pore as he looked up to greet the two new arrivals.

From the depths of a huge armchair he nodded distantly towards Melanie, a clear indication that he had made her acquaintance on earlier visits, but his gaze lingered longer on Alison, his eyes devouring every inch of her. Inside her rubber facemask Alison was already hot, but the way in which he smiled at the spectacle she presented made her feel hotter still.

'What did you say this one was called?' he asked Marcia, casually waving a lazy finger in the general direction of Alison and speaking as though she were not really there at all.

'Mitzi,' Marcia drawled, matching his nonchalance, 'though that's just her slave name. Do you need her outworld name too?'

Hancock shrugged. 'It's unimportant,' he said. 'Later maybe, just for our records.' He continued to look Alison up and down for several agonisingly long seconds, before crooking his index finger in an unambiguous gesture of summons. 'Walk over here, Mitzi,' he ordered, straightening his position just perceptibly. Knees trembling and suddenly feeling very unsafe on her towering heels, Alison tottered slowly towards him.

'Turn around, girl,' he said, softly. Carefully, Alison performed a full circle, but Hancock clucked his tongue at her. 'Not like that, you silly little slut,' he rasped. 'Turn about so I can see you from behind.' Glad that the mask covered her embarrassment and confusion, Alison did as instructed.

'That's better,' she heard him say. 'Now, bend over and touch your toes – and keep your legs straight.' A natural athlete, this was not a task which Alison would ordinarily have found difficult, for it was part of her daily warm-up. However, for her warm up routine she usually wore gym shoes, whereas these shoes placed her toes several inches further distant. By the time she finally managed to force her gloved fingers into contact, every muscle in the back of her legs was screaming out in silent protest.

What was more, Alison rapidly realised, the position she'd been ordered to adopt meant that her brief flared skirt, together with its layers of supporting petticoat frills, was now sticking almost straight up. It left her buttocks, as well as the tops of her stockings and the narrow band of bare thigh flesh above them, clearly on view. She grimaced, biting on her gag, as she realised that was exactly what Ralph Hancock intended and yet, despite Alison's earlier claims at being a liberated woman, there was once again the cold thrill of being treated like no more than a piece of meat.

Staring back between her slightly parted thighs, her view partially obscured by the dipping front hem of her uniform skirt and the cascade of blonde curls that now fell forward like twin curtains, Alison could see Hancock's feet and legs as he rose silently from his seat and moved towards her. She held her breath, listening to her heart thundering in her chest, determined not to react with anything other than calm obedience, but she still jumped at the first cool touch of his fingers on her right buttock.

The room fell eerily silent as he gently probed her flesh, stroking and pinching in a none too gentle fashion. The rasping sound of her own breathing inside the rubber cocoon now almost drowned out her heartbeat, but after that first slight reaction Alison remained stock still, like a bizarre statue.

'Nice arse,' Hancock conceded at last. 'Very nice. And good long legs. Are the tits all her own, Marcie, or have you padded them?'

'What you see is what you get, Rafe,' Marcia retorted. 'If I get a flat one, that's how they stay, apart from the girlie boys, of course.'

'Of course. So, what's the face like?'

'Very pretty. A natural English rose and a natural blonde as well. Hair's not as long as that little lot, of course, but what there is of it is thick and healthy, so it could be grown out to something like you see.'

'Or we could shave it off altogether,' Ralph said, his off-handedness sending a shiver of dread running through every nerve in Alison's body. Her head shaved! He couldn't! Only by a massive exercise of self-control did she manage to stop herself jumping up in horror at the prospect.

'We have a few clients with a penchant for bald beauties,' Hancock was continuing. 'I think it's something to do with the fact they all seem to have spent time in the colonies, and the black women have almost no hair at all.' He paused, considering for a few seconds. 'No, if she's a natural blonde, we'll keep her with hair.' Suddenly his finger was insinuating itself between the leather crotch strap and Alison's plugged sex, probing arrogantly until it came into contact with the base of the dildo.

'Do the collar and cuffs match?' he demanded, and Alison felt her stomach lurch at the dismissive way in which he was talking about her. Marcia laughed.

'They do indeed,' she confirmed. 'In fact, she's almost white down there. As you know, I like to shave my girls, but I've left her intact for the moment. I thought you might like to make that decision for yourself, later.'

'When I've seen her naked,' Hancock agreed. His free hand now moved to the crotch strap immediately over where the second phallus was embedded and, with his finger at the front pulling Alison's weight backwards, he pressed hard against it, thrusting the dildo even harder home. Despite herself, Alison could not prevent a groan from escaping past the gag. Hancock chuckled, mirthlessly.

'Thorough job as ever, Marcie,' he commented, a note of approval in his voice. 'How long has she been getting used to taking a cock behind?'

'As I said,' Marcia replied, 'she's very new to everything. All things considered, she's doing very well.'

'A natural, you think?'

'Quite so. Another week or two in training and she'll be perfect.' Suddenly, Hancock's hands were gone and Alison saw that he was stepping back from her.

'You may stand up now, Mitzi,' he said.

With a sigh of relief Alison struggled into an upright

stance, but she dared not turn back to face him until ordered. Behind her, the big man was continuing to discuss her with his ex-wife as though she were an inanimate object.

'She has a lovely pale complexion, from what little I've seen of it,' he said, laughing. 'It should redden up well under the strap and whip. My clients will like that.'

'I'd exercise a little restraint in that direction, if I were you,' Marcia suggested. 'Keep it to broad straps and paddles, otherwise you'll have marks that'll take months to fade, if at all. A badly marked slave loses value rapidly, as you should know.'

'Perhaps, but the effect at the beginning is quite dramatic.' He stepped around to stand in front of Alison and grasped her lower jaw between powerful fingers. 'How do you fancy having a pretty pink pattern laced all over your body, little Mitzi?' he sneered, putting his face close to hers. 'I can place fifty lashes down a slave's back and legs without a single crossed stripe.'

Alison felt her blood running like ice in her veins, the thought of what he was suggesting making her feel weak again, but she defiantly kept her back straight and stared back unblinkingly though the narrow eye openings. Hancock leaned even closer and kissed her full on her rubber lips.

'I think you could be fun, Mitzi,' he breathed. 'And I think I shall keep you inside this rubber head for a while. It'll add to the fun; trying to imagine what you really look like. One of my handlers can take you out of it to feed and drink, but we'll keep you as the anonymous slut slave to begin with.' He turned to Marcia.

'How much are you asking in commission?' he demanded.

Marcia shrugged. 'Two thousand.'

'Ridiculous. Call it a grand. She's not even fully trained,

by your own admission.'

'No way. This is a very valuable piece of merchandise,' Marcia retorted. 'And the rest of her training is a bonus. She's a natural, but she hasn't been schooled to any particular preferences yet. Bringing her to her peak should add to the value, if I know anything about you, Rafe. It's two thousand or no deal.'

Listening to them haggle, Alison wasn't sure whether she liked the way the conversation was going. Marcia really sounded determined not to give ground, but if she didn't and Hancock wasn't prepared to meet her price, the deal would fall through, which was not the object of the exercise. On the other hand, a small voice in the back of Alison's head was telling her it would be better if there was no deal after all; then Hancock would go on his way and she could return to her normal routine without any loss of face, or loss of bonus.

But then again, whatever devil Marcia's treatment of her had unleashed was almost eager to discover what being helpless in this arrogant beast's hands would be like.

'I'll go to one and a half,' Hancock reluctantly conceded, but still Marcia shook her head.

'I'll give you ten percent, for old time's sake,' she said. 'That's eighteen hundred and you've got the deal of your life.'

Alison held her breath.

'Seventeen fifty,' Hancock said, finally.

With a smile, Marcia held out her hand. 'Deal,' she said. 'Only bring cash.'

Slowly, Hancock grinned. 'I already did,' he growled. 'So, get some restraints on the little whore and I'll radio Thomas to bring the Land Rover around.'

Alison's eyes opened wide in horror. This wasn't how it was supposed to happen. She had assumed that there would be a date fixed and time for her to prepare for whatever perils might lie ahead.

Clearly, Marcia too was taken aback.

'But what about her outfit?' she protested. 'That little lot isn't exactly bargain basement stuff, Rafe!'

He shrugged. 'I'll have it sent back to you,' he said. 'Or else, as it seems to fit her and suit her so well, let me know what it stands you in and I'll add the cost to your price. I won't see you out of pocket.'

'Maybe so,' Marcia stumbled, 'but what about dinner? And where are the people who were supposed to be coming with you?'

Hancock waved the idea airily away. 'Oh, I forgot to tell you, they couldn't make it. Flight problem at the last moment.' He turned back to Alison, a broad grin on his face. 'And as for food, I'm afraid my appetite tonight is definitely for something else!'

Dennison Hall was much as Alison had expected it would be. It was a Victorian pile set in its own grounds, well off the beaten track and at least two miles from the nearest habitation; a small village which comprised perhaps a dozen houses, an antiquated pub and a workshop-cum-garage that advertised mostly agricultural machinery repairs.

Sitting upright in the back of the Land Rover, unable to speak and with her arms strapped to her sides by the cunning restraint harness which was hidden beneath the cape she now wore, Alison was only just beginning to regain her composure after the rapid series of events at Marcia's. Her first reaction to Ralph Hancock's suggestion had been something akin to panic, for immediate transportation to his lair had not been part of the original plan – or at least, not any part of it she had expected.

78

Rather, Alison had envisaged completing her two day tutorial and induction session and then having at least a day or so more to digest everything and prepare herself mentally for the potential ordeal ahead. To be suddenly plucked from the relative safety of Marcia's establishment – okay, her experiences had been bizarre and extreme, but at least she knew the dominatrix would only take things so far – and spirited away to the citadel of the enemy, without any opportunity to reflect, reconsider, or even to confer again with Mike, was more than a little traumatic.

When Melanie had led her away to prepare her for the trip, Alison, as soon as the rubber facemask and gag had been removed, had tried to protest.

'I can't just *go*,' she wailed. 'Not just like that. There are things to be done, things that need taking care of. Look, I reckon this is all a bad idea!'

Melanie stretched out a calming hand. 'Take it easy,' she soothed. 'Marcia will see to everything.'

'But I need to talk to Mike!' Alison persisted.

The maid cocked her head a little to one side. 'Look,' she sighed, 'I don't know much about all this, but I gather the idea was to get you inside Dennison Hall, one way or the other. Well, kiddo, you've just cracked that. The man's impressed with what he's seen and he's taken the bait, but one thing I do know about him is that he won't be pissed about. Not only that, if you try to backslide or put things in his way, he'll just get suspicious, which is the last thing you want.

'So, the way I see it, either you go now, or not at all. Hancock will probably just walk away from this otherwise and, if he should agree to a delay, it'll make your job a lot more difficult when you do get there.'

'But nothing's been properly prepared yet,' Alison protested. 'I'm supposed to have a back-up in place, and I don't have a camera or anything else.'

Melanie eyed her seriously. 'From what I know about this crowd, you wouldn't want to risk smuggling any sort of camera into Dennison Hall,' she said. 'I don't care what you've seen in these spy movies, but there isn't a camera you could safely hide under what you'll be expected to wear most of the time. Now, we're wasting time,' she said, picking up a bottle of water and offering it to Alison.

'Make your mind up quickly,' she continued. 'Have a few mouthfuls of that and then let me get your face and hair back on you. If I don't take you back in there, all ready as expected, then you might as well kiss your scoop goodbye – amongst other things,' she added, grinning wickedly.

Alison took the bottle, looked at it uncertainly, and then raised the neck to her lips, gulping down several mouthfuls. Melanie grabbed it off her.

'Not too much,' she warned, 'you've got a long journey in front of you – always supposing you're still game for it.'

Alison let out a long, deep breath and closed her eyes.

'Go on then,' she eventually said. 'Quickly, before I change my mind.'

Ten minutes later it certainly was too late for her to change her mind. Once the rubber head and facemask, complete with its fantastic blonde tresses, had been replaced and the gag re-inflated, Melanie buckled a broad leather strap about Alison's waist. On either side of this belt had been stitched a narrower strap and these were quickly buckled and locked about Alison's wrists, immobilising her hands completely. Additional straps were buckled around her upper arms just above her elbows, and a chain clipped between these, pulling her shoulders back and forcing her breasts forward even more noticeably. Finally, a rippling black rubber cape was fastened about Alison's throat, the rustling folds adjusted so that they hid the bondage, though not falling beyond the brief hem of her skirts so as to interfere with the view of her spectacular legs and thighs.

When Melanie steered her charge back into the lounge, Ralph Hancock nodded his approval and was on his feet almost immediately. From his pocket he drew a short length of chain, which he clipped to the wide rubber collar that was again in place about Alison's throat beneath the collar of the cape. He gave it an experimental tug, almost overbalancing her.

'You'd better be as good as you look,' he hissed, his lip curling back into a savage smile. 'For what I've already paid and what you get a month for yourself, I expect only the best. Do you understand, Mitzi?'

Slowly, Alison nodded, though even that gesture was made difficult by the collar which encircled her neck. Hancock's grin faded.

'That's good, my little dumbfuck,' he said with menace. 'Now, let's get you to your new home.'

Alison was eased into the rear seat of the vehicle and a seatbelt tightened across her chest, further adding to her feeling of helplessness. Still not satisfied, however, Hancock drew two tightly joined leather manacles from beneath the seat and buckled them about her ankles, adjusting the chain to which they were attached so that Alison was unable to move her feet more than a few millimetres in any direction.

'Comfortable, are we?' the big man taunted, backing out of the vehicle and closing the door. He came around and climbed up into the front passenger seat, turning to look back over his shoulder at his newly acquired captive. 'We like our girls to maintain a decent posture at all times,' he said. Alison grimaced, for with her costume and all the added straps, there was little else she could do but sit rigidly upright. Hancock stretched back an arm and tweaked one of her breasts through its latex molding.

'Bet you can't wait to get a few more hands on these beauties, can you?' he chuckled. 'Well, my little Princess Mitzi, you won't have to wait too long. Like I said earlier, we'll keep your mystery face on you for a while yet, but I think we should give everyone the chance to see what the rest of you is really made of at the first opportunity.'

The gates that defended the driveway at Dennison Hall were operated by some sort of electronic remote control, and swung silently open as the Land Rover approached them. Ahead, the dark silhouette of the house was spotted by the occasional blaze of light from a badly curtained window, and there were two brass lamps lighting the three steps up to the front door. Slaves, it seemed, however, were not permitted to use the main entrance. Instead, Thomas steered the vehicle around to the side of the house and drew up with a scrunching of tyres on gravel, level with a darkened porch.

Hancock turned to his driver and nodded. 'I'll leave you to take the slut inside,' he said. 'You can leave the keys in the ignition. I need to take a little trip, but I'll be back within the hour. Give her over to Kristin and tell her I expect to have her properly prepared by midnight. Oh, and remember that Kristin is to be the only one who sees her without the facemask on.'

'Right, boss,' Thomas replied, opening the door alongside Alison and stooping inside to release her ankles. Peering through the eye slits, Alison studied him, trying to make out his features in the gloom. She had seen nothing more than the back of his head since Hancock had hustled her out of the rear exit at Marcia's, but her scrutiny produced little more information until he finally led her inside the house itself.

Once there, Alison saw that he was a pleasant-featured individual in his early or mid-thirties, with dark hair, dark eyes, and muscles that would have been impressive, but for their recent comparison with Ralph Hancock's physique. He tugged on the leash and motioned with a jerk of his head for Alison to move ahead of him. Her legs still stiff from the journey, Alison battled bravely to retain her balance and was grateful that the remainder of their journey was very brief.

Thomas restricted his conversation to monosyllabic orders such as left, right, halt, and punctuated these with brisk prods between her shoulder-blades to indicate that he was not altogether impressed with the speed of their progress.

Their final destination proved to be an austere square room, the floor of which was flagstone slabs, and the walls tiled in plain white ceramics, although the lower half of one wall was lined with a series of oak-panelled cupboards. The only other furniture in the room was a slatted oak bed, a heavy upright oak chair with unpadded armrests, and a sinister-looking chain, which dangled from a round aperture in the otherwise featureless ceiling.

The room was illuminated by a series of uplighters set on the walls. In any other situation the lighting might have been considered soft, or mellow, but here it simply leant one additional element of menace to the oppressive atmosphere.

Thomas steered Alison directly towards the chair and, as they drew closer, she saw there were strategically placed straps to secure limbs and torso. It was a similar piece of equipment to the one she had seen earlier at Marcia's; the one that had set her heart racing when she sat in it. But now, as her captor turned her around and pressed her down onto the seat, Alison experienced a different concoction of emotions altogether.

Her ankles were rapidly fastened to each of the seat's front legs and then her wrists released from the waistbelt and secured to the armrests. Alison was then forced to lean forward while Thomas released the straps from her upper arms, but these were just as rapidly replaced by another set which were anchored to the back of the chair. Glancing to either side, Alison saw there were even more restraints available, but Thomas seemed satisfied to leave things as they were.

And to be honest, she had to concede anything else would have been superfluous, for there was not the slightest chance of her getting free of the chair without outside assistance.

Thomas picked up the original elbow strap and chain restraint, tossed it onto the top of the row of cupboards with a clatter that reverberated about the bare walls, and turned back towards the door.

'Mistress Kristin will get to you… eventually,' he said. 'In the meantime, amuse yourself.'

As the heavy door banged shut behind him Alison tried to ease her position, though she had little latitude. The dildoes which plugged her felt even larger than ever; every single movement on the hard seat thrusting them deeper into her, and her nipples felt as though they might very soon explode, constricted as they were by the uncompromising rings Melanie had clamped onto them.

However, despite her extreme discomfort, Alison was forced to admit that the entire situation was again beginning to trigger some hidden mechanism that she would never have dreamed existed some twenty-four hours or so earlier. She screwed her eyes shut, trying to force down the tide that was welling up within her, but she knew it was a losing battle and, a few moments later, she was writhing helplessly in the throes of another shattering orgasm.

'Why the fucking hell didn't you stop her?' Mike Hallet's face was purple with rage and frustration as he stormed back and forth across the lounge. Marcia Davenport gave an eloquent shrug, drew a cigarette from the silver-trimmed case and placed it between her carmine lips.

'You wanted to get her inside Dennison Hall,' she said quietly. 'Now she's there. You should be pleased; after all, there was no guarantee that Ralph would take her on.'

'I know that!' Mike snapped. 'But she's not ready yet.'

'I'd say different, from what I've seen of her,' Marcia countered. 'Your Alley Cat's a natural, just so long as she holds her nerve.'

'That's not what I meant,' Mike persisted. He stopped his pacing, turned to face Marcia and pounded his fist into the palm of his other hand. 'I wanted to brief her properly, tell her what to look out for. And there's a special camera coming I wanted her to take with her.'

'And just where was she supposed to hide this camera, Michael?'

'It's only small; a special thing, a bit like the gadgets you see in the spy movies. And it cost a small bloody fortune.'

'I don't think you've thought this through, Michael,' Marcia said, flicking her lighter into flame and bringing it to the tip of her cigarette. 'Unless they've invented cameras the size of shirt buttons, Alison would have been rumbled straight away. The girls at Dennison Hall don't wear much that isn't like a second skin, you know.'

Mike heaved a heavy sigh. 'Yeah, maybe you've got a point,' he conceded, 'but that still doesn't help. At least I could have organised a rendezvous point for her to contact Johnny McCoy somewhere in the grounds.'

'Is this before or after Ralph's Dobermanns tear them both to shreds? Always assuming your Mr McCoy doesn't rip himself apart on all the barbed wire and other nasty surprises Ralph's had installed there, that is.'

'Shit!' Mike raised his hands and ran them down his gaunt face. 'So what do we do now?'

'We?' Marcia's tone contained just a hint of amusement. 'My dear Michael, I've done my bit. I gave Alison a crash course in bondage and I got her inside the place for you. That's as far as our arrangement went, as I recall.'

'Maybe so,' Mike agreed, 'but that was before all this happened.' His face took on an earnest, plaintiff look. 'Listen please, Marcia, you've got to help me – help Alison, if you like.'

'In what way?'

'You can get inside the place yourself, can't you?' he replied. 'You could get messages to Alison, tell her it's probably a bum steer if the security is as good as you reckon it is.'

'I could get inside, sure,' Marcia nodded. 'But whether or not I could get anywhere near Alison is another matter. I do have a sort of excuse, but Ralph's a cute one, I can tell you.'

'What sort of excuse?' The sudden hope in Mike's voice was unmistakable.

'Well, Ralph pays his slave girls – pays them well, as it happens – and Alison will need a bank account for her ill-gotten to be deposited in.'

Mike's expression showed his alarm. 'But he still thinks she's called Mitzi, surely? If she gives him her right name he might well discover her real identity and what she does for a living!'

'Calm down,' Marcia said, soothingly. 'I've already thought about that. Ralph won't expect her name to really

86

be Mitzi; all the slave girls use working names, as it were. But she's already been warned about using her real name. Melanie had a few minutes alone with her before they took her away, so she knows to call herself Louise MacIntosh. She also knows to say that she doesn't have a bank account.

'I can phone Ralph and tell him that and say that I'll open one for her. The real Louise MacIntosh is working in Canada for the next few months, so there won't be any problem there if he does run any checks. Melanie gave her the right date of birth to memorise and they're near enough the same age, so no problems there either.'

'So, will you use the real Louise's bank account? Who is she, by the way?'

'My goddaughter,' Marcia replied. 'And no, it wouldn't be a good idea to use Lou's own account. If Ralph wanted to he could check back and find out that she's had the account for some years. No, I'll open a new account for her, locally.'

'But won't that be a bit difficult?' Mike protested. 'Surely the bank will want references and the account holder to turn up in person?'

'Not at this bank they won't,' Marcia assured him, grinning widely. 'The manager is an acquaintance of mine and everything between him and me is in strictest confidence… with the emphasis on "strict", believe me!'

Mike relaxed. 'So when can you get in to see Alison?'

Marcia treated him to another of her languid shrugs. 'I'll phone tomorrow,' she said, 'but it'd be best if I give it another day or two before I go up there. Don't want to arouse any suspicions unnecessarily, after all. In the meantime, if your Alley Cat is half the girl I think she is, she'll already have started using her eyes and ears. I can't see her hanging around, can you?'

Chapter Five

The Lion's Den

Alison, however, certainly was hanging around, though not in the metaphorical sense that Marcia had intended. The thick cuffs that had been locked around her wrists were heavily padded, but after twenty minutes suspended by them from two chains, Alison's arms were beginning to ache terribly. However, with the facemask and its integral gag still in place, there was no way she could communicate her discomfort to her present tormentor, not that she thought it would have helped one iota had she been able to do so.

Mistress Kristin was a tall, willowy blonde, with pinched features, severely drawn back hair, and legs that seemed to go on forever. She was not exactly pretty, but she was certainly not unattractive, though her thin lips were permanently set into a rigid line and her expression seemed to be a fixed scowl for most of the time. Alison wondered exactly how old Kristin was, but the best she could narrow it down to was somewhere between her late twenties and mid-thirties. The way in which she handled her captive, however, made her chronological age seem irrelevant, for her mastery of the shackles and chains bespoke an age of experience.

'The mystery slave girl, eh?' she had said, upon first entering the room some half an hour or so after Thomas had left Alison strapped to the chair. She stalked slowly around the helpless figure, her high heeled knee boots clacking on the stone floor, the short riding crop slapping against their leather with a menacing sound. Peering through the eyes of her rubber face, Alison took in the tightly corsetted waist, the leather corset buckled over the skintight rubber leotard, the black net tights and the severe makeup. Where Marcia's appearance had been elegantly severe, this woman's was intended to convey the full theatrical effect, be it to a slave or any onlooker.

Mistress Kristin raised the crop and placed the tip beneath Alison's chin. 'The Master has instructed that I am to be the only one to see your face… at least for the moment,' she said. 'He tells me you are supposed to be really pretty, but we shall see.' She removed the crop and slapped it against the frame of the chair with savage ferocity.

'I do not like sluts who are too pretty!' she hissed. 'Even this pretend face is too pretty for the likes of you. I think I shall find something more suitable for when you are with me. And if your own face is not to my liking, I shall have our makeup girls change it. How would you like to look like a wizened crone, eh?'

Alison closed her eyes and breathed slowly, trying to force back the wave of panic that was threatening to overwhelm her. This was not what she had anticipated at all, for there was little doubt in her mind that Kristin was completely unstable.

'Yes,' Kristin was continuing, 'we have clients who like that sort of thing; a nice young body and a face that looks as though it's been in collision with a thousand ships, rather than launched them. You'd be surprised what a real makeup artist can achieve, and we have two here who have worked for films, theatres and television companies.' She leaned over Alison. 'In fact, I shall suggest to Master Ralph that we let them loose on you without delay. When they've finished with you, you won't even recognise yourself, so there'll be no need for this mask to hide your real features.

'However,' she continued, straightening up again, 'for the time being we must get you more suitably attired for what the Master wishes for tonight. This outfit is perfectly suitable for domestic duties, but it covers far too much for other things.' She stepped back, resuming the tapping rhythm of crop against boot.

'Now, before we go any further,' she said crisply, 'I want to make one thing clear. Whatever else you might think you have learned, or whatever you might have thought your position here would be, all the time you are here you are treated just as though you were a real slave. You may be an overpaid whore in the real world, but in this world – our world – you can forget about that.

'Here the illusion is everything. Otherwise, when you are with the guests you might let the façade slip. No, my girl, here a slave is a slave is a slave, and any misdemeanours or slips in discipline are punished severely. Do you understand?'

The now familiar spiky fingers were spreading rapidly throughout Alison's nervous system as she struggled to nod. It was crazy, she thought. No, she was crazy. She was sitting there, totally helpless, unable to move or even speak and faced with a bitch whose mental state was open to more than just idle speculation, and she was getting turned on by it! By all rights she should be terrified.

Certainly she was more than a little apprehensive, but the tight knot in her stomach owed itself as much to anticipation and impatience as it did to trepidation. Two days before, Alison would never have believed herself capable of such a reaction to the situation in which she now found herself, but they had been a long and revealing two days.

My God, she'd turned into a real slut! Mistress Kristin evidently thought so.

'I am now going to release you and strip you, slut,' she barked. 'If you do not cooperate completely I shall summon extra help, and then you will be whipped thoroughly. In fact,' she added, stooping to tackle the first strap, 'a summons for help would be totally unnecessary; there are three cameras recording events in this room and they are being monitored continuously by our security personnel.'

Alison tried to spot the cameras, but wherever they were, assuming Kristin wasn't bluffing, they had been well camouflaged. Presumably, she thought, whoever had installed the system had to be an expert at disguising his hardware, or else the blackmail victims would catch on to what was happening straight away and Ralph Hancock's scam would never have worked.

Best to work on the assumption that the woman was telling the truth and, in any case, apart from earning herself a thrashing – and she was totally sure that Kristin wasn't bluffing on that score – she would only succeed in drawing unwanted attention to herself, getting branded as a troublemaker and, even worse, thrown straight out as an unsuitable candidate for the role she was expected to assume.

Kristin worked quickly and methodically and with little consideration for Alison's comfort. Her slender frame belied the strength she possessed, Alison realised, and it was unlikely that Kristin would have to rely on assistance to overpower her. Besides, with the whip in her hand she made an even more formidable opponent, and there was little doubt in Alison's mind that she would know how to employ that weapon to the most devastating effect.

Five minutes later Alison stood completely naked apart from the head mask and wig, the cool air inside the barren room raising little goosebumps all over her bare flesh. Kristin stalked around, examining every inch of her as though she were some animal on the auction block, and with a flash of comprehension Alison realised that that was exactly how the woman regarded her; a prize filly being prepared for sale – or lease – to the highest bidder… or highest *bidders*!

'Not bad,' Kristin muttered, grudgingly. 'Not bad at all.' She patted Alison's buttocks with her free hand and then kneaded the firm flesh experimentally, before repeating the same process on each of her breasts in turn. To her chagrin, Alison felt her nipples stiffen, and that fact was not lost on her handler. 'As I said,' Kristin remarked, standing back again, 'a thorough slut. Are you wet, girl?'

Indeed she was. Alison could feel the moist heat radiating from her sex. She tried to press her thighs closer together, but Kristin was having none of it.

'Legs apart, slut!' she snapped, tapping Alison's thighs with the end of her crop. It was not a hard blow, but even so the contact stung and Alison could only imagine the pain the implement could inflict if it were used seriously. Not wishing to find out at first hand, she quickly moved her feet apart. Kristin peered downwards.

'Hah!' she exclaimed, triumphantly. 'As I suspected. Dripping.' Before Alison could react the older woman thrust the end of the crop up between her thighs, pressing the braided leather between her labia. Alison's immediate instinct was to jump backwards, but she knew that reaction would have dire consequences. With a superhuman effort she managed to retain her pose and position.

Slowly, Kristin drew the crop back and forth and, despite the gag, a groan escaped Alison's throat. Much more of this and she would climax, she knew, but that was not Kristin's objective. With a flourish she withdrew the crop and lifted the tip to her nose, sniffing at it fastidiously.

'Very sweet,' she murmured. 'A regular little honey pot.'

She flourished the end of the crop under Alison's nose and Alison was forced to inhale the aroma of her own excitement for several seconds. She could feel her cheeks burning and was grateful that the latex face hid her own features.

'Yes,' Kristin said at last, casting the crop aside. 'I think you and I are going to have some entertaining times in the future. However, for now there is work to be done.' She turned and walked across to one of the low cupboards, throwing the doors wide, though the exact nature of its contents was obscured by the fact that they all appeared to be black. Kristin soon returned brandishing two items. One of them, Alison saw, was made of latex, the other of leather, comprised mostly of straps and buckles.

Putting down the latter, Kristin held up the former, and Alison saw it was a pair of what were best described as panties, though their design was unlike anything she'd seen before. Her first impression was that they were far too small. Indeed, they looked as though they had been designed to fit a child of four or five, so little was there of them.

But their elasticity proved phenomenal. So much so that, once in place, Alison felt as though she were being held in a vice. Furthermore, the oval cutout over her sex had the effect of thrusting her mound into even greater prominence, the black latex serving to highlight its nudity even more. At the back the garment was no more than a thong that passed between her buttocks, pulling up between them with a ferocity that was going to take some getting used to. Alison peered down at herself and realised that she felt even more naked than when she had actually been naked, and could not suppress a shiver of delight at the picture she knew she presented.

'Now we'll do something with these tits,' Kristin announced, retrieving the arrangement of leather straps.

Alison stood obediently while it was fitted to her upper body. Ostensibly, it was designed as a sort of brassiere-come-halter, but it was intended to emphasise, not cover the breasts. A wide collar was buckled about the neck, from which two straps descended at the front, joining a circle of leather at either side, through which Alison's firm orbs were pushed. The two circles were joined by a large metal ring and, at the bottom of each, was joined another strap which passed around to be buckled at the back. Once that had been done Kristin turned her attention back to the two leather circles, which Alison saw could be made smaller or larger by means of two buckles.

It was no real surprise to her when Kristin began tightening them, forcing Alison's breasts up and out, until they looked as though they were nothing to do with the rest of her body and took on an elongated and swollen shape. It felt strange, but not painful and not really even uncomfortable, once Alison had grown used to the sensation. Kristin examined the effect she had created and nodded, pursing her lips.

'Much better,' she said. 'A slut should have herself properly on offer at all times, and you are certainly on offer now.' She grinned maliciously. 'Play with yourself!' she suddenly snapped.

Alison stood there, too shocked to move, and Kristin slapped her painfully across each breast in turn.

'Are you stupid, girl?' she hissed. 'Play with yourself – nipples first and then that juicy little cunt. I want to see you come and I haven't got all day, so move it, slut!'

Slowly, Alison raised her hands to her breasts, fingering her nipples tentatively. They felt distorted and full, each teat alive even to her own touch, and the heat which was already building inside her turned itself up another notch. As she rolled the distended flesh between fingers and thumbs, Alison could hear the sound of her own heart pounding and the rasping of her breath in and out of the nostril apertures. Kristin, however, was clearly not a patient soul.

'Get a hand down on that cunt!' she ordered. 'I want to see you come, not indulge yourself.' Alison's right hand dropped instantly, her middle finger sliding easily into her slit and moving upwards to nestle against her clitoris. Yet again she was grateful for the mask to hide her embarrassment. She had masturbated herself to a satisfactory climax on many occasions in the past, but never had she thought that she would do it with an audience. Fleetingly, she thought of the unseen watchers observing her performance on the television monitors, and was suddenly seized with a fit of mad abandon.

With a long groaning sigh, she began to gyrate her hips slowly in time to the movements of her fingers. If they wanted a show, she'd give them one. But then they were all forgotten as the tide of orgasm surged over her and, with a choked cry from behind the gag, Alison toppled forward onto her knees, the juices of her passion seeping traitorously between her fingers.

Kristin allowed her only a minute or so to recover, while she returned to the cupboard and began selecting more things.

'Up!' she snapped, dropping her burden onto the floor. 'Kneel up and hold out your arms. Mutely, Alison obeyed, and thick padded cuffs were buckled and locked around both wrists, the single connecting link holding them close together. As soon as the second lock had been snapped into place, Kristin turned her about and guided Alison to stand beneath the dangling chain. 'Raise your arms,' she commanded. 'No, higher than that. Damn!' she cursed as it became evident that the chain did not extend low enough, even when Alison's arms were lifted at full stretch.

For a moment Alison thought she had escaped this particular part of the ordeal, but it was not to be. Kristin spun on her heel and strode across to the wall opposite, flipping open a cunningly concealed panel to reveal a small control panel. At the touch of a button a motor somewhere above began to quietly hum and the chain descended another foot. Closer to it now, Alison could see that the lowest link was in fact some sort of snap catch and, within seconds of the motor stopping, Kristin had attached it to the link between her manacles.

Once again the motor started, but this time the chain began to ascend, rather than descend. What little slack there had been was soon taken up and Alison felt her arms being dragged and stretched until finally, standing on tiptoe, she saw Kristin shut the mechanism off. The position Alison now found herself in was painful in the extreme, the muscles in her arms, shoulders and calves screaming out for relief. She closed her eyes and prayed that Kristin would not keep her like this for long, and indeed the woman did not. There was worse to come.

From the small pile of accoutrements Kristin had brought from the cupboard, she now selected a steel bar, about eighteen inches in length, at either end of which was fastened a heavy leather strap. Bending down, the woman quickly buckled one of these about Alison's left ankle, then pushed her legs roughly apart and repeated the process on the right. The effect was to deprive Alison of almost all of what little support her feet had been able to offer her, transferring even more strain onto her arms. Yet still Kristin was not satisfied, for the tube proved to be two tubes, one telescoping inside the other. With a grunt, Kristin began extending the bar, locking it off when about fifteen inches of the inner bar had been extended, so that Alison's ankles were held about two and a half feet apart and her toes now completely out of contact with the stone floor.

Kristin stood up, and with a derisive sneer she raised one boot and thrust it against Alison's left heel, setting her slowly spinning like a grotesque marionette.

'A satisfying sight,' Kristin laughed. It was a thin, mirthless sound. She allowed Alison to continue turning for a minute or so, before sticking out a leg to halt the sickening motion.

'Just one more thing to do,' she said, walking back to the cupboard. The chain started to rotate again, only this time far more slowly, so that Alison was left dangling with her back to her captor, unable to see what she was doing. It was not long before she found out, though.

She felt a hand on her buttocks, the fingers forcing their way between the taut rubber of her thong, pulling it down and to one side, and then another pressure against her bottom hole, cold and slippery. For a second her muscles tensed, resisting, but Alison realised it was a futile gesture. She forced herself to relax and grunted into the gag as the oiled dildo was pushed up inside her and the crotch of the panties snapped back into place over it.

'We'll leave your cunt,' Kristin said, turning her around to face her again. 'The Master will want to attend to that himself.' She reached out and tweaked Alison's nipples and Alison felt them hardening once again. Kristin laughed her reedy laugh. 'Oh yes, you really are a dirty little whore, aren't you?' she taunted. 'I wonder how randy you'll be when Master Ralph's through with you.'

Marcia Davenport surveyed the naked figure stretched out on the bedframe before her. The man's limbs were spreadeagled and cuffed and chained to the four corners of the sturdy timber construction, the body face down so that the bare metal diamond mesh pressed hard into the chest muscles and the softer flesh of the somewhat flabby stomach. The man's penis and balls, although blocked from her view as she stood, had been threaded through one of the gaps and Melanie had then secured the thin strap about the scrotum and attached the small lead weight to its hook.

Her actions had elicited nothing more than a muffled grunt from their victim, for beneath the all enveloping leather hood his mouth was efficiently gagged with a large, soft rubber ball. Marcia smiled to herself, wondering what the various employees of the local branch of Marston's Bank would think of their usually so prim and austere manager if they could see him now.

Simon Ffoukes-Baker instilled something akin to terror in the various young females who worked under him, Marcia knew. And she could imagine some of the reactions if they ever discovered his secret vice. But then Marcia knew a lot about a lot of people and their secret vices.

Like the mousy nursing sister who enjoyed being tied, spanked and blindfolded and then being left in a room to be taken and used by men she could not see, satisfied only when she had been ravished by at least three unknown assailants. The fact that the three parts were usually played by one man, with half hour or so intervals in between, did not matter. The woman would never discover the truth and the man in question would leave well satisfied himself, his contribution helping to swell Marcia's already formidable coffers.

There was always a greater degree of satisfaction for Marcia if she could pair up two clients like that. If she couldn't, there was no shortage of paid volunteers no more than a telephone call away. But Marcia, businesslike to the tips of her elegantly manicured fingers, was always aware of overheads, and if both parties were paying rather than one being paid, so much the better.

Marcia beckoned Melanie, who walked around the bed and handed her the riding crop.

'You see to him,' she said, her voice barely more than a whisper, though it was doubtful whether the banker would have been able to make out what she was saying even if she had spoken in a normal conversational turn. Beneath the hood, in addition to the gag, Simon's ears had been plugged with soft rubber inserts and covered with thick leather and foam pads. All he would hear, Marcia knew, was a distant and very vaguely muffled sound. Apart from that, his only audio stimulation would be the pounding of the blood in his heart and head and the sound of his own breathing.

'Mistress?' Melanie's big eyes opened wide in query. Marcia winked.

'It's a bloody freebie and I'm tired,' she said. 'Besides, he'll never know the difference. Just make sure you don't forget to put a sheath on him before the second session, otherwise I'll have you licking the floor clean afterwards.'

'And if the second session doesn't bring him off,' Melanie asked, 'should I masturbate him to a finish, or do I have a free rein?'

Marcia regarded her maid severely. 'You wank him,' she said, sternly. 'This is a valued client and I don't want you giving him any unwanted shocks.'

Melanie looked a little crestfallen, but Marcia was adamant. Simon Ffoukes-Baker was a masochist who got his kicks from being subjugated and maltreated by women and, as far as she knew, that was it. If he ever found out what the demur little maid really had hidden in her knickers, the banker would probably run a mile!

'See to him efficiently and you can have one of the girls during tonight's little cabaret,' Marcia promised. 'And maybe one of the boys as well,' she added, 'depending on who actually turns up.'

'Maybe it'll be Robin,' Melanie suggested, wistfully. Marcia shrugged.

'It's quite possible,' she agreed. 'He only missed out on the part last time because he was in New York. Now, be a good little transvestite and get on with it. When you're through, leave him for ten minutes before you release him, then you can tell him I've already gone upstairs. And remind him I want to see him before he leaves.'

'Very nice,' Ralph Hancock murmured, echoing the sentiments expressed by Kristin not so long before. He slowly turned the helpless Alison around, his hands travelling lightly over her exposed flesh, fingers probing and exploring. Alison stared mutely ahead, determined not to betray any apprehension, though her heart was pounding like a steam hammer.

The cock inside her rectum seemed to have grown and her sex was hot and soaking, and she wondered how long it would be before Hancock finally filled it for her. There was little doubting that the man was massively endowed, for the costume he had donned left little to the imagination.

He wore thick, heavy ankle boots, above which was a pair of what could best be described as black leather chaps, which left his groin and buttocks fully exposed. His cock had been laced into a sort of sheath, which also enclosed his testicles and, while it was in place, he was unable to attain anything like a full erection. However, what was already on view was impressive and Alison felt her vagina twitching at the thought of what it would look like when it was fully aroused.

'It doesn't look as though you've had a taste of the whip, little girl,' the big man said. 'At least, not recently. What

100

did your Mistress use on you? Strap? Paddle? Bare hand?'
He continued to stroke her, his hands cupping her buttocks.

'It would be a shame to mark these lovely things,' he said, 'so I hope you've learned obedience properly. Meanwhile, we'll just warm them up a little.' He moved out of Alison's field of vision and, when he returned, he held up the long paddle for her to see. The handle was made of braided leather, similar to the crop, but instead of the vicious tapering end, there was fixed to it a broad rectangle of thick rubber. It would sting and no doubt it would make her flesh turn a bright pink, but it would not cut into the skin and any marks it left would fade quite quickly.

What followed, however, was far more painful than Alison had expected, for Hancock was clearly a master of his art. Stepping behind her he delivered two hard whacks, one across each cheek, drawing a muffled yelp from behind her gag. Two more blows were then aimed at her upper thighs, making Alison buck wildly in her bonds, for they hurt even more than the first strokes. What she was not prepared for was the third pair of strokes.

Hancock stepped back around in front of her and, with two deft flicks of the wrist, delivered a stinging whack across each breast in turn. He employed far less force than for the first four strokes, but his aim was unerring, landing square across each nipple, and Alison shrieked through her gagged mouth like a cat with its tail caught in a door.

'Obviously not so experienced as that bitch led me to believe,' Hancock murmured, as much to himself as to Alison. He raised the paddle again, but this time it was only to draw it softly across Alison's now bright red globes, pressing it down on each nipple and bringing an involuntary groan from deep within her. 'However,' he added, with evident satisfaction, 'the pain does seem to turn you on.'

With his free hand he reached out, cupping the mound of her sex, his middle finger sliding into her wet slit. Alison could feel the beginnings of another orgasm building and shuddered uncontrollably.

'Oh yes, indeed,' Hancock breathed. 'Very promising. *Very* promising.' The finger found her clitoris and began massaging it slowly. Alison writhed helplessly to his touch, all thoughts driven from her mind except one. She peered down through misty eyes, fixing her gaze on that massive, leather sheathed organ, wanting it, needing it, wishing she could beg for it. Hancock understood, but he was not about to give her the release she so desperately desired.

'Not yet, my moist little Mitzi,' he laughed, withdrawing his finger and breaking the contact with her. 'Soon, yes, but not yet.' He stepped back and swung the paddle again.

'I think we shall have to take a hand,' Marcia sighed, replacing the receiver onto its cradle. Across the desk Melanie stood demurely, hands together in front of her, like a naughty schoolgirl waiting to hear the verdict from her headmistress. 'Michael doesn't quite seem to understand what he's up against here, and for all I've said, young Alley Cat is probably in way over her head.

'She's a natural submissive, despite her modern Sixties Miss appearance and attitude in her normal life, but that may not be enough. If my – no, *when* my delightful ex-husband gets carried away, she will almost certainly find things a bit too much for her. He was bad enough ten years ago, but he's been getting progressively worse. Quite frankly, I think he's now completely lost the plot.

'I don't know how much money he's raking in from all his scams, but I do know it's a lot. All that wealth and power has turned his head completely and I wouldn't put anything past him now. He's got so many influential people in his pocket that he probably believes he can get away with anything, and he may even be right.' Marcia stood up and walked slowly around the desk, placing her hands upon Melanie's shoulders.

'I need your help, my little buttercup,' she said. Melanie's eyes betrayed nothing.

'In what way, Mistress?' she said. Marcia paused, looking for the right words to express what she wanted to say.

'Despite everything,' she began, 'I have no right to demand you do this, but I am asking you.'

'Asking me what, Mistress?'

'Asking you to go into Dennison Hall as backup for Alison.'

'Me?' Melanie said. 'In Dennison Hall? What good would I be?'

'To be honest, I'm not entirely sure,' Marcia admitted. 'But I have a few rough ideas. Firstly, when I take the bank details to Ralph, I'll tell him that I have to go away on business for a few days and ask him if I can leave you with him for safekeeping. I think he'll jump at the chance of having your special talents available for a little while. I'll insist that he is not to use the whip on you as that is my prerogative, though I'm afraid I'll have to agree to him using you in other ways – his clients too, no doubt.'

Melanie's lips twitched in the ghost of a smile. 'I don't think that would be too great a chore, Mistress,' she said, her voice deadpan. Marcia's own face broke into a real smile.

'No, I don't suppose it would, would it, you little tart? In fact, I imagine the thought of getting those lips around a few nice juicy cocks has all the appeal in the world.'

Melanie's face was a picture of innocence. 'I try to please, Mistress,' she said.

Marcia laughed out loud. 'You certainly do,' she agreed. 'But this will also be very dangerous. Firstly, you will have to carry in Michael's special camera, plus a set of lock picks.'

'Lock picks?' Melanie echoed. 'But I don't know how to use them.'

'Not yet you don't,' Marcia said. 'But you will after I've given you a crash course. It's surprisingly easy, once someone shows you the knack. I learned years ago. It's a handy skill to have in this game, just in case keys get broken or lost. Your average lock is easy pickings, if you'll pardon the pun. Security locks are a lot harder, but then Ralph wouldn't spend out on that sort of lock any more than I would.

'Basic two and three lever locks are more than enough to hold any slave, willing or unwilling, and I can open a three lever padlock in thirty seconds flat. In a couple of hours time you'll be able to match that, I should think.'

'But how am I supposed to get the camera and picks in?' Melanie asked. 'You told Michael that they'd have been on to Alison if she'd tried.'

'I know,' Marcia nodded. 'But you're not Alison. Remind me, what bust size are you naturally?'

'Thirty-six A, Mistress,' Melanie answered. 'They don't seem to have grown much in the last three months, even though I take the tablets every evening and use the cream every morning.'

'I'm told that's not unusual,' Marcia said, soothingly. 'But I'm also assured that it's only a temporary state. You'll have nice big boobies eventually, my little narcissus. In the meantime, that's to our advantage. I want you to go and search out one of your original corsets that you used to wear when you first came to me, one with soft rubber padding, not the fancy so-called lifelike inserts.'

Light dawned in Melanie's eyes. 'Ah, I see,' she said, slowly. 'Very clever, Mistress. Very clever indeed.'

Marcia smiled, but grimly this time. 'Let's just hope it's not being *too* clever,' she said.

Sprawled face down on the cold stone floor, Alison felt as though her entire body was on fire, but at least there was now relief for her arms and shoulders. Her hands were still manacled and the spreader bar was still forcing her legs wide, but she no longer cared. There was only one thing she wanted now, and she knew it would not be long in coming.

'Up!' Hancock barked. 'Kneel up!' It was an awkward position, kneeling with her ankles so far apart, but gamely Alison struggled to obey. She watched as Hancock slowly undid the laces that held the pouch about his genitalia, sliding it off to reveal his manhood in all its naked glory.

'That's the only disadvantage of keeping you gagged,' he smirked. 'A nice soft mouth is the best aid to full arousal.' He stepped closer to her, so that the semi-tumescence was only inches from Alison's face. 'However, you still have the use of your hands,' he growled. Tentatively, Alison reached up and took the steadily thickening shaft in her right hand, twisting her left to keep it out of the way. Slowly, she began massaging him, a gentle masturbatory action which instantly began to take effect. Within a matter of seconds Hancock was fully erect, and a staggering sight it made, for now Alison could not close her fingers about his shaft by some way.

She caught her breath, staring at his organ in dread fascination. She knew that books often held tales of men endowed to ridiculous proportions and that the reality was that very few boasted more than six or seven inches, and many far less, but this was really something else. Hancock's shaft reared rigidly upright to a length that had to be between nine and ten inches. Alison wished the gag was not in her mouth, for she would have dearly loved to replace it with what was now on offer.

'Like what you see, little slut?' Hancock chuckled. Alison nodded, meaning it sincerely. 'Then let's try it out, shall we?' He reached out, seizing Alison by the neck and forcing her head down to the floor as he walked around behind her. 'Keep that arse well up, tart, or I'll beat it again... with a proper whip this time.'

Alison needed no such threats to convince her. She just hoped that Hancock wouldn't waste any more time.

He didn't.

Dropping to his knees between her splayed calves, he took his manhood and guided it unerringly to her gaping slit, pushing its head in without ceremony or consideration. Even though she was as well lubricated to receive it as she could ever hope to be, Alison still gasped at its size as it entered her.

'Now, you push back, bitch!' Hancock rasped. Alison needed no second bidding, but she did so slowly, savouring every inch as it penetrated her, until finally her buttocks thrust hard against his groin so that the anal plug was pushed even deeper inside her and she was fully impaled. His powerful hands grasped her hips, holding her rigidly for several seconds, and she guessed he was savouring her wet heat in the same way she was savouring him.

Dimly, Alison remembered that this man was supposed to be the villain of the piece, an unprincipled extortionist and much worse besides, but right then it didn't seem to matter. Right then, Ralph Hancock was simply a damned good looking man who was, she hoped, about to give her the fucking of a lifetime. She braced herself and was not kept waiting long.

Slowly, deliberately, Hancock began to piston in and out of her, one hand coming around and down to seek her clitoris and begin stimulating it in time with his rhythm. It was too much for Alison and she came immediately, groaning and slobbering into her gag, her whole body convulsing helplessly, so that Hancock was again forced to grip her with two hands in order to prevent her from collapsing altogether.

The man was relentless and a second orgasm quickly built and exploded, followed by a third. Alison lost count as her world dissolved into one long roller-coaster pleasure-ride, and then finally sunk into a black velvet pit just as Hancock's own climax began jetting hot streams deep into her belly.

It was necessary for Melanie to change into something a little more conventional for the drive to Dennison Hall. Marcia drove a car with heavily tinted windows, but unlike her ex-husband, she did not believe in taking unnecessary risks. One nosey policeman looking into the back seat and seeing a figure dressed in such an obviously outlandish costume as Melanie's maid uniform certainly was, would not on its own be too much of a problem. After all, there was nothing illegal in riding around dressed in whatever fashion you chose, so long as it did not offend public decency. And it was decidedly unlikely that anyone would suspect Melanie's real gender, but policemen, in Marcia's experience, tended to be more than just nosey.

The car was registered in her own name and address, and any copper with his fair share of inquisitiveness might be tempted to take a closer look at the house. On the outside there was nothing to mark it from any other house in the area, but if any sort of watch were to be mounted, the number of callers might just arouse the suspicions another notch. The growing drug culture also meant that it was quite easy for the police to obtain search warrants, often just on some so-called suspicion. Okay, they wouldn't find any illegal substances anywhere on any of her property, but Marcia could imagine their faces if they saw the basement area, especially if they just happened to burst in during a major session. She suppressed a little laugh at the thought as she climbed into the back of the Daimler herself.

No, much better to let Melanie do the driving; that was part of what she paid the prissy little tart for anyway, and the simple white blouse and white leather miniskirt were nothing if they weren't fashionable. With her long hair swept up and a pair of very expensive gold and diamond rings in her ears, the maid would look like a little rich girl driving her daddy's big expensive car with the driver's window wide open. She would turn a few heads, but she wouldn't arouse anything other than the odd manhood.

'I've told Ralph that I don't expect him to use a whip on you,' Marcia said, as Melanie eased the powerful car out into the main stream of traffic. 'And neither is anyone else to, though they may well use a paddle or a strap instead... unless they find the camera and lock picks, of course.'

Melanie instinctively looked down at her now well endowed figure. 'I think they should be all right where they are, Mistress,' she said. 'Even if someone removes the corset, they would be very lucky to find anything, unless they knew in advance that something was there.'

'Let's hope you're right,' Marcia said. 'Now, it's still not too late to change your mind. This could be very dangerous for you, not to mention the fact that it'll probably be a bit of an ordeal anyway.'

Melanie stifled a little giggle. 'Nothing I haven't seen before,' she said. 'And I'm a big girl now.'

'No, you just wish you were,' Marcia laughed, trying to

ease the tension she was feeling. 'But I mean what I say. I wouldn't want you to go through with this just because you thought that a refusal might offend me. That wouldn't be at all fair.'

'No, Mistress,' Melanie agreed. She changed lanes and then half turned her head back towards Marcia. 'Actually,' she said, 'it's quite exciting. A bit like that Cathy Gale woman on the television. Did you see that episode where she had that gorgeous leather catsuit on?'

'No, but I've heard about it,' Marcia said. 'Just remember though, this isn't a television programme. Cathy Gale isn't really a judo expert, and there's no John Steed waiting to pop up at just the right moment. There's just me and Michael's Irish laddie, and there'll be a twelve foot fence and a pack of vicious dogs between us and you.'

'I know, Mistress,' Melanie said, cutting back into the left hand lane again. 'I will be very careful. I've got more to lose than a real girl, after all!'

'That's not funny!' Marcia snapped. 'I wouldn't put anything past Ralph.'

'No, Mistress,' Melanie said, soberly.

'All you have to do is await the right moment and then try to get one of you into a position where you can get photographs that we can use to put paid to his nasty little operation. You've got two spools of film and there are fifty exposures on each. According to Michael, you just point it and press the top and it does the rest itself. The round bit at the bottom contains the film, and when you've used it all you just twist and pull. The replacement cartridge goes on by reversing the process.

'And, assuming you get the chance, you must tell Alison not to take any risks at all. You'll be bringing out the films and then I'll work out a way to get her out of there afterwards. An ailing granny or sister, something like that.'

'I'm still not sure what we're supposed to be looking for,' Melanie pointed out.

'Nor am I, but then I'm not a trained journalist,' Marcia said. 'Alison will know and she'll tell you, but be on your toes for any opportunity if it comes along. I'll be collecting you again in three days, and there won't be a second opportunity.'

Chapter Six

Old Maid

The sound of Kristin's voice finally penetrated the fog and Alison forced her eyes open. She was still lying on the hard stone floor where she had finally passed out, and by the feel of her joints she had been unconscious for quite some time. She automatically made to roll over on her back, only for the attempt to be brought up short by the leg spreader, which was still in place, as were the wrist restraints.

With a groan she managed to haul herself up into a kneeling position, but it needed Kristin's assistance before she could stand. The tall blonde looked her up and down, her narrow features an impassive mask.

'All a bit too much for us, was it?' she taunted. 'We'll have to work on building up your stamina. Master Ralph is good, I know, but you'll be expected to handle far more than that if you're to remain here.' She stooped and began unlocking the ankle cuffs and Alison gratefully assumed a less strenuous position, though the woman made no attempt to remove the wrist straps. Instead, she produced a broad leather belt, which she looped about Alison's waist and buckled in the small of her back. Then, with a small padlock, she secured the link between the cuffs to a sturdy ring sewn into the front of the belt, holding Alison's arms tight against her body.

'That should keep you out of trouble,' Kristin remarked. 'And now I suppose we'll have to feed and water you, so 'let's have you sitting down while I take that mask off.'

To Alison the relief of being able to close her mouth again and to breathe without the rasping sound of air going in and out the nostril apertures was almost as ecstatic as a minor orgasm. And the bliss of being able to feel the cool air on her cheeks again!

'Thank you, Mistress,' she said, quietly. Kristin glared at her.

'You were not given permission to speak, slut!' she barked. 'I will overlook the transgression, as you're new here, but remember in the future. Slaves do not speak unless directly asked a question, or expressly told to make a certain statement. Do you understand that?'

Alison nodded fervently. 'Yes, Mistress. I'm truly sorry Mistress.'

'Make sure you are,' Kristin said, laying the mask with its blonde tresses on the top of one of the low cupboards. She turned back and regarded Alison critically. 'Yes, very pretty indeed,' she conceded, acidly. 'But I'm sure we can do something about that. You'll be on basic domestic duties for your first three or four days, so your facial appearance won't be that important.

'You should thank me, really. The makeup will disguise your true features, which is what Master Ralph wants for now, so you won't have to wear that hot mask for a while. You'll be gagged most of the time, naturally, but even that will be less arduous than what you have been wearing.

'Meanwhile,' she said, fumbling for the zip at the crotch in her leotard, 'I will let you thank me in a suitable fashion. After that, assuming I'm satisfied with your performance, you shall eat. Now, down on your knees and get that pretty little mouth open, slut!'

Ralph Hancock was feeling extremely pleased with himself. Not that this was an unusual state of affairs, for Hancock almost always felt pleased with himself. But today was extra special. He turned the small package over in his hands and patted it contentedly.

'Smart bastards, the Yanks,' he said to the empty room. 'I wonder what they'll come up with next.'

The new recording technology had cost Hancock a pretty packet, but already it was paying for itself in spades. Inside the brown paper wrapped box was a flat tape cartridge, upon which was recorded three hours of frenzied activity from inside one of the deep cellar rooms. It clearly depicted the "star" of the show in an exhausting series of depraved escapades that he would not want made available for general consumption.

And it was all so much better than using the old-fashioned cine camera. Not only was there no developing – the results were available for perusal immediately – but the cameras were completely noiseless as the images were transmitted to the recording system electronically. The people being filmed thus had no idea at all that their antics were being filed away for future use.

The subject of this particular "video", as the Americans called it, was a fairly senior man in the Foreign Office. Not quite the Foreign Secretary himself, but not that far down the ladder and quite likely to assume the top job when the present, somewhat aging, incumbent finally settled for the peerage that all Westminster knew would soon be offered him. When that day came Ralph's library footage would become even more valuable, but already it was worth its weight in diamonds.

Just one copy of the tape before him – he kept several copies of each and had them safely stored at a variety of locations about the country – had been more than enough

113

to convince his victim that a certain shipbuilding contract really ought to go to a certain firm, which in turn had already rewarded Ralph more than generously for his part in the affair. And that was just the beginning. The Ministry of Defence was about to order a completely new style of army camouflage jacket and Ralph's man also sat on its budgeting committee, along with another of Ralph's regular clients, who was now also the proud possessor of a living colour record of his time at Dennison Hall.

They really should be grateful to him, Ralph mused. After all, he had even supplied them with the machines to play their tapes on and they would not be available in the UK for another year or so at least, according to the company that was developing them. At present they were so large, cumbersome and expensive that only wealthy organisations could afford to use them, which had started another train of thought in Ralph's devious brain.

He grinned to himself and put the package into the top drawer of his desk, locking it as the light knock came on the door. He barked out the permission to enter and the door swung open to admit the tall figure of Kristin. The dominatrix was clad in her working outfit – or one of them – but then she never wore what Ralph referred to as "civvies" when she was at the house. In fact, as far as he knew, she always dressed in the same bizarre fashion, simply donning a long leather coat to hide the fact whenever she drove out beyond the high gates at the end of the drive.

'Has the new girl recovered yet?' Hancock asked.

Kristin gave him one of her rare smiles. 'She's having a little difficulty sitting down at the moment,' she replied, 'but she's basically okay.'

Hancock nodded. 'What do you think of her?' he asked. 'I presume you've had a look at her face now?'

'You won't be disappointed,' Kristin assured him. 'She'll

prove a big hit, I'm sure. Why don't you just take a look for yourself?'

Ralph chuckled. 'It's all part of the game, sweetie,' he said. 'You ought to know me by now. I like to do things differently. That's why you and I get on so well. Apart from me, you're the most devious and ingenious bugger I know.'

'I'll take that as a compliment.'

'It was meant as one. Now, tell me, what have you got lined up for little Miss Mitzi?'

'I thought I'd keep her on basic household duties for a few days, you know, all nicely plugged and so on. And I also thought of another nice little touch.'

'Go on.' Ralph eased forward in his seat a little. He liked it when Kristin came up with her "nice little touches", and he knew he would enjoy whatever it was she was planning. Kristin pulled back the chair opposite and lowered herself onto it.

'Well, you know little Lord Fauntleroy's particular predilection?' She was referring to a certain peer of the land who had inherited his title, together with an estate the size of Oxford at the tender age of seventeen. The young man was still only twenty-five, but certain experiences from his youth had made a lasting impression on him. Apparently, his sexual awakening had come courtesy of one of his late father's housemaids; not the usual pert little madam so favoured by novelists, but a rather older femme fatale and one with looks that conjured up expressions concerning buses and their back ends.

Sadly for the young lord, the front end of a bus had finally terminated the poor woman's earthly tenure and he had never been able to find a replacement. The trouble was, as he once confided to Ralph, although the woman was in her sixties and looked it, she had somehow retained the figure of a woman half her age.

'No problem,' Ralph had assured his new young friend, and no problem it turned out to be, especially as Hancock's retinue had recently been joined by a girl who was an expert makeup artist, as well as a died-in-the-wool dominant lesbian. In the space of a few hours she had taken one of the regular slave girls and transformed her pretty and youthful features into a face that should have been atop flannelette knickers and bodices, rather than basques, stockings and suspenders. The young aristocrat had been delighted and had since savoured the favours of most of Ralph's stable.

None of the girls were that keen, however. Not because of the client, who was always gentle, courteous and kind with them, but because of the long session beforehand with the makeup artist and the fact that, if they caught sight of their reflections in a mirror, unless they were prepared for it it came as a horrible shock.

'You're thinking of giving her over to the noble lord, then?' Ralph said. Kristin grinned, lopsidedly.

'Not just that,' she said. 'I thought she could stay that way for the time she's doing domestics. That way his lordship can re-enact a few old memories. I believe he's due here tomorrow for a short break. Perhaps he'd care to extend his stay a little longer.'

'And increase his subscription accordingly,' Ralph said. 'Yes, I'll put it to him.'

'And I thought you might like to try her again when she's ready,' Kristin added. 'Her own mother wouldn't recognise her, after all, so you'll still be keeping your little air of mystery.'

'Very true,' Ralph agreed. 'Yes, I like it, and furthermore, we can try another little experiment. My dear ex-wife will be arriving tomorrow. She's brought some papers to do with the girl – her real name's Louise MacIntosh, by the way. It's quite a drive, so I've offered her dinner. We can have Mitzi to serve at table and see if dear Marcia recognises her.'

'She won't,' Kristin said, confidently. 'Linda's too good at what she does.'

'There's no such thing as being too good,' Ralph told her. 'In fact, you've given me another idea. Tell Linda to see to Mitzi first thing and be on standby for another job around teatime. I think we'll have two maids tomorrow night.'

Kristin regarded him quizzically. 'Who have you in mind for the second one?'

Ralph laughed and put a finger to his lips. 'That'd be telling,' he said.

Mike Hallet crouched beside the open door of the Daimler and spoke quietly to Marcia.

'I've been thinking,' he said, seriously. 'I'm only going to give it another four days and then, unless I've heard from Alison that everything's okay, I'm going to blow the whistle on the whole thing.'

Marcia looked at him dubiously from the back seat of her car.

'Knowing Ralph, that might not prove as simple as you imagine,' she said, darkly. 'It's one thing to pop along and spill the beans to the local plod, but quite another getting something done about it. Ralph's got contacts everywhere. The Met, the local country lot, magistrates, judges, lawyers – the lot. I'd rate your chances at getting that place raided as marginally better than that of a snowball in hell.'

'Haven't you got any more contacts of your own?' Mike pleaded.

Marcia shrugged. 'Plenty, but they're strictly second

division compared to what that bastard can call on. There is one possibility, but I wouldn't want to try it unless there was absolutely no other way. For a start it's not legal, and I do mean not legal. Secondly, it could start something akin to world war three and a lot of people could get hurt in the crossfire, in more ways than one.

'No, I reckon we'll just have to keep our fingers crossed. If the girls can come up with the evidence, you can at least force a few of his stooges to resign from the various positions of power they hold. That would at least weaken his set up to start with, and maybe start some sort of domino effect in motion.'

'Meanwhile I feel so bloody helpless,' Mike groaned. 'There's absolutely nothing I can do at my end until I hear from Alison.'

'They also serve, and all that,' Marcia soothed him, extending a gloved hand to pat his arm. 'Your turn will come. Meanwhile, have a bit of faith in your Alley Cat and Melanie here. I reckon they make a formidable team – our A Team, we should think of them as.'

'That sounds like the title of some TV show,' Mike grunted. 'I'm surprised no one's thought of it before.'

Marcia smiled. 'Oh they will, sweetie,' she said. 'They will.'

Alison stared at herself in the long mirror and shuddered, not just at the picture she presented, but at the devious mind that could think up something like this and at the even weirder minds that actually found something like this exciting. She shook her head slowly and the grey-haired old maid in the glass copied her.

A few hours earlier, Alison would not have believed such a transformation to be possible, despite what Kristin had said to her the previous day. She had been allowed to sleep during the night with only a minimum of restraint; a chain locked from the foot of the bed and then locked about her left ankle, and her wrists shackled to either side of her waist belt.

'Just enough to keep your fingers out of temptation's way, slut,' Kristin had told her. Alison was too tired to think about such things and grateful, as well as surprised, that the mattress on the bed was very comfortable. It would not have surprised her if she'd been left chained to a bare frame, or even made to sleep on the floor. But then, she reasoned, it would not be to their advantage if they had a bunch of slave girls all crippled with bad backs and stiff joints.

It appeared that all the slaves slept at the cellar level, but in a different area from where the "games" rooms were. Each girl – and boy too, for all she knew – had a separate cell about eight feet by six, in which was a single bed, a hand-basin and a bare toilet pedestal. The ankle chain was just long enough to enable Alison to reach the latter facility, though she was forced to sit upon it with her left leg stretched out before her.

She was awoken by a new face at what she later discovered was seven in the morning. This time the woman was slightly older than Kristin, possibly in her late thirties, and was built on an altogether different scale. Her corset was having to work hard to restrain her massive breasts, which threatened to overflow their cups at every movement. And her hips and upper thighs, where they emerged from the high leather boots, would not have looked out of place on a wrestler. Only her waist, constricted by the tight lacing, was dainty, giving her a curious hourglass figure that was almost comic. Alison wondered how much of that shape was really due to the leather corset and how much was natural. Surely no one could endure being laced that severely?

The woman, whose black hair was pinned up and back in a severe style, introduced herself as Mistress Paula, speaking in a surprisingly soft voice as she unlocked the ankle chain. However, she was not so gentle as she buckled the leather collar about Alison's throat and jerked on the leash.

'Come along,' she chided. 'We don't have all day, and you'll need feeding again before I dress you. Only first, we need to strip and shower you. You really do smell disgusting.'

Alison had not really noticed, but now as her foggy brain began to slowly clear, she realised the woman was right. The combination of stale sweats, bodily fluids and warm rubber really was awful and she was glad to be stripped and pushed under the showerhead in the tiled room at the end of the corridor. Paula, who had only removed the belt and wrist restraints once they got into the shower room, tossed Alison a bar of soap.

'Better do a thorough job,' she warned. 'It may be a few days before you get another chance.'

After the shower, belt and cuffs once more in place, Alison was led back along the corridor, past her cell and on towards the other side of the subterranean complex. On the way they passed a curious looking couple coming in the opposite direction. The handler was a tiny Chinese woman with black hair and deep, dark eyes, dressed similarly to Alison's handler and with a stunning figure. Her tiny feet looked as though they might break at any moment and her ankles were far too slim for the towering heels, but she walked with perfect poise and the grace of a born dancer. The two women exchanged brief nods as they passed, but Alison's attention was more taken by the figure on the end of the Chinese woman's leash.

It was female, without a doubt, its shaven sex more

prominent than anything Alison had imagined possible. The swollen nipples at the tip of each heavy breast was pierced with a thick gold ring, a chain hanging between them and jingling at every awkward step the girl took in the high shoes which were locked about her ankles. However, it was not the shoes that were the biggest impediment to the poor creature's progress, but the thick leather hood that encased her head. For apart from a horizontal zipped opening, currently closed over the mouth, and two tiny steel-ringed holes to admit air to her nostrils, the mask had no other openings and its wearer was forced to stagger along completely blind.

Not only that, but her arms were bound behind her, fastened cruelly together inside a curious leather glove or sleeve affair, her elbows all but touching, so that she was denied even the use of her hands to navigate the narrow passageways.

Paula sensed Alison's curiosity.

'Punishment,' she explained. 'She got too carried away and used her teeth on a client who doesn't go in for that kind of thing. As a result she wears that lot for five days and nights, and spends any time when she's not needed for anything more productive by sitting on a punishment perch. She's only got one day left to go, but of course she won't know that.

'She hasn't seen any light for four days, and the helmet is padded over the ears, so she won't have any way of calculating time. I'm told that after even an hour or two in one of those it feels like a day already.'

Alison wanted to ask what a punishment perch was, but she had already taken in Kristin's instructions about not speaking unless directly spoken to, and kept her tongue firmly under control. She wanted to cause as few waves as possible, working on the theory that the less noticeable she was, the more chance she had of getting about the house and trying to prise its secrets from it. No doubt she would learn what a punishment perch was in good time, and just hoped it wouldn't be at first hand!

They saw nobody else before Paula eventually ushered Alison into a room that looked not unlike the sort of dressing rooms found backstage in thousands of theatres throughout the world. There was a long dressing table with a mirror set about by bare light bulbs running the length of one wall, and two large wardrobes set against one end. From one of these Paula started selecting various items of clothing, all, Alison noted, made from black latex, other than a set of white latex petticoats similar to those she'd worn beneath her maid's uniform the previous day.

A heavy corset came first, not that Alison was at all surprised. In her few days' experience of this strange subculture she had already understood the significance of tight lacing. It not only produced a far sexier figure, but the wearer was constantly reminded of her status, though she wondered what the psychological effect of wearing something like Paula's corset was on a dominant personality. She gave a mental shrug and gave up the struggle, concentrating instead on regulating her breathing as Paula steadily hauled in her waist.

The big woman was no Melanie and the garment was designed to be even more severe than the corset Alison had worn beneath her uniform at Marcia's and, by the time it was completely closed, Alison really felt as though she had been cut in two. She stared down at the narrow strip of leather that hung from the lower edge of the corset. No prizes for guessing *its* purpose, she thought, grimly. The two D-shaped rings, one stitched into either side at waist level, were more curious, but there were other things to occupy Alison's mind and she soon forgot about them as

Paula continued to prepare her.

Apart from the tightness of the new corset, the rest of Alison's uniform was quite similar to the original one, except that her stockings were not fishnet, but thin latex. They required a lot of effort and concentration to get into place, not to mention copious dustings with talcum powder to help the clinging fabric slide up her legs. But finally it was done and they were attached to the array of suspender straps that encircled the bottom of her corset, holding the tops high up her thighs, almost to crotch level.

Rubber gloves were then eased carefully up to her shoulders, their tops tucked out of sight beneath the white frills around the bottom of each puffed sleeve when the dress was added after the petticoats, and then high heeled ankle boots locked onto each foot in turn. The white latex apron, bedecked with even more extravagant frills, completed the ensemble, or so Alison thought. But Paula was not through yet.

She made Alison bend forward over the back of the seat and then carefully inserted two black dildos into her, drawing up the dangling strap to hold them in place and locking it to a ring in the back of the corset. She patted Alison's naked buttocks before allowing the petticoats and skirt to fall back into place.

'You'll enjoy those,' she promised, grimly. 'Meanwhile, don't sit down, apart from on a padded ring, or you'll turn the back one on.'

She reached inside the wardrobe again and, sure enough, withdrew an inflated rubber ring, not unlike the ones Alison had seen advertised for sufferers of piles. She placed it on the seat and laughed at Alison's confusion.

'They're vibrators, sweetie slut,' Paula explained. 'And there's a switch in the base of each one. The switches are stiff to operate, otherwise the crotch strap might start them up. But they're not that stiff, and banging your stuffed butt down onto a hard surface will set them off as sure as we're standing here.'

Alison lowered herself onto the ring very gingerly. Already the effect of all the rubber and the dual plugging was beginning to work its insidious spell, and she knew that if she set off either of the devices accidentally she would almost certainly climax before it could be turned off again. She didn't know what the penalty for having an unauthorised orgasm was, but she doubted it would be pleasant.

Still Paula was not through with her. Again from the cupboard she produced a pair of leather wrist cuffs, which were quickly locked into place. From inside the wrist of each one projected a steel staple, from which in turn hung four small metal links. Now, at last, Alison discovered the significance of the D-rings attached to the corset, for aligned with them in the rubber dress and previously unnoticed, were two narrow slits, through which Paula now deftly extracted them, locking each to one of the chains. In this fashion Alison retained sufficient use of her hands to be able to carry a tray, or wield a duster, but was unable to raise her hands above the level of her bust, rendering her unable to reach the lacing at the back of her uniform or corset. Even eating and drinking, she realised, would prove difficult, and she soon had the chance to test her theory.

The slave girl who brought the breakfast tray in was barely out of her teens, and wore a maid's uniform identical to Alison's own, except that there was also a cute little white latex cap perched atop her mop of red hair. She laid her burden carefully on the dressing table and stood back, looking at Paula questioningly. The big handler nodded curtly.

'You may go,' she told the girl. 'This slut can take her

own tray back to the kitchens when she's finished with. Then she can spend an hour washing up and scrubbing the floor.'

The food was not exciting; scrambled egg on toast with two rashers of grilled bacon and a large tumbler of a thick orange juice concoction, but Alison had not eaten for what seemed like a lifetime and she wolfed everything down as rapidly as her hampered hands would permit. Her appetite was not lost on Paula.

'The orange contains all sorts of vitamin and mineral substitutes, and a little something which helps suppress your appetite. Fat sluts are generally worthless, except for the odd client with a leaning in that direction. Right, if you're finished, get yourself over to that basin and clean your teeth.'

It was no easy challenge, bending her neck down towards her hand, and the handle of the toothbrush was barely long enough for the task. But somehow Alison managed and rinsed her mouth thoroughly, glad to be rid of the stale feeling and running her tongue around her teeth and gums appreciatively.

'Feeling better?' Paula demanded. She had something concealed in her hands.

Alison nodded. 'Yes, Mistress,' she replied, meekly. 'Thank you.'

'Then get your mouth open.'

Alison obeyed, and had only a brief glimpse of what Paula raised to her lips before it was inserted. What she saw resembled a segment of an orange, except that it was white and made of some sort of hard rubber or nylon. It fitted between Alison's teeth, and when she bit down as instructed she felt an extension piece between her teeth on either side. Another projection from the front reached back and held her tongue compressed into the bottom of her mouth.

Without the use of her hands Alison would have been hard enough pressed to expel the device, for it fitted snugly and tongue pressure alone would have been insufficient to force it out, but whoever had designed the contraption was leaving nothing to chance. By means of a small Allen key, Paula tightened a small clamp onto the inside of two upper and two lower molars on either side, holding Alison's jaws clamped immovably. Looking into the mirror, she saw that her lips were now held slightly apart, but all that was visible was a thin strip of white that would easily be mistaken for teeth.

Despite the fact that the gag was so complete, it was nowhere near as uncomfortable as a ball gag and totally undetectable in place. Alison had to admit it was an ingenious piece of work, even if it was her mouth it was in.

'All the maids wear these when they're on domestic duties,' Paula told her. 'We cannot be everywhere at once and it prevents idle chatter when sluts think they can't be overheard. Someone will remove it every few hours for you to eat, but it remains in place for drinking. You will find special cups in the kitchen fitted with thin tubes and these fit into this small hole here.' She inserted an index finger between Alison's lips and parted them to reveal a tiny aperture.

'It takes a little practice and concentration, but it works fine,' she concluded. 'Now, we'll just take care of your ankles and then Linda should be along to take care of your makeup. I'm sure you'll enjoy that.'

The ankle chain clipped between rings set on the insides of Alison's boots, and was little more than twelve inches long. To prevent it dragging on the floor a vertical chain was clipped to the centre link and drawn up and clipped to her crotch strap, immediately where it covered the vibrator in her vagina. All very neat, professional and carefully thought out, Alison was forced to admit, trying to keep her attention focussed away from the steadily rising heat deep inside her.

Paula motioned for her to stand and walk back and forth across the room, while she carefully checked that no further adjustments were needed. Eventually, the older woman signalled that she could stop.

'You'll do,' she said. 'Now you can sit there and stare at your pretty face until Mistress Linda gets here. You won't get the opportunity for such narcissism again for a few days.' She studied Alison carefully. 'Seems a waste to me,' she confessed, 'but then, as they say, it takes all sorts.'

She moved towards the door. 'I'll be back to collect you later,' she said. 'In the meantime, if you give Mistress Linda any trouble, I'll give you even worse.'

'How the hell am I going to give anybody any trouble like this?' Alison asked her reflection when the door had closed behind the big woman. She experimented a little with her shackled hands, but didn't manage to find any way of giving herself more freedom. No, the little outfit had been well thought out, she realised even more. They could put her to work and not have to worry that she was getting up to any mischief. Mind you, for the time being all she needed was her eyes. As long as she kept them open and her wits about her, she'd at least presumably be able to wander about the place and get some idea of where everything was. Trouble was, she could do with some sort of camera. She wondered what Mike was doing.

Alison's thoughts were interrupted by the arrival of the makeup expert. She had been half expecting someone in a white coat, or with some sort of professional looking apron, so she was unprepared for the figure who entered, and only the large case she hauled with her gave any indication as to her true role. Or maybe it was only one of two roles,

Alison thought, for her outfit was identical to those of the other handlers Alison had so far encountered there.

Mistress Linda was almost as tall as Kristin and nearly as blonde, though she was more rounded both in build and features. Her face might have been quite kind, but for the deliberately severe way in which she had made it up, arching eyebrows and deepening the eye sockets with lots of black and dark blue shadow. Her lips had been painted a purple colour that was very nearly black, and the white base makeup she had employed thus threw everything into even starker relief. All in all, Alison thought, Mistress Linda looked like something from a zombie horror movie.

She heaved the case up onto one end of the dressing top and stood back to survey the task in hand.

'Well, this will be a challenge,' she breezed, in a surprisingly hearty tone. Alison detected an Australian twang to her voice. 'Mind you, having said that, I've had plenty of practice. Now then, honey pot, have they gagged you?'

Alison gave her a mute nod and tried to part her lips further to display the plastic segment, but to no avail.

'Very sweet you look, too,' Linda chuckled. She drew another chair up and sat down, crossing her booted legs with a flourish. 'Now then, before I start, let me assure you that none of the procedures I use will cause you any pain. Oh, you look surprised that I should want to set your mind at ease?' She laid a gloved hand on Alison's rubber sheathed knee.

'Well, don't be. I'm a handler here, it's true, and I like to dominate, but usually I prefer doing it to men rather than women… and I'm rather good at it. I'm also rather good at what I'm about to do to you, but if I wasn't I doubt I'd have much contact with any of the female slaves here. So, I'm not going to hurt you and it's not my place to frighten

128

the pants off you, always supposing you're actually wearing any under that lot. No? Doesn't surprise me. Probably got you all plugged and ready for action, eh? Yes, thought so.' She chattered on, barely pausing for breath.

'Seems a bit of a bugger of a thing to do to a girl, if you ask me,' she continued. 'Bad enough having to shuffle about in all those chains doing housework, just to lend a bit of authenticity to the atmosphere for the bloody punters, without having a bloody vibrator buzzing away in your cunt. Back too? Yeah, well you see what I mean. Still, dominant or slave, we're all bloody minions around here at the end of the day, and Lord Lovehimself and Lady Po-face make all the rules.

'Mind you, don't you go telling anyone I said that.' Linda laughed again. 'Not that you can tell anyone at the moment, of course. No, I promise you, if I had my way I'd take that gag off you while I'm working, but if Big Tits or Po-face happened to come back before I'd finished and put it back on you, there'd be a fucking big ruction.

'Can't see their problem myself. After all, the punters don't get to come in here, so what's the point. I reckon they just love being able to push people around and give them a hard time. Either that or they believe in getting their money's worth. Anyway, now I've seen to the introductions – you're Mitzi, aren't you? – time to get stuck in. It takes a good couple of hours to ruin a lovely face like that, and the meter's running.'

It was nearer two and a half hours before the bluff Australian zombie girl was done, but in that time she more than proved her boast that she was good. Layer by layer she applied strips of thin latex, working them skillfully with fingers from which she had now removed her gloves, delicately brushing in little lines of something gooey and touching pigments into it as it hardened.

All the while she worked she talked, and Alison had to force herself to drag her concentration away from what she could see in the mirror to listen properly. It was a worthwhile effort, for she gleaned much useful information, which she carefully stored away for future reference, especially those things Linda said about Kristin. The thin, austere blonde handler was the nearest there was to a number two to Ralph Hancock and, if Linda's summation was to be believed, every bit as tricky and potentially dangerous. Alison studied Linda's reflection in the mirror and wondered if the woman knew of Hancock's hidden agenda of blackmail and extortion. She concluded it unlikely, but would have been willing to bet a week's salary that Kristin did.

At last Linda eased the grey wig into place, stretching the base so that it covered every trace of Alison's own hair, and then stepped back. Alison sat stock still, unable to move or to tear her gaze from the glass, for what she was now seeing was not only unbelievable, but quite possibly a glimpse of fifty years into her own future.

The woman that stared back at her still had all the appearance of youth from the neck down, but the face was that of a female nearer seventy than sixty, the features lined with age, the cheeks drooping, the double chin very unflattering.

'There you go, sport,' Linda shrugged. 'Just what the doctor ordered, though I can't see the point myself. Any bastard fancies a woman looking as haggard as you do must be some bugger of a weirdo. Still, aren't we all, in our own little ways?' She began packing things back into her case.

'One word of caution,' she advised. 'Even if you do get left with your hands free, don't try to take that stuff off. Apart from the bollocking you'll get, you'll like as not do

130

yourself some damage. There's special solvents I use for that, so I'll be seeing you when it's time to get your youth back. In the mean time, see you around, old girl,' she laughed.

Too bloody right, sport, Alison thought, continuing to stare at her new old self in fascinated horror.

Chapter Seven

Dinner for Two

'It's very decent of you to accommodate Melanie for me, Ralph,' Marcia Davenport purred. 'I could take her with me, I know, but I've several meetings and she tends to be a bit of a liability. I'd thought of leaving her in the hotel room, but you know what these places are like. Chambermaid lets herself in to do a bit of dusting, finds girl chained to bed, screams for manager, manager blows whistle.'

'You hadn't thought of leaving her unchained, I suppose?' Ralph Hancock suggested.

'You are joking?' Marcia exclaimed, throwing her hands up in an exaggerated gesture. 'The last time I tried that I came back to find the little slut in bed with said chambermaid. I was too late to stop the girl discovering Mel's little secret, so I had to find us a different hotel. I couldn't imagine that sort of gossip being kept quiet for long, and I didn't fancy the thought of all those eyes watching and so on.'

'What about a chastity belt? Out of sight, under the skirt, undetectable in place.'

'Except that wouldn't stop Melanie. She doesn't have to get it up to get it off, so to speak. She'd be just as happy lying with her head between some slut's thighs, tonguing her for hours at a time. Then when I need her she's too damned exhausted to be of much use.'

'I'm surprised you don't take the whip to her more often,'

Ralph grunted. 'I wouldn't let the deviant little bastard get away with half the things you do.'

Marcia smiled. 'No, I know you wouldn't, but then I'm not into not sparing the rod the way you are.' It was one of the main reasons behind their original splitting up. Marcia was not averse to administering a little pain in the course of bringing eventual pleasure, but Ralph was a dyed-in-the-wool sadist. He enjoyed thrashing a helpless slave for its own sake, and only Marcia's intervention had saved one particularly unfortunate girl from genuine harm. As it was, the whip marks had not faded for more than two months.

'In any case, darling,' Marcia continued smoothly, 'Melanie is something of a special case. She's my version of Kristin, except I can't trust her libido. Of course I could always leave her behind at my place. But then she'd just take advantage to laze about, and one call to my friendly locksmith and she'd be free to get up to all sorts of nonsense.

'No, as long as you promise not to let anyone whip her, I know she'll be better off here. I'm sure you can find plenty for her to do and it's a little more variety for your menu, so to speak, if only for a few days.'

'I might even make some use of her myself,' Ralph drawled.

Marcia looked surprised. 'You?' she said. 'I didn't think you were in to—'

'Men?' he finished for her. 'I'm not, but then Melanie's more female than male, isn't she? And she's got a mouth and at least one other orifice.'

Marcia looked dubious. 'I know, but that other orifice has its limits, and I'm not sure that you might not push it beyond them. You're not exactly lacking in that department, as I remember.'

Hancock laughed uproariously. 'You think I'd be too

much for the poor little slut to accommodate, do you? Well, you may be right, but it could be fun trying.'

'Not for Melanie,' Marcia pointed out.

Hancock gave her a crooked smile. 'In which case it might teach the tart to behave herself in future. Anyway, I've got a lot on my plate these next few days, so it probably won't come to it. Did you bring those papers, by the way?'

Marcia snapped open her handbag and extracted a long brown envelope, which she passed across to Hancock.

'How's Louise – I mean Mitzi – coming along?' she enquired. 'Do you think you've got your money's worth?'

'Early days,' Hancock said, tucking the envelope inside his jacket. 'But so far she's very promising, and Kristin confirms your opinion as to her looks. I shan't be tempted myself for a few days yet, so Kristin's come up with a good idea in the meantime.'

'Such as?'

Hancock tapped the side of his nose with an index finger. 'Stay to dinner and you'll see for yourself,' he told her.

Marcia looked uncertain. 'I don't know,' she said. 'I've got a long drive ahead of me. A good three hours.'

'Then stay overnight,' Hancock offered. 'There are plenty of free guest rooms at the moment, and we can even offer you a little light relief, on the house, of course.'

'Of course,' Marcia smiled. 'Well, I suppose I could, as long as I get away early in the morning. My first meeting isn't until ten o'clock.'

'Phone ahead and put it back an hour or two and save yourself the rush,' Hancock said, walking across to the drink cabinet and selecting two tall glasses. 'I'm a great believer in doing things to suit my own convenience.'

'I remember,' Marcia replied, and she did. Ralph Hancock considered that the rest of the world had been created to revolve in an orbit of which he was the centre, and she had known him threaten to let a deal go rather than be put out of whatever routine he wanted to adopt. Strangely enough, he never seemed to lose out in the end, as the other party always seemed to come running back, tail between legs.

'Then it's settled?' Hancock said, pouring two healthy measures of champagne. 'I must say I'm pleased,' he continued. 'We really don't see enough of each other, and I've always enjoyed your company more than anyone else I've ever known.'

'Including Kristin?' Marcia said.

Hancock raised his eyebrows as he passed one of the glasses to her. 'Do I detect a hint of jealousy?' he retorted. 'That I wouldn't expect from you. But in any case, it's not quite the same thing. Kristin has something about her I find... interesting. But she's not in your class once she moves outside the dungeon territory. She's very inventive and very loyal, but I could never love her, and especially not the way I once loved you. To be honest, Marcia, I still am in love with you.'

'But you can't control me the way you would like to,' Marcia returned. 'You'd rather have had me as your love slave, rather than as your partner, your equal.'

'It wouldn't have been quite like that,' Hancock protested, but Marcia raised her hand to silence him.

'It would have been exactly like that,' she insisted. 'You'd only have been happy if I'd been prepared to play the Mitzi role for you, and there was no way I was going to spend my days wandering around in gags and chains and baring my backside for you to cover in welts.'

'No, I must admit that now it's rather difficult to imagine you in the role of a submissive, though I did flatter myself back then that I might be able to bring you round.'

'Well, that's all in the past now,' Marcia replied. 'And

there's no reason why we shouldn't be able to remain friends, just so long as we both know exactly where we stand.'

'Quite so,' Hancock agreed. 'Now, I'll just go along to the kitchens to make sure everything is coming along nicely, and leave you in private to make your call. It's a separate line, without any extensions, so you won't be overheard.'

'My call?' Marcia echoed, furrowing her brow, before remembering. 'Oh yes, of course.' She opened her handbag again and took out the little gilt-edged address book. 'And I know you won't mind if I help myself to another glass of this delicious champagne. It really seems like a decent vintage.'

'Glad you approve,' Hancock said, airily. 'And of course, help yourself. There's plenty more where that came from.'

Marcia watched him leave the room, flicked open the address book, rose and crossed to where the telephone sat on an elegant Edwardian walnut sidetable. She picked up the receiver and listened for the dial tone, as well as for any strange noises that might indicate that Ralph had been lying about it being a separate line. All seemed in order, but Marcia knew her ex-husband's methods of old. She would not put it past him to be listening on the other side of the door, apart from which, she already knew that parts of the building were bugged.

She dialled a number and listened, as though waiting for a reply, though she knew she would not get one at this hour. The girl who worked under the slave name of Honey would be at the house overnight, keeping an eye on things for her, but was unlikely to arrive for at least another two hours. Marcia would phone her later to tell her that she was likely to be delayed, but for the moment, anyone watching or listening would believe that she was talking to someone other than the unanswered ringing tone of her

136

own telephone number.

'Yes, hello,' she called out, after what she calculated was a suitable delay. 'Is that Eric? No? Oh, Brian. Yes, you'll do. You might be a darling and pass a message on for me. Yes, it's Marcia Davenport. Yes, tell Eric I'll not be arriving until one in the afternoon, okay? If there's a problem with that, you can reach me on...' She paused, looking down at the little round circle in the centre of the dial, and then read off the numbers written there. 'If I don't hear anything, tell him I'll assume it's okay. Yes, fine. Thank you, darling. Byeeee!'

Marcia dropped the receiver back onto its cradle and walked slowly across to retrieve the champagne bottle from the ice bucket, dropping her address book into her handbag first and snapping it firmly closed. She refilled her glass and took it back to the long sofa, settling herself back and relaxing into a pose which would convey mild interest in her surroundings to any watching eyes, though what she was really looking for, as she had been ever since she had first entered the room, was any sign of hidden cameras.

As something of an expert in this field herself, Marcia reckoned she would be able to spot anything out of the ordinary, but, to her chagrin, she saw nothing to indicate that the room was under surveillance. Perhaps, she reasoned, Ralph kept certain areas of the house free of cameras and microphones. This room was, after all, his private domain, a sitting room, study and dining room all in one, so it would be logical to assume that he would not want mere employees being able to oversee and overhear what he did here. On the other hand...

Marcia smiled to herself. You never knew with Ralph, apart from in certain well defined areas, so it did not pay to take chances. Ah well, best to just relax and enjoy the evening. One never knew what little titbits one could pick up during conversation over a good dinner. And it would be a good dinner, that much she could be certain of.

And a good dinner it was, although Marcia had not been prepared for the two maids who served it. Both were clad in brief and very sexy rubber uniforms, mostly black, but with white aprons and frilled trimmings and caps, and both had the figures and movements, allowing for the chains that hampered them, of course, of youth. Their faces, however, belied that first impression.

Both looked as though they should have been drawing pensions rather than waiting table, and for several minutes Marcia was somewhat nonplussed. She wanted to say something to Ralph, but she could tell from the way his eyes watched her every movement that that was precisely what he was expecting, and she was determined not to give him the satisfaction. Then, suddenly, the penny dropped.

'What an excellent makeup job!' she exclaimed, clapping her hands delightedly and beaming across the table. 'My, but you nearly had me going there. One of these haggard looking crones is Mitzi, isn't it?' She looked from one grey-haired head to the other. Both pairs of eyes were trying to tell her something. Now she understood why.

'And the other one is my own dear little Melanie, isn't it?' she challenged. Ralph grinned and laughed.

'It most certainly is,' he said. 'Bang on in both cases. It was Kristin's idea to do the aging bit on Mitzi – we find it's an excellent way of humiliating a pretty slave who's too fond of her looks. And it's a warning that she can be returned to that state and kept looking that way indefinitely. Somewhat undermines the old ego.'

'I should think so,' Marcia concurred. 'But what about Melanie? Was it my saying about her getting herself into trouble?'

Hancock shook his head. 'No, not at all. That makeup takes a couple of hours and I had Linda start on it as soon as you handed over the little tart. It really only started as a bit of a joke. I didn't think you'd recognise Mitzi, but you know Melanie a whole lot better, and it was a good test of Linda's talent.

'On the other hand, what you said about the little tart did give me another idea. Lift your skirts, Melanie,' he said, turning to the nearer girl. Obediently, the figure raised the front of her skirt and petticoats. 'Now, walk around to your mistress. Now my dear,' Hancock said to Marcia, when the little transvestite maid was standing before her, 'feel between her legs.'

Hesitantly, Marcia extended a hand and probed gingerly between the tops of Melanie's thighs. To her astonishment there was no sign of the usual lump that was Melanie's male parts, albeit scrunched up inside a very elasticated cache sex. Instead, her fingers traced the unmistakable outline of a female vulva, complete with soft labial lips and defined opening. She recoiled from the touch, turning on Ralph.

'You haven't—?' she began, but then relaxed again. Of course he hadn't, that was impossible. 'So okay, clever clogs, how's it done?'

'More stage stuff,' Ralph explained. 'I had a quick word with Linda and she used this sort of liquid rubber that hardens quickly to a jelly state as soon as it gets out into the air. She just dipped the little slut's cock into it, pressed it back into place and did a bit of sculpture before the reaction set in. There's a tube so she can take a pee, but that's it. She can't get hard and she won't get any stimulation through it, so for the duration of her stay, Melanie's not going to be doing any sly seduction scenes.

'From what you tell me about her, in a day or so she'll

139

be begging for someone to fuck her just about any way that's left to them. Isn't that right, Melanie?'

Dumbly, the poor maid replied with a slow nod. Marcia wondered why she did not reply audibly, for she could see no sign of a gag. Presumably, Ralph had given both maids instructions to remain silent throughout the evening.

The day leading up to Ralph and Marcia's dinner party had been a hard one for Alison. Paula, the handler, had returned to collect and inspect her soon after Linda had departed. The sight of her cunningly aged face amused the woman no end.

'Hard to see how anyone could fancy you now,' she laughed, 'unless they put a bag over your head. Mind you, there's plenty around here that would screw anything female.'

She led Alison upstairs to the ground floor level and showed her the way to the kitchen. It was a huge old room, still with an old-fashioned range in place, though the cooking now was evidently done on an ultra modern electric system that glittered and gleamed from the wall opposite. There were two other maids already in attendance, both dressed in identical fashion to Alison, though their faces remained in their naturally youthful state. Alison found herself idly wondering if, beneath their skirts, they had been treated as she had.

The cook was the first sign of normality Alison had seen since her arrival. The woman was somewhere in her late fifties, very matronly, scrubbed clean features and powerful forearms, a floral apron tied about her ample waist and a florid complexion beneath a mass of iron-grey curls. As Alison entered, carrying her breakfast tray, she looked up from the dough she was kneading and offered her a sad smile.

'Oh dear, another one of those days, is it?' she sighed, a faint Welsh lilt to her voice. She looked past Alison and addressed herself to Paula. 'Which one is this?' she asked. 'I can never tell when they have this done to them.'

Paula let out a short, mirthless laugh. 'You haven't met this one before, Meg,' she said. 'This is a new slut, name of Mitzi. Mistress Kristin thought this'd be a good way of getting her in her place right at the start. So you can have the use of her for the next few days. Send her out with one of the others when she's not needed down here – the boss wants her kept busy.'

'I'll bet he does,' the cook said. 'Well, if it's work she's to do, there's plenty of it down here. Lord Whatsisname is having one of his special parties tomorrow and that always means lots of extra preparation work. So, just leave her here and I'll make sure she doesn't slack off.'

Paula paused in the doorway. 'One bit of good news then, Meg,' she said. 'I'm told we're getting another new girl, though only for a few days. I'll put in a word and see if I can't get her allocated to your team. Apparently his lordship is staying for a few days, and this one's earmarked to provide his special services, so that'll take up a fair bit of her time.'

The heavy oak door closed behind Paula with a dull thud that set crockery rattling on a nearby dresser, and the cook shook her head in exasperation.

'That woman,' she said to Alison, 'just doesn't know her own strength. Now then, just put that tray down over by the sinks, fill that big kettle, and we'll all have a nice cup of tea and get to know each other. Sandie love, you get some mugs organised.'

The slightly taller of the two maids, who was also slightly darker, nodded and turned to open a cupboard. Alison walked across and deposited the tray as instructed and then

141

turned back to face the cook, who smiled encouragingly at her and beckoned for her to approach.

'Now then,' she murmured, fumbling in the pocket in the front of her apron, 'let's have that thing out of your mouth while you're in here. If anyone comes in, just keep your mouth shut and they won't notice a thing, all right?' Her hand reappeared and Alison saw that she was holding one of the little Allen keys and, a few moments later, she prised the gag free from Alison's grateful mouth. 'There now, that's better, isn't it?' she said, placing the thing into her voluminous pocket. 'Better keep this out of sight,' she added. 'Now, Mitzi dear – or do you have another name?'

Alison opened her mouth to reply, and just remembered the alias she had agreed with Marcia. She nodded.

'It's Louise,' she said. 'But I thought we were always to be addressed by our slave names?' Meg laughed.

'Load of old nonsense, that,' she said. 'I never bother with it, except when one of the bullies is about. In this kitchen I call you what your mothers called you, and there's an end to it.'

'Aren't you worried that you might get into trouble?' Alison asked.

Meg winked. 'Anyone who wants to start trouble in my kitchen will end up with a frying pan-sized dent in their silly heads,' she said, and Alison could believe she meant it. 'All this old rubbish is all right for them as wants to play silly games and make-believe, but not for the likes of me. I expect you'll be wondering why I bother to stay on here, what with all the silliness and all?

'Well,' she continued, before Alison could confirm whether she was or not, 'it's just a case of money, and that's a fact. Mister Airs-and-Graces Hancock and his weird friends like their food, see, and you don't find too many cooks with my experience and expertise who accept all this parading about in leather and rubber. Too hot for a start, see? You'll find that out for yourself, once you've had an hour or two down here. Can't understand why you young girls do it, though I suppose that's all about money too.

'Well, you take their money, same as I do, but use it wisely. Me, I've got two lovely granddaughters lost their parents in a road accident, so working here lets me give them a damned good education. Mind you, they'd have twenty blue fits if they ever found out exactly what sort of a place their gran cooks in.'

'They must wonder,' Alison said, 'how you can pay for them on a cook's salary?'

Meg tapped the side of her head. 'Ah well, there's crafty, see?' she said. 'They think it's from a legacy left for me to see to them till they're twenty-one. Eldest one's nearly nineteen already and Emma's turned seventeen, so it won't have to be for that much longer. Mind you, I wouldn't mind putting a bit extra away for my retirement, and it's not so bad really. I never mix with them lot up there, and I've got my own quarters well away from everyone. All I ever see is you young ones in your funny clothes, and I've got used to that after all this time.'

A sudden thought occurred to Alison. 'What would you do though, if one of your granddaughters appeared in your kitchen dressed like this?' She moved her fingers to indicate her own garb. The cook looked sternly at her, her expression changing in an instant.

'You ever suggest my girls would do such a thing,' she said, dragging the gag from her pocket, 'and I'll have this back on you before you can say Jack Robinson. There's wicked you are!'

'I-I'm sorry,' Alison blurted, realising her error. 'I didn't mean anything, honestly.'

'Well, you make certain I don't catch you saying such things again, young lady. I'm not blaming you for what you do, any more than I'm likely to feel guilty myself, but all this is unnatural, I'm thinking, and my girls have been brought up proper like.'

So had Alison, but she let the subject drop.

The tea was welcome, although Alison realised, as she was draining the mug, that drinking it might not have been that wise a move, considering her current inability to relieve her bladder without causing a mess. But as the day wore on she began to suspect that the orange drink had contained something to suppress more than her appetite, unless it was the amount of bodily fluid she was sweating under all the rubber.

When their stint in the kitchen was finished, Alison found herself paired with the dark-haired Sandie and, gags firmly back in place, they set off on a long round of dusting, hoovering and polishing. It was still presumably too early in the day for the guests to be about, and Alison reasoned that they probably confined most of their exertions to the evenings. But every time a handler appeared it meant a problem.

Every single one of them lifted their dresses and activated the vibrators, before walking away laughing, or occasionally standing about to watch the results. With both devices buzzing merrily away there was only ever going to be one outcome; two rubber maids clinging to each other in the throes of enforced orgasm. On the first occasion when the handler, a statuesque redhead, calmly walked away and left them to it, Alison started to panic, for even had her fingers been able to reach, she had no idea how to deactivate the infernal machines.

She need not have panicked, however, for inside each shaft, in addition to the mechanisms and batteries, was fitted some sort of timer device which cut the power automatically after about fifteen minutes. Even so, Alison had not realised just how long fifteen minutes could seem and, by the time Sandie indicated they should return to the kitchen, there were telltale rivulets staining the insides of the tops of both girls' stockings.

Meg removed their gags again and they made more tea, which they drank while they ate a large ham sandwich. Whatever was in the orange drink though was quite effective, for Alison only managed to eat half of hers, and she noticed that Sandie did little better. She sighed. Six orgasms, eight rooms cleaned, her feet were killing her, and so far she had not had a single opportunity to look around properly. And unless the regime eased considerably, she realised, opportunities were going to be far rarer than any of them had calculated.

The makeup made her face muscles feel stiff and unnatural and Alison wondered what it would feel like after three or four days. So far it had only been a few hours since Linda had finished applying it, though it felt like a lifetime. She sighed again and thought back to when she had been given the final opportunity to change her mind about this assignment. It had seemed like a good idea at the time, but now Alison was not quite so sure.

When Paula reappeared to take charge of her again and removed her gag to give her another glass of the orange concoction, Alison decided to risk asking her a question, first asking the big woman's permission to do so. Paula nodded and Alison took a deep breath.

'What would happen, Mistress,' she began, 'if I was to say that I'd changed my mind? About staying here, I mean.'

Paula laughed. 'Not much,' she replied. 'But you wouldn't be able to leave. Not yet, anyway. The Master insists that all new slaves must remain a minimum of one month, as they often get cold feet during the first period. After a while, you'll settle into the routine and feel happier about it.'

'And if not?'

'Then you'll be paid off and sent on your way. Why? Having a change of heart?'

Alison quickly shook her head. 'No,' she said. 'It was just idle curiosity, Mistress. After all, this must be a bit harsh for some people's taste.'

Paula nodded her agreement. 'It is at first, which is why the minimum period. It wouldn't do to have slaves coming and going all the time, and we find that at the end of a month very few still want to leave. You get hooked by it all, and the money's pretty good. You can also pick up some handsome tips, as you'll discover when you meet the noble lord.'

She went on to explain about the young peer with a taste for older women. 'If you play your part right, he'll like as not tell the accounts department to add an extra three or four hundred for you personally.'

Alison gasped in genuine astonishment. 'Three or four hundred pounds?' she repeated in disbelief. 'And what am I expected to do for that sort of money. That's several months' salary!'

'And paid in cash, so it's tax free,' Paula reminded her. 'And it won't be anything you haven't done before, unless you've never caned a man?' She saw Alison's perplexed look. 'With this one you sometimes have to play a bit of both roles. You've got to be the humble maid, getting fucked and thanking her lord and master for the privilege, but then sometimes he wants the girl to play like the stern nanny and give his naughty bottom a good thrashing. It all depends. It's not difficult, anyway.'

'But how hard do I hit him?'

'As hard as you like; the harder the better, usually. He'll certainly repay the compliment, if he doesn't cane you first in any case. And he'll lay it on pretty good, though not enough to cause any damage.'

'Sounds a bit peculiar to me,' Alison said, before she realised the stupidity of that statement. Paula grinned.

'Everything here is peculiar, girlie,' she retorted. 'Now, mouth open and let's shut this inquisitive little mouth of yours. It's beginning to grate on my nerves.'

The new maid, her face as aged as Alison's own, was waiting when she was finally sent back to the kitchen. Meg was still working, together with another two young maids, but this time she didn't remove the gag. The younger girls were free to talk, Alison noticed, but the newcomer was restricted as she was herself, and remained mute as they loaded up the food trolley.

'I'm told that Millie here is experienced at waiting on table,' Meg said, 'so just take your lead from her and don't make any mistakes. Rumour has it that he's got his ex-wife for dinner this evening, and he likes to make a good impression on her. Rumour also has it that he'd give his right arm to get her back.'

Alison felt her pulse quicken at the mention of Marcia; always assuming that Marcia was Hancock's only ex-wife. For all she knew Hancock could have been married any number of times.

However, it was Marcia, and Alison wondered why she'd turned up so soon, unless it was just to check that she was all right. She wondered if she should try to let Marcia know that it was her beneath the makeup, but reasoned there was no advantage to be gained from that. Instead, she concentrated on the task in hand, watching Millie closely and avoiding any clumsy mistakes.

Marcia's astonishment when she learned the identities

of the two maids was matched by Alison's own at discovering that Millie, her companion in rubber restriction, was none other than Melanie. Once again she wondered what was going on. Why would Marcia's personal maid be there and forced to undergo the same treatment that she had received? As Alison turned away to load the empty dishes into the bottom of the trolley, Melanie caught her eye and winked. Alison tried to smile back, but the gag made it extremely difficult.

As the conversation across the table continued, Alison realised that Melanie was going to remain in the house for three or four days, and slowly began to comprehend. Obviously Marcia thought that Alison needed an ally, some sort of back up and support, and it didn't seem at all like a bad scheme. Alone, mostly chained and gagged and still suffering from the shock of having her inner self revealed to her so graphically, Alison knew she was out of her depth. But with Melanie there, the odds against some sort of success had tilted considerably, although when they would get to communicate with each other was anyone's guess.

In fact, Alison thought, anything that happened at all was anyone's guess.

Chapter Eight

Age Before Beauty

The dinner party continued late into the evening, but Alison's part in it ended as soon as the sweet course was over. Hancock pressed a button on the wall and a few minutes later the figure of Kristin, resplendent in shining red leather, all boots and studs, strode into the room.

'The temporary slut can cope on her own now,' Hancock said. 'So take the new one and get her ready for his lordship, seeing as how he's turned up early. He'll only want her for an hour or so this evening, if he's been travelling all day, so make sure she gets a relatively early night. I've got plans for this pair for tomorrow morning. Lloyd-Jervis and his little group are coming up and I thought we'd stage a little lunchtime cabaret for them. I'll explain my outline ideas to you later.'

To Alison's relief, before Kristin led her upstairs she took her back to the cellar level, removed her waterlogged stockings and towelled her lower limbs dry, before talcing a fresh pair of rubber hose and easing them up her legs.

'One day,' she muttered, 'someone will invent a latex that will let moisture through and save all this aggravation. Right then missy, up you get and make sure you put on a good performance. The gag stays in for this one, so you can't ruin the illusion by speaking. Your voice is far too young sounding and besides, this one doesn't expect women to talk to him. As far as he's concerned, females are only good for one thing.'

Mike Hallett did not recognise the tall blonde who opened the door when he rang Marcia's bell. Cool and beautiful, she wore a simple white mini dress with shoestring shoulder straps, and it was obvious that she wore no brassiere underneath. Mike started to introduce himself, but to his surprise the girl seemed to know exactly who he was.

'You'd better come through to the lounge, Mr Hallett,' she said, stepping aside. 'The Mistress isn't back yet, which is a little worrying.'

In the lounge the girl indicated for Mike to sit down on the sofa, while she stretched decorously in one of the sumptuous armchairs.

'Having said I was a little worried,' the girl continued, 'I know I shouldn't be. The reason Mistress asked me to sit the house tonight was in case anything cropped up and she was delayed from returning.'

'And you've heard nothing from her?' As Mike spoke, right on cue the telephone began to jangle. The blonde rose effortlessly and swept across the room as though her six inch heels were ice skates. She picked up the receiver, listened for a few seconds, and gave an affirmative reply, before replacing the instrument. When she turned back to Mike her expression seemed easier.

'It's all right,' she smiled. 'That was Mistress phoning to say she'll be spending the night at Dennison Hall, and that any urgent enquiries should be referred there on her ex-husband's private line. She's definitely up to something, judging from the funny way she was speaking. I guess someone was there in the room with her, because she made some remark about remembering to feed the cat.'

'What's funny about that?' Mike asked.

The girl's eyes crinkled. 'The cat ran off about five months ago and we haven't seen him since,' she said. 'Now, seeing that Mistress isn't coming home tonight, is there anything I can do for you?'

'Not really, thanks,' Mike replied. 'I only called in to see if Marcia had found anything new while up there. I wonder why she's staying overnight?'

The girl shrugged. 'Who knows? That's the other reason why I'm sure she's up to something. She's a very clever lady, the Mistress.'

'Yes, don't I know it,' Mike murmured. He started to rise, and the girl looked disappointed.

'Are you sure there's nothing I can do for you, Master Michael?' she persisted.

Mike looked at her quizzically. 'Do I know you?' he demanded. 'You evidently seem to know who I am. What's your name?'

'Sally Anne Crichton-Thomas,' she purred, extending a perfectly manicured hand. 'However, around here people usually just refer to me as Honey.' Mike froze, her hand still in his, and stared at her.

'Honey?' he echoed. 'Not the Honey who—'

'Gave you the blow job you seemed to enjoy so much?' Honey offered. 'Afraid so, in the flesh. I hope I'm not a disappointment now you can see the rest of me.'

At last Mike managed to retrieve his hand and his composure.

'No, not at all,' he blustered. 'I should say not.'

'Then how about letting me pour you a drink,' Sally Anne Honey suggested. 'I wouldn't mind one myself and, as Mistress isn't coming back tonight, we have the entire house to ourselves... including the basement.'

Mike opened his mouth, about to decline the invitation, but his mind was suddenly filled with images of a helpless slave girl, clad in almost transparent white latex, her shapely legs perched on high white sandals, her eyes –

151

which he now knew were green – hidden by those curious tinted lenses. And he remembered the urgent caress of those full lips.

'I could manage a small one,' he ventured.

Honey pulled a wry face. 'Now I know you're being modest, Master Michael,' she cooed.

The young pillar of the aristocracy was not what Alison had expected, not that she was really sure what she had expected, though it certainly was not what confronted her when she was pushed into the bedroom. The figure lounging in the deep armchair in the bay window on the far side of the huge four-poster bed turned as she entered, and fixed her with a pair of the darkest brown eyes she had ever seen.

As he stood, Alison suppressed a gasp, for the brief leather pouch hid little of his fantastically well muscled body. And his handsome face and careless long dark hair would have melted the hearts, not to mention the underwear, of any girl with red blood in her veins. The young lord, whose name she had not been told, presumably because she was not going to be in the position to address him as anything anyway, certainly seemed to disprove popular theories about inbreeding in the aristocracy producing weedy, chinless wonders. Alison felt her vaginal muscles clenching around the vibrator and her knees started to tremble. She wished fervently that she had not been made to look like a haggard old woman, until she remembered that this was apparently what the man desired most.

How on earth, she thought, could a man like him have turned out so? But then she had already learned more about what went on inside people's heads in the past four days than she had learned in a lifetime, or would ever have believed there was to learn.

'I hope my new underwear meets with your approval, nanny,' the young nobleman said, a distinctive little boy sound in his tone. 'I brought it with me especially for you.' He suddenly laughed, baring a set of perfect white teeth, and walked towards her, looking her up and down.

'Oh yes,' he breathed, his voice sounding much more normal now. 'Perfect as usual. And apparently you're new here, is that so?' Alison nodded and he copied her action. 'Not that anybody can tell, with all that makeup. Nice legs, though,' he added, appreciatively. 'And nice tits and a firm bum by the looks of it. Nanny had the loveliest legs you could imagine, and a nice bum too.' He stooped down, produced a small key from the palm of his right hand and quickly released her ankle fetters, unclipping them from the vertical chain, which he left dangling between her legs. 'Now then, as you're my nanny for today, let's see how you walk. Back straight now; remember, posture is everything and we mustn't slouch or stoop.'

Throwing her head and shoulders back, Alison walked slowly back and forth, feeling rather foolish, but determined to give a good account of herself. If that's what it took to get him excited, then fair enough. She concentrated on the fact that he would eventually take her, and hoped it would be sooner rather than later. After a few minutes the young man seemed satisfied. He ordered Alison to stop and then, with a wail that made her jump, fell to his knees in front of her, burying his face in the folds of her rubber skirt and clasping her buttocks to draw her in closer.

As he did so, his right hand caught the base of the rear vibrator, which immediately hummed into life. Alison let out a low groan and grasped his hair in her hands, thrusting her crotch as hard against his face as she could and grinding against him. He reached up beneath her petticoats, his fingers seeking the buckle that held the crotch strap in place.

Moments later he was withdrawing the larger dildo from her front opening, the dangling chain clattering to the floor like a metal snake, and trying to tug the dangling strap out of the way.

His head disappeared under the layers of rubber and his mouth sought her sex with unerring precision, his tongue pushing in between her already well lubricated lips. Alison groaned again and tried to fight against her passion, desperate to make the moment last, pushing his face away with all her strength.

But he was having none of it. He was far too strong and determined and, after only a fleeting effort, Alison surrendered to the inevitable and came in a torrent of weak-limbed abandon. She was still climaxing when he broke away, stood, and scooped her effortlessly into his powerful arms.

'Naughty nanny,' he chided. 'You'll have to be punished for such wicked thoughts. But first...' He tossed her casually onto the bed, climbed up between her outspread thighs, flipped up skirt and petticoats with one hand, and tugged the brief leather pouch clear with the other. He was already half erect, only the restraint having prevented him from becoming fully aroused, but Alison had never seen a penis swell and grow so quickly.

By the time the leather thong hit the carpet near the window his member was rigidly at attention and, without further ado or ceremony, he entered her with one powerful thrust. Alison choked and screamed, bucking furiously, as the end of one orgasm instantly became the start of another. She grabbed his hips with her gloved hands, urging him into her, but he needed no telling. He pounded in and out of her with a manic ferocity, supporting himself with one hand only, the other moving from breast to breast, massaging, kneading, tugging and pulling, until the pleasure pains became as one in the depths of Alison's stomach. Despite her gag, her shouts of abandoned ecstasy reverberated around the walls as he began to spasm, jetting his hot seed high into her womb, and then collapsing on top of her with a strangled cry of exaltation.

The next hour was little more than a blur for Alison. She was vaguely aware of his weight on top of her, but even more aware of the fact she did not care, for even after the second incredible orgasm had faded, it was followed up by a series of minor after shocks, each of which brought a delicious feeling of disorientation. When the young man finally recovered enough strength and purpose of mind to withdraw from her and kneel up, Alison saw that his erection was still as firm as ever, glistening with a mixture of both their juices. Only the gag prevented her from sucking the throbbing pole into her mouth. Instead, she had to be content with wriggling herself into a crouching position in which she could place a kiss on his purplish plum with her already parted lips.

She looked up into his eyes, waiting for a reaction. He was studying her quite calmly, though his chest still rose and fell more than normal. Gently, he reached out and brushed at the silver curls.

'That was beautiful, nanny,' he said softly. 'But you know I must still punish you. If not, Daddy will find out and make Mummy dismiss you. Then where would you go? And what would your darling Teddy do without you then, eh?'

Assuming he was not referring to a stuffed toy, Alison at least knew now the name of her lover. Teddy. Edward. Teddy Edward. She stifled a giggle, remembering her own teddy bear, for that was what she had always called it. Teddy Edward had always been her closest friend, her confidante, her confessor. From little girl to rebellious teenage student, he had always been on her bed. She remembered how she used to talk to him, telling him of all the injustices, all the nearly romances, all...

Well, everything.

Teddy Edward – the human one – was on the move again. He swung his legs off the bed and stood up, padding across to a chest of drawers on the far wall. From it he extracted a steel bar about three feet long, at either end of which was forged an oval loop. In addition he pulled out two leather straps, each less than half the length of the bar.

'Stand up please, nanny,' he said, gently. Alison struggled to obey and he held out a hand to assist her. 'Turn around,' he instructed, still in the same soft tone. Alison shuffled around so that she was facing away from him. Deftly, he inserted one end of the rod between her arm and her body, settling it into the crook of her elbow, and threaded it across to repeat the same manoeuvre with the other arm. The effect was to drag Alison's shoulders right back, forcing her to thrust out her breasts alarmingly. Her wrists, meanwhile, were still secured to the chains at her waist and these chains were now replaced by a single link, leaving her no movement in her arms at all.

Satisfied of this fact, Teddy Edward now put the two straps to use, threading one through each of the metal loops and buckling them tightly about Alison's upper arms, precluding any chance there might have been of her dislodging the bar to ease her position. He reached out, took hold of her shoulders and turned her back to face him. There was a peculiar, almost saintly smile playing about his lips as he looked at her.

'Always posture, nanny,' he whispered. 'You see, I haven't forgotten.' He reached up and cupped a breast in each hand and her nipples seemed to jump to meet his touch.

The vibrator, which had now resumed its dormant status, felt huge inside her rectum, and Alison could feel the damp trickle from her vagina as gravity did its work. She fought to control her pounding heart and wondered what was coming next, as he massaged her rubber-covered globes in silence.

At last he stepped back from her, letting his arms fall to his sides, before suddenly grasping his rampant shaft with his right hand.

'Nanny would like to wank this for Teddy, wouldn't she?' he said, with unexpected savagery. 'Well nanny can't, can she? Teddy's taken care of nanny's wicked hands and now Teddy's going to take care of nanny's naughty bottom, too. Turn around and bend over, you wicked woman.'

Alison quickly did as he wanted, the bar through her elbows pressing harder against her spine as she bent forward. She desperately hoped that she wouldn't be required to maintain the position for long.

'Legs apart, you old whore!' he snapped. Dutifully, Alison shuffled her feet wider and grunted as she felt the vibrator being withdrawn from her. She felt her skirt and petticoats being lifted and felt the pressure against her spine and realised that Teddy was pushing the latex between the bar and her back, thus holding it up out of the way. His hands, when they caressed her exposed buttocks, felt warm and surprisingly soft. Whatever else Teddy Edward was, he obviously wasn't a manual worker.

'Now you can stand up again,' he told her, breaking the brief physical contact. He did not tell her to turn again, so she remained facing away from him, unable to see what he was doing, but conscious of the sound of some kind of activity.

Suddenly her buttocks exploded in a surge of fire, to the accompanying crack of bamboo against bare flesh. She shrieked through the gag and staggered forward, only to be rewarded by a second stinging cut just below the first.

'That's it, you old whore!' Teddy roared. 'Let's see you dance. In a circle, you dirty old bat. See what you get for playing about and corrupting innocent boys.' He delivered more than a dozen blows in all, forcing Alison to run in a rough circle about the large room, following her with unerring accuracy until her backside and upper thighs were throbbing with unbelievable pain. And yet even the pain was turning her on. The sheer helplessness of her situation, the feeling of being completely under the control of another human being, the punishment and the humiliation, all, she knew, were driving her back towards that beautiful, awful chasm, and she suspected he knew that too.

The bamboo tattoo ceased as suddenly as it had begun, but Alison was given no time to recover either her breath or her senses. Teddy tossed the cane onto the bed, grasped her about the waist and spun her so that her back was to him. At the same time he pushed her head forward and down, and kicked her feet apart with such force that had he not already established a firm grip on her waist, Alison would surely have fallen on her face.

She guessed what was coming and, four days before, she dimly remembered, she would have fought with all her strength to prevent it. But now she just hung in his grasp, panting like a bitch in heat, waiting for him to take her and to take the place so recently vacated by the second vibrator. What she had not realised, however, was how big he was in comparison to the artificial phallus, and only the fact that he had greased his erection – presumably just before he had picked up the cane – enabled him to enter her. Even so, it was a struggle and Alison felt certain he must rip her in two.

Her muffled shriek of protest quickly became a groan of

satisfaction though, once the head was in, and she pushed backwards greedily as his full length bored home. She wished she could reach her clitoris, or that he would reach for it, but it ultimately did not matter. As he began thrusting in and out of her those now familiar waves began their inexorable approach towards her beachhead, and the pattern on the carpet before her eyes began to slowly dissolve into a meaningless mist.

'I thought people were supposed to pay for all this sort of thing?'

Mike leaned back against the piled up pillows, admiring Honey's sleek figure, once again confined in the white latex bodysuit. So far her face and head remained bare, but Mike had not missed the crumpled piece of white rubber laying on the dressing table. He had not asked her to wear it, but Honey seemed to understand the effect she had had on him when wearing it before, and had slipped away to don it after showing him into the bedroom and opening a second bottle of wine.

Mike himself remained more or less fully dressed, having removed only his jacket, tie, shoes and socks. He had considered stripping completely, but was unsure exactly what was expected of him. Honey grinned.

'Feeling cold?' she teased, filling a glass for herself. Mike looked sheepish.

'Well, I wasn't sure—' he began.

'Whatever you prefer,' Honey said. 'Personally, I think you'd look great in black rubber. As I remember, you've got a very good body.'

'Oh, well, thanks,' he mumbled, and began unbuttoning his shirt. 'But what about—?'

Honey laughed. 'Money?' she said. 'This isn't about money. I fancy you and you evidently fancy me, so that's

159

it. I also love fucking in rubber and I get the feeling you quite enjoyed the idea, but if you'd rather be naked yourself, that's fine too.'

'But aren't you... I mean, don't you rely on—?' he stammered. Honey's smile remained as wide as ever.

'You mean, am I a prostitute and do I need the money and can I afford to give you a freebie, as the Yanks call it?' she said. Mike felt his cheeks reddening, but Honey continued unabashed.

'My dear Master Michael,' she said, 'it's quite true that the Mistress pays me well for my services, so technically yes, that does make me a prostitute, but I don't do it for the money. I do it because I get a kick out of being dressed up, chained up, hung up and then screwed stupid. Some people are just born that way, I guess.

'But I do have a day job, as it were. I'm the Marketing Director for Richmond Records, a company in which I also hold a thirty percent shareholding. Thanks to the success of groups such as The Downtowners, Whizzkid, Zaramaya and The Fallouts, I am a millionairess in my own right.

'In addition, when I told you my name earlier, I was being a little economical with the truth. The family surname is Crichton-Thomas, but my father is better known as the Earl of Estbury, which makes me Lady Sally Anne Crichton-Thomas, or, if you like, Lady Sally Anne Margaret Lucinda Alicia Crichton-Thomas. But if I used that, I'd never be able to fit my chequebook into my handbag.'

'And I suppose people call you Honey because of your hair colour?' Mike said.

Honey snorted. 'Actually, not quite. My mother's American and she always used to say things like "Honey do this" or "be a real Honey". And then a certain gentleman of my acquaintance suggested that a certain part of me tasted like honey and that was it.' She eased herself onto the bed and slithered towards Mike like a white snake. 'Perhaps you'd care to judge for yourself?' she suggested.

Alison came out of her comatose state to see Teddy standing over her, a glass of wine in one hand and one of the little Allen keys in the other.

'Sit up and I'll take the gag out for you,' he said. 'I'm sure you could use a drink.'

Nodding, Alison struggled to sit upright, but it was not easy with her arms and hands still bound rigidly by the steel bar and cuffs. When she finally made it, the young nobleman placed the glass on the bedside table and went to work with the key.

'There, I expect that feels better,' he said, but Alison noted that he made no move to release her hands or arms. Instead, he proffered the glass to her lips and she sipped from it gratefully.

'Now,' he continued, settling himself on the edge of the bed, 'would you like me to release you for half an hour, or would you rather stay as you are? I know some of the girls prefer to remain completely helpless, otherwise it ruins their concentration.'

Alison gave him a wry grin. 'I would appreciate a little respite from all this,' she admitted. 'Okay, I get a kick out of being tied up, but if this is some sort of interval, I'd rather take advantage of it to be comfortable.'

Teddy nodded, placed the glass alongside the bed and turned away to retrieve the keys from the dressing table. A minute or two later Alison's arms were back under her own control.

'Thank you, Master,' she said, dutifully. Teddy smiled at her.

'You can forget the "Master" bit for a while,' he said. He passed the wine glass back to her and went to fetch the bottle again. 'I may have a bit of a kink,' he told her over his shoulder, 'but I'm not that far gone that I don't know reality. Tell me, would you mind our just having a chat for a while?'

Alison almost choked on her wine, but managed to regain her composure.

'Mind?' she said. 'No, of course not. But what exactly did you want to chat about?'

Teddy waved his free hand airily. 'Well, this and that,' he replied, walking back towards the bed. 'You know how it is.' This time Alison did splutter, and he looked quite taken aback. 'What have I said wrong?' he demanded.

Alison shook her head sadly. 'I'm afraid, my dear Teddy,' she said, 'that I don't know how it is. A few minutes ago, unless I've been unconscious for longer than I thought, you were screwing the shit out of my arse. Before that you had me prancing round the room to the tune of your bloody cane, and before that again you fucked me near to oblivion.

'I'm a reasonably attractive female in my middle twenties and yet I've been made up to look like my own grandmother, purely because you want to fuck old women. And I've been tied, chained, gagged and God knows what else, and now you sit here calm as you like, and tell me I know exactly what sort of small talk you want to make! I'm sorry, Teddy, but I think you're just a teeny bit fucked up!'

Teddy cast his eyes downwards and Alison saw that his cheeks were becoming redder by the second.

'I'm sorry,' he mumbled. 'It's just me, I suppose.' He looked up again. 'I really am sorry,' he repeated. 'Look, I'm not so bloody gone that I don't know this is just a game for my benefit. Christ knows, I pay that bastard Ralph enough for the privilege. And don't think I'm being all superior, just because you do this for money. Of course, that's never mentioned, but there's no way you'd do something like this with me if you weren't being paid – and paid well.' He peered at her earnestly, and suddenly Alison felt her heart melting. She turned, placed the wine glass on the bedside table, and leaned close to him.

'Look at me,' she urged. 'Look at this face. It's not my face and I'm really sorry that my own face isn't good enough for you.' She reached out and stroked his cheek with a rubber-sheathed hand. 'And do you know why I'm sorry, Teddy?' she hissed. He jolted back, surprised by the sudden vehemence in her voice.

'N-no,' he stammered. 'Why?'

Alison crawled even closer to him, straddling his lap and cradling his head in her hands, before planting two little butterfly kisses on his forehead.

'Because, you silly Teddy Edward,' she whispered, 'I would give everything I've got to be screwed by you. You are absolutely gorgeous and I could get wet just thinking about you and I would dearly love to fuck you without this haggard bloody face between us. The rubber's okay, the chains I love, but the face is something else.

'I would give my right tit to have the opportunity to show you that this is not necessary. You could have me do almost anything and it wouldn't cost you a penny, but then I doubt you'd be interested because you're Lord Fuck Knows Who and I'm just a... just a slut,' she finished, lamely. She had nearly said journalist, but stopped herself in the nick of time. As she finished speaking she slid backwards off his lap and remained squatting on her heels, awaiting his reaction. Teddy seemed confused.

'Please,' he began, 'I don't think of you as a slut. Nor as a prostitute, nor anything else.' He stared at her. 'You said you... fancied me?' he challenged.

Alison nodded. 'Like a bitch in heat,' she replied, fervently. 'I never thought I'd hear myself saying this, but if you just clicked your fingers, I'd be there.'

'I don't understand,' Teddy protested.

Alison shrugged. 'Me neither,' she confessed, 'but I don't really care. Listen, you stupid gorgeous man, I'm trying to tell you that I'm in love with you… No!' she added fiercely. 'I don't know if I'm in love with you, but I'm certainly in *lust* with you.'

'Oh!' Teddy exclaimed, his hand flying to his mouth. 'But why?'

'Because you're beautiful and have the sort of body any red-blooded girl would lie down for. Listen Teddy, this is the sixties, and girls are allowed to say what they feel. And right now I feel like another fuck!' She reached out and cupped his balls in one hand.

'I don't even mind if you want to chain me again,' she added, 'but I have to tell you that my arse is sore, both inside and out, so I'd appreciate a bit of consideration.'

Teddy shook his head. 'I'd never want to hurt my nanny,' he whispered, reaching behind her.

Alison grabbed one of the pillows and hurled it at him from point blank range. 'And I'm not your nanny!' she asserted. 'Okay, I can't help how they've made me look, but I'm not! Listen Teddy,' she continued, her tone softening, 'why don't you try doing it with your eyes closed and I'll describe what I really look like as we go? And no cheating by peeking.'

Teddy looked nonplussed, but only for an instant. 'You're on,' he said. 'But just hang on a mo. I've got a blindfold here somewhere. That'll make sure I can't cheat!'

Chapter Nine

About Turn

It took Kristin only five minutes to appear from the time Teddy replaced the receiver on the bedside phone. She looked from him to Alison and back again.

'Has she been giving you trouble, sir?' the blonde dominatrix asked, an unmistakable hardness in her voice. Teddy shook his head.

'Quite the opposite,' he replied, smoothly. 'In fact, I must say that this young woman has possibly done me more good than anyone else I've ever met. Now, I'd like you to take her down to wherever it is you have to take her and have that makeup stuff removed. I would then like her made up properly, if perhaps a little vampishly, and returned here to me.'

'Any changes in her costume you would like?'

Teddy shook his head. 'None whatsoever,' he replied. 'She's fine the way she is. I've replaced both vibrators and I'd like them activated just before you get back to this door.'

Kristin's alert gaze spotted the white segment alongside the phone. 'You don't wish her gagged?' she asked.

Again a shake of the head. 'No, not this time. I want her mouth eager and ready the moment that door opens. I've already explained to her what will be required. Oh, and tell accounts to debit me a thousand and credit it to her account.'

Alison, who had been standing quietly, nearly fell over

when she heard this. A thousand pounds! Good grief, she was in the wrong job!

At first Mike had felt very self-conscious, allowing Honey to help ease him into the skintight black catsuit. But as his body heat rose inside the latex cocoon so too did his libido, and he didn't even protest when she pulled the mask over his head, covering everything except his eyes, nostrils and mouth. The thigh length rubber boots were a bit much, but at least they had only two inch Cuban heels, rather than the slender, six inch feminine spikes that adorned the white pair Honey changed into.

The lithe blonde pulled a white latex mask over her own features, and Mike recognised it as being the same one she had worn during their first encounter, the blue lenses hiding her eyes completely. She placed her hands on her hips and took up a suggestive stance, thrusting her hips forward.

'Does my Master approve?' she cooed.

Linda, the makeup artist, made it quite clear to Kristin that she did not approve of being summoned at such short notice.

'I spent hours doing this lot and now you tell me it's all got to come off again,' she snapped. 'I've got two lovely lads nicely trussed up back there, too,' she added. 'I was halfway through thrashing the first one and wallop, it all has to stop. They'll be aching like buggery by the time I get back to them.'

'You could have let them down,' Kristin pointed out.

Linda gave her a withering look. 'Sod that,' she sneered. 'If they want punishment, then punishment they can have. Let them find out what it feels like to really be helpless.'

'Except that George is capable of getting free from almost anything,' Kristin replied.

'Not this time he won't,' Linda assured her. 'I've put a

mitten glove on each arm and locked them with a harness. Then I doubled the fingers and locked them to the wrists and put a spreader bar between them for good measure. Finally, I used a clever little thing I only discovered last week. It's a sort of leather mitt, lined with foam rubber. You put it over the hand, tie off the drawstring and the fingers are totally useless. It's not supposed to need the mitten first, but I decided to go belt and braces with Georgie Porgy this time.'

'Sounds all very efficient,' Kristin agreed. 'Well, I'll leave you to it,' she said. 'I'd be obliged if you'd return her to Teddy afterwards, and he says not to bother with a fresh gag.'

'Snotty bitch,' Linda muttered, as the door closed behind the blonde. 'Well then, what's been going on with his lordship? I've never known him request a young looking maid. You must have made some sort of an impression there.'

'I sincerely hope so,' Alison replied. 'He's absolutely gorgeous.'

'I know,' Linda agreed. 'I just wish he was into something else. I'd love to have that hunk strung up for a sound whipping, but he only likes to play at the odd caning with his little maids.'

It took Linda nearly an hour to remove all traces of her handiwork and carefully restore Alison's makeup to something resembling what it had been upon arrival. The one embellishment she added was a pair of long false eyelashes, which she darkened with a lavish application of mascara.

'Bat your eyes at him now, hon,' she laughed, 'and you'll blow him over.'

Back in Teddy's room, the young lord seemed uncertain at first. He stood regarding Alison carefully for a full half minute before speaking.

'You are certainly very beautiful,' he said at last. 'But it's just that... well, you know...'

'I think I do,' Alison said, 'but I've been thinking about that. You'll need to trust me, though if I get it wrong I want you to promise faithfully that you won't complain about me to them. I'd get into big trouble.'

Teddy thought about this for a few seconds. 'Okay,' he eventually said. 'I'll trust you. What do I have to do?'

'Nothing, yet,' Alison replied. 'But you must go along with everything, regardless.'

Teddy grinned, nervously. 'I see, fair enough... Do your worst.'

'I intend to,' Alison returned, also starting to feel nervous. 'Now, get out of that robe if you don't mind, my beautiful Teddy Edward.' She turned her back on him and went over to the high chest of drawers, which it seemed were standard fixtures in all the guestrooms. She pulled open a drawer at random and nodded, satisfied, for like all its counterparts she had encountered during her round of domestic chores, it was filled with all the paraphernalia to ensure the clients did not run short of ideas.

After only a few seconds she found what she wanted and took it back across to where Teddy now stood, naked and looking more than a little apprehensive. She held up the leather blindfold for him to see, showing off the velvet lined internal padding that would ensure that no light whatsoever would penetrate to his eyes.

'It's even better than the one you used earlier,' she said. 'That worked okay, but this time I want to try something even better.'

'You're the boss,' he said, and stood quietly while she buckled the blindfold in place. 'I say,' he said, as she tightened it, 'this really is efficient. A bit spooky, too.'

Alison patted him on the shoulder. 'Just don't try to move around,' she said. 'I'll be right back.' In the very bottom drawer she found exactly the right thing and hauled it out amidst a jingle of buckles. It was much heavier than she had anticipated, and as she carried the leather straitjacket over to its intended wearer, she half expected Teddy to protest. However, either he was determined to keep to his side of the bargain, or whether he did not fully realise what Alison was putting him into, he meekly held out his arms and let her guide them into the sleeves.

Determined to get past the point where Teddy could change his mind, Alison worked feverishly with the buckles at the rear. There were eight of them in all, including one that fastened the high collar, but she was finished in what she reckoned must have been close to a record time. Now she took hold of the trailing straps in which each sleeve terminated, passed them around behind his body and began pulling on them. Understanding what she wanted, Teddy dutifully raised his arms and crossed them over his stomach. Within seconds Alison had buckled the ends tightly together and stood back with a little grunt of triumph.

Now he couldn't resist her, though he could always shout out. She wanted his mouth unhindered eventually, but for the moment she decided to do something about that. From another drawer she found a ball gag, but discarded that in favour of the next item she found. She held it up to the light, nodding in approval.

It consisted of a thin collar, to which was attached a carefully shaped leather half mask, designed to cover the lower portion of the wearer's features from below the nose. There were three small buckles at the back to pull it tight, and at the front there was an opening over the mouth, but at either side of this was a small buckle to which a double-ended strap supporting a ball gag could be attached. In addition, there were three smaller buckles wider still, to which a padded leather rectangle could be fitted, thus eventually covering the mouth completely and making it impossible to expel the gag.

Stepping behind Teddy, Alison instructed him to kneel and then loosened off the straitjacket collar so that she could fit the collar of the gag first. When she had tightened all three buckles, she fastened the straightjacket collar over the other, forming a snug bond between the two.

When she presented the rubber ball to his lips, Teddy made to draw back, muttering a stifled protest, but Alison tapped him smartly on the shoulder.

'Remember the deal,' she said. 'It won't be for long, but I don't want you trying to make me change my mind. Personally,' she added, in a whisper, 'the first time I was gagged it terrified me, but then I realised it made me free. It was the last bit of control completely taken away from me.' She shuddered a little, recalling how quickly she had come to adore the feeling of helplessness and how easily Marcia had moulded her in that basement.

With a sigh, Teddy opened his mouth and a second later it was too late to go back. Alison carefully fitted the padded cover and stepped back, walking around her new slave and almost wishing she could change places with him.

Abruptly, she brought herself back to the task in hand and told him to stand, leading him over to the bed and guiding him down to sit on the edge. She had seen something in one of the other rooms earlier that now gave her an idea, and she hoped she would find its twin there. With a grin of delight she did exactly that, hauling the heavy leather sheath out from beneath a double arm glove.

Placing Teddy's feet together, she struggled to draw the sheath up his legs, but finally she managed it. The leather stopped just short of his groin area, but there were vertical

170

straps at either side that ran up to a waist belt which, once secured, would ensure there was no way the slave could wriggle out of the sheath. Having taken care of that detail, Alison set to work drawing in the laces, compressing his legs tightly and rendering him finally completely helpless.

She bent close to his ear. 'How does that feel?' she whispered. 'Is it a nice safe feeling?'

Teddy gave a little grunt and tried to nod, but the two layers of collar limited his head movement considerably. Stooping further, Alison lifted his feet and swung them onto the bed, rolling him over first onto his face and then onto his back, until he lay face up in the very centre. She climbed up and crawled alongside of him.

'I think you've been a very naughty Teddy Edward,' she said, 'and you deserve to be soundly punished. The first part of your punishment is to lay there for a while, all in the dark on your own, and think about your naughtiness.' She reached down and took hold of his member, which was already beginning to swell. At her touch it began to respond even more rapidly. Alison leaned closer to his face.

'Teddy wants a wank, doesn't he?' she teased. There was another muffled grunt. She waited a few more seconds, by which time he was fully erect. 'Well,' she laughed, releasing her grip. 'Teddy will have to wait for the nice things, because first he has to think about his sins, and then he will have to have his bottom attended to.' She gave his rigid penis one final, playful pat and slid off the bed again. She heard him sigh in frustration from behind the gag.

'I know, my beautiful Teddy,' she cooed, 'but you have to learn to fancy nice young ladies again.' Especially this nice young lady, she thought, although she wasn't sure whether the adjective really applied to her any more.

Originally, Alison's plan to render Teddy helpless had

been no more than a way of trying to break through whatever barriers were encasing his sexual drive. She reckoned she'd already learned enough to ensure that he gained as much satisfaction out of her without the gruesome makeup as he had with it. And her plan had been to whip off his blindfold at some crucial stage, so that he climaxed with her own features in full view.

She wanted him to feel about her the way she suspected she already felt about him. Okay, it was animal lust first and foremost, but there was also something else about him that she found irresistible. Perhaps it was his emotional helplessness, perhaps it was something else, she didn't have time for psychoanalysis. What she did know was that she could easily face a life where she woke up every morning next to him. But she was not going to go through a long-term relationship looking like one of MacBeth's witches, even for the pleasure of being able to screw simply the most beautiful male she had ever laid eyes on.

No, she thought grimly, that was one habit she was going to break him of. But in the meantime the situation had developed into a stage where she could take advantage of it in a different way, one which would suit the purpose of her original reason for coming to Dennison Hall. Right now, with Teddy securely trussed up, blindfolded and gagged, she was freer than at any time since her arrival, and she was determined to make the best use of the little time that would seem reasonable within the rules of the charade they were acting out.

'I think you should be alone with your thoughts, Teddy,' she said sternly and loudly, mindful of the fact that there were probably cameras and microphones monitoring the room. 'I'm going out to find a toilet, otherwise I shall be tempted to pee on you instead. In fact, I might do that later anyway. Naughty boys need to be humiliated.' There was another soft sigh from the bed, but he made no move at all. 'I'll be back when I think you're ready,' she concluded, and spun on her heel to cross to the door.

She nearly jumped out of her skin, however, when she swung open the door to reveal the tall figure of Kristin standing in the passageway outside. Alison opened her mouth to explain, but the blonde raised a finger to her lips, motioning her to stay silent, and waved her to come out of the room, reaching past her to close the door when she had done so. Alison swallowed nervously, waiting for the expected tirade, but it didn't materialise. Kirsten instead gave her a rare smile.

'That was most impressive,' she said. 'I was told you were a natural slave, but it appears you have talents in the opposite direction, too. Have you had much practice at playing mistress?'

Alison shook her head. 'None at all,' she replied, truthfully. 'I just thought of what my last Mistress would have done and tried to copy it.'

Kirsten's eyes widened a little. 'Then you are a quick learner, young lady,' she said. 'We must think about helping you develop more in that field, although I would have to consult with Master Ralph first. He paid a lot of money in commission for you and he may not like the idea of his slave turning into a mistress half the time.'

'Of course,' Alison replied, as meekly as she could manage. 'It must be up to the Master. A slave knows her place.'

Kristin laughed. 'You're very good, girlie,' she said. 'Yes, very good indeed. Now, where did you intend to go while you were letting Lord Teddy stew for a while.'

Alison tried to keep her voice natural. 'I don't really know,' she said. 'I do need to use the loo, but after that I wasn't sure. I thought I might go down to the kitchen and get a cup of coffee or something. Would that be all right?'

Kristin's face softened a little. 'I can do better than that,' she said. 'The main guest lounge is empty now, except for a certain young lady who's been left on a whipping frame for the amusement of any bored guests who happen by. Let's go down and get ourselves a proper drink, and then you can practise on her arse before you try your skills on Teddy.'

For the first time in her adult life, Alison Katt was not attracted by the offer of a free drink. She groaned inwardly. There went her chance to snoop around on her own for a while. Outwardly, she managed to keep a grateful expression on her face.

'Thank you, Mistress,' she replied, dutifully. 'I would like that, but I must use the toilet first, if you don't mind?'

Kristin nodded. 'And do you really think you could bring yourself to pee in Teddy's mouth later on?' she asked.

Alison started. 'I-I didn't mean to go that far, Mistress,' she said.

'Why not?' Kristin smiled, laconically. 'A lot of men and women like it. I can see you're not quite as experienced as we were led to believe. Come on, my little Mitzi, let's start furthering your education. And you can stop calling me Mistress until you go back to being a slave.'

Mike had to admit that being enclosed from head to toe in tight rubber did produce a strange sensation of surreality, and as he watched Honey continue with her preparations, he knew also that the bulge of his throbbing cock would not have escaped her attention.

It was like a ritual sacrifice, he told himself, with the victim preparing herself for the altar with loving care. With her eyes hidden behind the opaque lenses, Honey presented a perfect picture of anonymity and detachment as she fitted the waist belt, wrist cuffs and ankle cuffs to herself, locking each one carefully and tugging the locks to ensure they were properly secure. Finally, she held out the neck collar to Mike.

'I think you should do it from now on?' she whispered and turned to face away from him. Fingers trembling, Mike lifted the studded leather and eased it around her throat, threading the end through the locking buckle. Slowly he tightened it, making sure that he left enough slack not to interfere with her breathing, examining the article closely as he did so. The two rows of studs ran around the top and bottom of the leather, which was perhaps three inches wide. But there were also four D-shaped metal rings stitched onto it, as there were also on the belt about her waist.

'Is that comfortable?' he asked, trying to keep his voice steady. With the collar in place, Honey could no longer nod, but she turned to face him and smiled.

'Perfectly, Master,' she purred. She pressed herself up against him and Mike felt the firmness of her breasts through the combined two layers of latex, and the heat of her was unmistakable. His gloved right hand travelled down to where her hairless mound protruded through the cutaway and one rubberised finger slipped easily inside her. She moaned and pressed her lips against his.

'I think you should secure me now,' she breathed, pulling her head back, 'otherwise I might do something a slave girl should never do.'

'It wouldn't worry me,' Mike replied, trying to sound lighthearted, but his entire being ached for her. He looked around and saw the little collection of locks alongside the bed. Swiftly he grabbed two of them, the rubber covering his fingers making things a lot more difficult than he had expected. He seized her left wrist, drawing her arm behind her, and threaded the open lock through the ring on the cuff and then through one of the two rings at the small of her back. A moment later he completed the same manoeuvre with her right wrist, rendering her completely helpless. He reached up and cupped her breasts, and Honey groaned softly.

'I'm not quite sure what I'm supposed to do next,' he whispered.

'Anything you like, Master,' she said. 'You might like to spank this slave, or maybe use a paddle. There are all sorts of things in the chest over there.'

Mike turned away and walked uncertainly to the chest. Pulling open the top drawer, he was confronted with a bewildering array of black rubber and leather, including paddles, straps, gags, blindfolds and...

He picked up the highwayman style mask and peered through its opaque black lenses. They made the room look a smoky grey, but other than that they afforded perfect vision, while from the other side they hid the wearer's eyes completely. With a hesitant grin he fumbled the buckle open and put it on.

'I think that's only fair,' he muttered. 'If I can't read your eyes, you shouldn't be able to see mine.'

He turned and peered across the room at his reflection in the long mirror, and the anonymous black creature stared back. A sudden little tremor of a chill ran up his spine. He rummaged through the rest of the drawer's contents and drew out what at first looked like a deadly weapon in the shape of a cat o'nine tails, but on closer examination he realised that the thongs were made from some sort of soft suede-like material. He placed it on top of the chest, closed the drawer, and opened the next one down.

This was less cluttered, but the strange collection of straps he pulled out at first baffled him, although the bright red rubber ball gave at least some clue.

'It's a harness gag,' Honey said, from where she had remained standing. Mike untangled the webbing and held it up for examination. Yes, he could see now how it was supposed to be fitted, with one strap running around the forehead, another passing over the top of the head and dividing to either side of the wearer's nose and rejoining again by means of a buckle beneath the chin. The strap connected to the ball also connected to these vertical straps and passed around to buckle at the rear. And there were rings to which, presumably, some sort of leash – no, reins, he realised! – could be attached. He looked over his shoulder at Honey.

'Would you like to wear this?' he suggested.

'That's not for me to say, Master,' she replied, coolly, 'but this part of the building is nowhere near as well soundproofed as the basement.'

Mike placed the harness alongside the whip. He also took out the extending chrome pole and tested the snap connectors at either end.

Five minutes later, safely gagged and with her ankles held a couple of feet apart, Honey lay face down over the side of the bed, her pert latex-covered rear delightfully presented to his aim.

Mike picked up the cat and swished it experimentally through the air. He saw Honey quiver slightly with anticipation.

'I can't believe I'm doing this!' he said, under his breath. But a second later the thongs cracked down onto their target with a satisfying sound, followed instantly by a groan of sheer lust from the helpless figure on the bed.

The guest lounge turned out to be more like a small hall, at least fifty feet long and nearly as wide, with thickly padded leather armchairs and sofas scattered about, low oak tables

177

serving each cluster of seats. The background lighting level, provided by a series of hidden wall uplighters, was low, but there was a circle of spotlights trained on an uncarpeted area in the centre of the room, which was dominated by the most strangely cruel tableau Alison could ever have imagined.

At one end of the boarded area were two upright pillars spaced about six feet apart. Alison realised immediately that these had to be what Paula had referred to as punishment perches, for one was already in use. And the other, whilst standing empty at present, showed precisely how the punishment was administered and also why the girl she had seen in the blind and deaf hood had had such prominent looking labia.

Each beastly contraption comprised the main upright, a round pole of approximately three inches diameter, standing about four feet high. On the top of each was a narrow plate of either wood or metal, covered with dull leather. It was some six inches long and maybe three wide and the two ends curved upwards. From its centre rose two ominous looking dildoes, which Alison very soon learned were actually vibrators. The smaller one was as large as the ones Alison had so far seen employed only to fill and stimulate the vagina, though its tip was very much tapered, presumably to effect easier entry.

The larger dildo was also tapered a little, but at its base it flared out to occupy the full width of the plate upon which it was mounted. Alison winced at the thought of how much it would stretch the unfortunate victim, and at how the rough rubber nodules set along its length would reduce her to a quivering jelly in seconds.

The second pole was a testament to the perches' effectiveness. Alison assumed the girl was the same one she had seen in the corridor, but it was only a guess, for the heavy isolation helmet precluded any chance of identification. Her arms were still trussed behind her in the long leather sleeve, but now a short chain ran from the steel ring at the bottom to a ring set in the pole, forcing the poor wench to sit bolt upright and thrust out her full breasts. The thick rings with which her nipples had been pierced now had large, pear-shaped gold weights hooked onto them, stretching her teats and dragging her breasts down.

Her legs, one each side of the upright, had been strapped tightly to it at thigh, knee and ankle, so that she was held rigidly like a marionette, blind, virtually deaf, dumb and completely at the mercy of whoever might happen by. And from the chain between her nipples, now hung a neatly printed sign. Alison peered closer and read:

I AM A DISOBEDIENT SLUT AND DESERVE
CONSTANT PUNISHMENT.
PLEASE TURN ME ON OR OFF
AS YOU SEE FIT
FOR I AM FIT ONLY
TO BE FUCKED BY A MACHINE

Alison turned away in horrified disbelief, but the other half of the display area contained an equally terrible tableau. The whipping frame had clearly been designed by a malicious genius, and a good deal of money had gone into its construction. Made mostly of shining stainless steel, it too was mounted on a sturdy four foot upright, but there all similarity to the punishment perches ended.

At the top of the upright was a curious looking universal joint mechanism, from which sprouted, like the spokes of a wheel, five steel arms of various lengths. The girl, who wore a thick leather mask identical to that worn by the perched slave, had been fastened to these like a pinned starfish, arms and legs strapped, each by means of three restraints, so that she faced the poles. The fifth pole, shorter than the rest, was the most maniacal effort of all. It reared up in front of the girl's mouth and Alison saw that it was adjustable to enable it to wreak its fiendish work no matter how large or small the victim.

On the end of it and set at right angles was an adjustable clamp that was designed to go inside the mouth. The zipper on the mask was open to facilitate that. A strap around the back of the girl's head ensured she could not free herself from it, which she must surely have yearned to do, for there was a small wheel that, when turned, opened the jaws wider, and they had currently been set so that her mouth was forced open as far as possible. When Alison, at Kristin's prompting, moved closer, she saw there were even little sub clamps that held the main ones to both upper and lower teeth, and a freestanding clamp had been tightened cruelly over the girl's tongue.

How she must have longed for the relative comfort of the ball gag she had worn while the mouth zipper had been closed, Alison thought, but then another awful thought took the place of that one. How did she know it had been a ball gag? Perhaps they left that clamp in place for the entire duration of the punishment. It was a terrifying thought!

The cruelty of the slave's situation did not end with the hood and gag, for about her waist had been laced a black leather corset, so tight that her body now seemed almost to be two separate halves. Her own lacing was severe enough, Alison thought, but what agony this poor creature must be enduring, even without the additional pain from the repeated floggings, evidence of which was clearly visible on her back, shoulders, arms, buttocks and thighs. How anyone had ever managed to lace her corset so tightly, Alison could not imagine, unless the girl's waist had been constantly reduced over a long period of months, or even years.

'How long does she have to stay like this?' Alison asked.

'It depends on who issued the punishment order and what for,' Kristin shrugged. 'I haven't checked on it this time. In fact, I'm not even sure who she is, though to judge from the waist, she's got to be one of only three.'

'And what sort of offence would merit such a severe punishment?'

'Oh, all sorts. But usually persistent disobedience or striking a handler or guest.'

'I should have thought you'd just get rid of anyone who didn't follow the rules,' Alison suggested. 'I thought the whole point of this place was that everyone was here as much for their own satisfaction as anything else.'

'Everyone starts that way,' Kristin said, 'but it doesn't always follow and, as for getting rid of anyone, we do, believe me. But as I told you before, it's not good policy to have different slaves wandering in and out of the system. Much better if we train them properly and put right any flaws in whatever training they may have had in the first place.'

'It... well, it does seem a bit extreme,' Alison said. There was a cold fist knotting itself into the pit of her stomach, and it was an effort to keep her voice steady as she spoke, for Kristin's revelations were awful. It was one thing to be part of a great big make-believe game, no matter how extreme some of the encounters were, but this was different. This was no pretend act, but deadly serious, and the poor girl spreadeagled before her was really suffering.

Alison turned back towards the girl on the perch, who remained as rigid and silent as when she had first seen her. She too, presumably, had no choice in what was done to her and Alison felt herself trembling at the thought that the same sort of fates awaited her if these people ever

181

discovered the truth about her.

'You can whip both these bitches if you wish,' Kristin offered. Alison was caught in a dilemma. She had no wish to inflict pain on someone who did not wish it, but on the other hand, to refuse might either arouse suspicion or make Kristin angry.

'I'm not sure,' she said, deciding that a certain amount of honesty was probably her best route. 'As you know, my only experience of these things has been from watching others, or from what has been done to me. I know how much I can take myself, but I've no idea how to administer the right amount of force.'

'It's easily enough learned,' Kristin said. 'As long as you don't rip their pretty hides to shreds, that's all that matters for a punishment flogging. These sluts haven't been put up here for their own benefit, just to fire up their fannies with a bit of slap and tickle. They're intended to suffer and that means they don't offend so easily in the future. Oh, it's quite likely that she may get off on the beating somewhere along the line. All our slaves are conditioned to the pleasure from pain syndrome, but the pleasure won't be sufficient to make the pain worthwhile.'

Kristin walked across to the edge of the boarded area, to where a low table stood before a semi-circle of five armchairs. There was an ashtray in the centre of it, overflowing with cigarette butts, evidence of a fairly long occupation of these ringside seats by several people, and a long whip lay coiled next to it. Kristin picked it up, turned, and with a flick of the wrist cracked the rawhide expertly in midair. The girl on the punishment frame did not twitch, although Alison was sure she must have heard the noise, even through the padded helmet.

Coiling the whip again, Kristin walked back to rejoin Alison. 'This,' she said, indicating the whip, 'is a skill that *does* take some learning. A cane, a strap, or a crop can't do too much damage, but a proper bullwhip can peel the skin off even the toughest hide. As I said, we don't want to do that, even for the most serious offenders, so the trick is to get it just right.'

She flicked the whip again, but this time aiming it at the helpless figure, and as the leather cracked against skin Alison saw, as though drawn by an invisible red pen, a perfectly straight welt appear on the girl's right shoulder. A strangled, gurgling wail came from the gaping mouth, repeated as the whip produced a mirror image mark on the left shoulder. A third and fourth line were rapidly added, one on each buttock. Kristin turned, saw the look of anguish on Alison's face, and began recoiling the whip.

'Perhaps we'd better leave your further education to another day,' she said. 'Best to start on something a little more basic. I presume you intended to redden Teddy's backside for him, though?'

'Only with a paddle, or maybe a light cane,' Alison said. 'I didn't want to really hurt him.'

'Oh, Teddy would take some hurting,' Kristin assured her. 'If he's in the right frame of mind, I've known him have a relay of girls paddling him steadily for an hour and come two or three times in the process, as long as one of them gives him a little encouragement at the same time.'

It was crazy, Alison thought, how if somebody had told her that about Teddy just a few days before it would have banished all thoughts of love, lust, desire or even liking for the man. And yet now, hearing that simply made her jealous that some other female might be able to satisfy him. Overwhelmed by a sudden lack of reason and a mounting anger she did not want to explain, she made a snap decision.

'Have you a cane I can use?' she asked. Kristin looked mildly surprised.

'Naturally,' she said, pointing to a rack of implements on the edge of the spot-lit area. 'Take your pick. What changed your mind?'

Alison strode across to the rack, speaking over her shoulder.

'I just thought I ought to make sure I don't disappoint my errant little boy,' she said. 'And if I don't cane her, someone else is certain to, so what's another six strokes one way or another. Besides, I don't even know her, and will probably never find out who she is.'

Chapter Ten

Trouble Brewing

By the time Alison returned to Teddy's room, she was astonished to discover that over an hour had elapsed and she was still no nearer getting started on her mission to expose Dennison Hall for what it really was.

Teddy still lay as she had left him, his chest rising and falling in a relaxed rhythm, and she wondered what sort of thoughts had been going through his head in her absence. A lot different from those in the minds of the two slaves she had just left, she was sure, for Teddy knew that his bondage ordeal was only short-term and was unlikely to be taken to any extreme he could not handle. She wondered how he would cope with hours on one of those perches, or strapped to the whipping frame with that cruel metal gag forcing his jaws apart. Alison was positive she would not handle it too well herself.

Teddy turned his head towards the door as Alison closed it behind her, but he made no sound and simply waited for her to approach. His cock was semi-flaccid, lying across his lower stomach. But once again, as soon as she touched it, it began to respond rapidly.

'Naughty boy,' she scolded quietly. 'We'll have to do something about this first.' Stooping over him, she took the head of it into her mouth and sucked gently until his shaft was completely rigid. She pulled back, still holding it in one hand, but now licking it in little flurries, eliciting a moan from behind the gag. 'I want to see this wicked thing do its stuff now,' Alison purred. 'Otherwise it doesn't get what it really wants. Come on you naughty boy, let's have you. Next time around I want you to have a bit of staying power.'

Whether it was the effect of her words, or the persistent masturbatory strokes of her fingers, Teddy suddenly went rigid, arched his back, and a geyser of milky whiteness erupted from his penis, splattering both himself and Alison. She continued to milk him as the secondary spasms subsided, until she was satisfied that she had drained him completely, and then lifted her rubber-sheathed hand to her mouth and slowly licked the spendings from it.

'Good boy,' she whispered. 'And now I think you've earned yourself a thorough paddling.' She patted his member, which still remained stoically upright, and slid from the bed.

The act of caning the anonymous slave girl in the guest lounge had done little for Alison, and she had not really put much effort into it, if she were honest with herself. The girl had shown little reaction to the cuts across her buttocks and thighs anyway, and Alison wondered if perhaps she had become inured to anything but the most severe pain by constant exposure to it. Alison's own beating of her had been terminated at six strokes by the arrival of three guests, two men and a woman, all in their thirties and all wearing very bizarre costumes made of red leather.

The woman, who looked Spanish or Italian, appeared to be the instigator in the group and quickly selected a long whippy crop. Then, as the two men stood back, she began to lash the girl with slow, deliberate strokes, seemingly increasing the venom with which she struck each time until, by the fourth, the slave girl was gasping and groaning, with saliva dripping from her open mouth. Alison had excused herself and watched no more, wondering what sort of mentality could derive pleasure from inflicting such genuine torture on another human being.

Confronted now with Teddy and the broad-bladed paddle she had selected for the next stage of her plan, Alison felt a different emotion from the distaste she had experienced earlier. This beating she was going to enjoy, but only because it was not a real beating and the strokes she laid on would be done with something akin to genuine affection, if not something even deeper. Teddy would enjoy his enforced suffering as much as she would enjoy being the cause of it, she knew – or at least hoped.

She stroked his rampant organ with the end of the rubber paddle and saw his body stiffen again. Yes, he was ready for it, ready for her. With a good deal of effort she managed to roll Teddy onto his stomach, presenting his lightly tanned buttocks for her attention. Gently, she stroked with the paddle blade again, caressing the area she intended to target. Teddy, helpless inside the laced leather cocoons, shivered slightly, and Alison saw his muscles tense in anticipation.

The sound of the flat rubber plate striking his firm flesh was far louder than Alison had expected and she started back in alarm, concerned that she might have put too much effort into her swing. However, unlike the cane or whip used on the slave girl under punishment, this implement was mostly show and very little effect. At least, very little in comparison to the more extreme choices that were employed in the house.

Certainly the paddle caused Teddy to jump visibly, and an area of his buttocks began turning pink immediately. But not a sound escaped from behind the gag and he lay still, awaiting the next stroke. Alison paced the round dozen blows carefully, waiting perhaps half a minute between each one, all the while employing both the paddle and her gloved hands to caress the beaten area in between times.

By now she noticed her victim was breathing quite heavily, his face turned to one side to avoid burying his nose in the bed covers.

Laying aside the paddle, Alison pulled herself back onto the bed and heaved Teddy over onto his back once more. The gag and the blindfold obscured most of his features, but what little she could see of his cheeks looked as flushed as the cheeks lower down. She smiled to herself, seeing his cock still rigidly erect, and eased her right knee over him, straddling the top of his thighs and grasping the massive shaft in both hands.

'Now I'm going to fuck you, Teddy Edward,' she cooed. 'I'm not an old hag and I don't look like one any more, though you can imagine what you want under that blindfold. But I'm going to keep reminding you of who and what I am, and whether you like it or not, you can't stop me from fucking you.' Beneath her Teddy remained silent as she eased herself forward, releasing her grip on him with one hand in order to lift her skirt and petticoats clear of the action.

She knew she was already wet and would have no trouble getting his thick rod into her, so she wasted no time on preliminaries or niceties. Instead, lining up the head of his organ, she dropped onto him in one swift movement, gasping with pleasure as his hardness immediately filled her, and reaching for her clitoris to stimulate it with her rubber finger. Leaning forward, she used her free hand to tug at the buckle on the blindfold, tearing it away from his face and tossing it across the room.

Teddy blinked at the sudden invasion of light, but as his eyes focussed again, he stared straight up into her face. Alison had half expected that he would either shut his eyes or try to avert his gaze, but he did neither as she began to move up and down on him. It was a wonderful feeling, knowing she was in total control; as good as when their positions had been reversed earlier, or maybe, just maybe, even better. Either way, Alison was in her own little seventh heaven.

The gag she would remove later, for she wanted to see all of his beautiful face when she took him for the second time. But for now just gazing into his gorgeous deep eyes was enough, especially knowing that he was not going to climax for quite some time yet; not after the number of orgasms he had so recently enjoyed. In fact, Alison thought, through the haze of sumptuous delirium, any normal man would have been pushed to raise the standard at all under the current circumstances!

'Well, my darling Teddy,' she breathed, 'how's this for a bit of therapy?'

Marcia slept alone, mindful of the likelihood of there being hidden cameras in her room. It was always a temptation when someone offered the services of a new slave, but she had no intention of leaving potential blackmail material in her ex-husband's hands. Besides, she told herself as she settled down beneath the covers, it made a pleasant change to enjoy an uninterrupted night's sleep.

She awoke to the knock at her door slightly after daybreak, and called out for whoever it was to enter. It proved to be one of the maids, a girl of about Alison's age, carrying a tray upon which was a pot of tea and a round of buttered toast. The maid placed it on the bedside table and bobbed a little curtsey, standing obediently to see if there was anything else she could do. Marcia smiled at her.

'Thank you,' she said and pointed to the connecting door that led through to the en suite bathroom. 'If you would be so kind as to run me a bath, I'll get myself moving early. I've a long drive ahead of me this morning.' The girl curtsied again and Marcia saw the telltale white strip between her parted lips. It really was a cunning little device, she had to admit, and had already decided to have a word with one of her specialist craftsmen the moment she returned home.

The ball gag had a much more dramatic effect, it was true, but with this invention it would be possible to take a slave along on a shopping expedition and keep him or her gagged throughout, and she knew several of her clients who would thrill at that prospect. As the girl went through to begin running the water Marcia poured herself the first cup of tea, stirred it, and picked up one of the dainty pieces of toast. She was on her second cup before the maid returned to stand in the doorway, signifying that the bath was ready for her.

Marcia never made it to the bath. Instead, she had taken only two or three paces from the bedside when the first wave of dizziness overtook her. Gasping, she shook her head and turned back to cling onto the bedpost, blinking furiously in an effort to clear her vision. She felt suddenly hot and then cold and clammy. She opened her mouth to tell the girl to fetch help, but all that emerged was a slurred jumble of sounds and in any case, as she began slipping into unconsciousness, she understood the truth. There would be no help arriving, at least, not the help she wanted!

Alison slept far beyond the dawn, exhausted at last by her efforts. Beside her Teddy also slept the sleep of innocence, freed now from his bondage and also, if his efforts of the latter part of their encounter were anything to judge by, freed of a lot of the emotional baggage he had brought with him.

Alison awoke first and, after a minute or so staring up at the canopied covers above her, she turned and raised herself on one elbow to gaze at Teddy's sleeping features instead. He really was quite beautiful, and she was definitely well on the road to falling in love with him totally. It could prove quite a relationship, she thought with a grin, and probably a lot more liberal than the majority of people would think possible. But then this was nineteen sixty-eight, and the world outside was changing its moral viewpoints at an amazing rate.

She reached down under the thin sheet and her fingers closed about his limp penis. He stirred and grunted, but did not wake. His organ, however, seemed to have a mind of its own and quickly grew stiff in her hand. Pushing the cover clear, Alison straddled him and took his full length into her eager sex.

'Wakey wakey, Teddy,' she purred, as he finally began to surface. 'This is your early morning alarm call.'

Ralph Hancock stared down at the naked, unconscious figure of his former wife, his face a mask of anger and hatred. Behind him Kristin waited patiently, not daring to interrupt his deep thoughts. Finally, when he did speak, his voice was barely under control.

'Get a couple of the boys up here and take her down to the stable block. She'll be out cold for two or three hours at least, and when she comes round I want her to have the shock of her life. Whatever's going on here I don't know, but I intend to get to the bottom of it. And lift the little transvestite whore and the slut she recommended to us.

'She's up to something and it means no good to us, whatever it may be. I'm going to give Sir George a ring and see if he's heard any rumours. Meanwhile, spread the word to be ready to clear everything out at a moment's notice. We'll use the barges on the underground canal and have the vehicles ready over by Sealey's Bridge. If we do get raided, as long as none of us are here, it won't matter.

'I've got documentation to prove I'm leasing this place to a wealthy Arab and I'll have alibis to say I was five hundred miles from here.'

'Where will we go?' Kristin demanded. 'We've got nearly forty slaves here, and about twelve guests at the moment. Shall I telephone and cancel all the impending arrivals?'

'No, but explain that we might have to drop everything and hightail it. Tell them we're well prepared, but to leave their own vehicles somewhere safe and either use taxis or hire cars – false names, of course – for the last leg. As to where we go, I've already made plans for such a situation. It's not as ideally suited as this place, but I've bought a somewhat rundown little castle in the wilds of Scotland. It'll do as a refuge until everything blows over, always assuming there is something to blow over at all.

'I may be overreacting,' he said, turning back to look at the unconscious Marcia, 'but you never know with this one. She'd do anything to get one over on me, even though we always manage to maintain a civil relationship. A pity,' he added, looking suddenly pensive. 'It could have been so different.' He turned and strode to the bedroom door.

'I'll leave her to you,' he said, turning the handle. 'Give her the full treatment. Even if there's no real danger involved, she's lied to me and I can't have that. It's about time she realised who's the master around here!'

Still blissfully unaware of developments in other parts of the house, Alison was collected by Paula mid-morning and taken below to be showered and then dressed in a fresh rubber outfit. She was given the same light meal as on the previous day, and then sent to the kitchen under restraint as on the first time. Expecting to be sent out on domestic chores again, she was somewhat surprised when Paula reappeared and beckoned for her to follow.

Hoping that Teddy had sent for her again, she was more than a little disappointed to be returned below stairs and locked back into her cell, a heavy steel collar secured around her neck, from which a chain ran to a ring set in the masonry. No explanation was offered and, with the clamp gag in place, Alison could not have raised any query, even had she dared do so. Instead, she simply had to lie on the bed and await further developments.

Kristin finally appeared, just when Alison was beginning to think she had been forgotten. The tall blonde released the gag and removed it, but left the chain in place.

'Now then, slut,' she rasped. 'I want to ask you a few questions. For a start, what's your name?'

Alison blinked. 'Mitzi, Mistress,' she said, eagerly. Her reward was an explosion of coloured lights and a stinging pain as the older woman slapped her hard across the face.

'Don't play games with me, girl,' she snapped. 'What's your real name?'

'Louise!' Alison gasped, shaking her head. 'Louise MacIntosh.'

'And what did you do before you came here?'

'Not… not very much,' Alison said. 'I was a waitress and a typist and I worked behind the reception desk at a hotel in Nottingham, the Regal, but that only lasted a few weeks because one of the supervisors was jealous of me. I also worked in a couple of pubs and went to France to pick grapes one year. I bummed around over there for a while,' she said, using her experiences during her university holidays.

'Then I came back here and worked in an office for a small building firm.' Her father had his own small business, so Alison reckoned she was on pretty safe ground there, as she had often helped out when he was short staffed.

'So, what brought you here, to us?' Kristin asked.

'I… I thought you knew,' Alison protested. 'I have, well you know, certain desires, needs, and something like this is ideal. Mistress Marcia suggested I needed something more severe than she was able to offer, plus I would get good money for it.'

'And how long have you known Mistress Marcia?' Kristin persisted. 'And how did you come to know her in the first place?'

'About a month, I think' Alison said, thinking fast. 'I met her through a friend, at a party.'

'Boyfriend or girlfriend?'

'Girl. I knew her as Honey, but I don't think that was her real name.'

Kristin's eyes narrowed. 'It's not,' she affirmed. 'Not if we're talking about the same one. So Lady Hoity-Toity introduced you?'

Alison nodded. 'She was never hoity-toity with me, though.'

'No, she wouldn't be,' Kristin muttered. 'She likes to prove she retains the common touch, though her family is so aristocratic it makes poor old Teddy look positively nouveau riche.' She paused, studying Alison's face.

'So, you'd have no idea why Mistress Marcia should pretend to be phoning a number up north and then phone her own house and carry out a conversation with the dialling tone?' she continued again.

Alison shook her head. 'None at all,' she confessed. 'Are you sure?'

'Positively. All calls on all the lines, both in and out, are recorded, and they go through a central exchange that keeps a log of all outgoing numbers dialled. Later she called the same number again, though this time she spoke to a woman,

194

probably her fucking Ladyship, though it wasn't a clear line.'

Alison tried to look blank. 'I'm sorry, Mistress,' she said. 'I can't help you, you must believe me.'

'Must I indeed?' Kristin sneered, her mouth twitching. 'Well, we'll see about that.' She opened the door and called out two men's names and almost immediately the cell was filled by the muscular figures of two leather clad handlers. Kristin nodded to Alison.

'We know something's going on,' she said, 'but not what, except that it's not to do with the police. Master Ralph knows the Assistant Chief Constable and he's certain that there's nothing brewing there. So, you're not a police spy. But you may have reasons for being here other than what you say. Of course, I could whip it out of you, but Master Ralph wants you kept in good condition. Senseless to ruin good merchandise, especially when there's another route. So, for now we'll just keep you where you can't get into any trouble, or cause any.' She turned to the two men.

'I could just leave her locked in here, but that would just be boring... for all concerned. But if she isn't kosher we can't risk letting her wander about the place, even under full restraint. She might see faces and hear things she shouldn't, not that it'll do her much good where she's going. Anyway, I've got a better idea and it'll give her time to reflect on whether she is the born masochist she'd have us believe.

'Get her stripped and prepare her for a perching,' she ordered, clearly enjoying the horror that spread instantly across Alison's face. 'A few hours of that might change her mind!'

Marcia came round very slowly, and for a minute or more could not remember where she was. Suddenly it all came flooding back to her and she opened her eyes wide, struggling to sit up, only to discover that she'd been totally restrained whilst unconscious and was forced to remain laying on the cold flagstone floor. She peered along her body and groaned at what she saw, for she understood only too well where she was and what was planned for her.

She was in a stall in a stable, with straw piled thickly on one half of its floor, and a collection of reins and bridles hanging from pegs set into the partition walls on either side. However, although she had never seen the inside of this building before, she knew that Ralph did not use it for four-legged horses; the ponies who occupied these stables were two-legged, human ones, probably all attired as she was now.

Her legs had been encased in thigh length white leather boots, not unlike the sort of thing that Honey would have favoured, but they did not boast stiletto heels as those in Honey's wardrobe did. Instead, although they were shaped so that the foot was arched in exactly the same way as it would have been in a conventional high heeled boot, the platform soles and heels had been welded into one piece and flared out and shaped to resemble a horse's hoof, to which, judging by their weight, had been nailed a heavy horseshoe.

Her arms had been laced together behind her in a single leather sleeve, identical to the ones used on the girls she had seen on the punishment perches, except that this one was white to match her boots. Her lower body was encased in something that resembled a pair of stainless steel, high cut panties. Inside these were two dildos, and Marcia could feel their insistent pressure in her lower orifices every time she tried to move. The front dildo was held in position by means of a short flat bar, for the main metal had been cut away to leave her vulva and labia completely on display.

From the rear dildo projected a luxuriant white tail.

Her head had been encased in a white leather bridle, although so far the two rings from which the bit would be attached hung empty at either side of her mouth. At least they had not risked her choking to death whilst under the anaesthetic. At either side of her eyes were fitted large blinkers, restricting her field of vision to what was immediately ahead. And she could feel that her hair had been drawn up into a high pony-tail, for it was exerting a pressure on the skin of her forehead, so savagely had it been tied up. In addition, someone had glued the longest false eyelashes imaginable over her own and applied thick mascara to them. The harness was buckled tightly and connected to a stiff collar about her throat, forcing her head up, unless she wanted to endure the discomfort of the inverted V-shape at the front constantly pressing into the soft skin beneath her chin.

She looked down again, being careful to move only her eyes, and sighed. She had pierced her nipples many years ago, but instead of the usual delicate gold rings, her swollen teats had been hung with heavy silver bells, and when she moved her head suddenly she knew that similar bells had been put through her ears.

'Bastard!' she hissed aloud. She could imagine the satisfaction that Ralph had taken from seeing her being degraded like this, for he had always wanted to find a way to make her subservient to him. And now he'd done it, though quite why he'd decided to act against her now, she had no idea. Unless...

No, she shook her head. There was no way he could...

And yet... the phone must have been bugged, though she'd been certain it wasn't at the time. Damn! She cursed her gullibility, but then just as suddenly realised it wasn't necessarily a fatal mistake. As her head cleared further she began to put together a story which she hoped, fervently, Ralph Hancock would swallow.

Time, for Alison, had ceased to have any meaning, and the only world she knew was the dark one into which she now found herself locked. It was a world where her every reaction was controlled by and centred around the twin invasions that reared up from the perch, and the constant drag on her newly pierced nipples from the heavy gold pendants that she'd seen hung on them in the last moments before they had inserted the soft plugs into her ears and drawn the padded leather punishment hood over her head.

She was dimly aware of the nagging discomfort of her arms being bound so cruelly behind her in the sleeve, and of the hard edges of the narrow plate on which they had balanced her. But they had quickly become as nothing once the two vibrators had sprung into life. Orgasm had followed orgasm until her existence became one long climax, draining her and shattering any chance of coherent thought, other than in the brief respites that arrived every now and then. Whether the little machines switched off at regular intervals, or whether it was a random pattern, Alison neither knew nor cared, and it came as a total shock when she suddenly found herself being unbuckled and lifted down.

As the hood came off and she blinked against the unaccustomed light, she saw the shadowy figures of the audience who had been watching her in such a wretched state, and shuddered as she collapsed against the nearer of the two handlers. There was a faint smattering of ironic applause as they dragged her from the room and into a small annex where they mopped her face with a cold cloth and allowed her to drink a beaker of water. The plugs were still in her ears, so her hearing was not very acute, and she didn't pick up the telltale rustle as the hood was pulled back into place again.

At some stage during her ordeal someone had unzipped the front opening in the mask and removed the rubber ball from her mouth, presumably so that those watching could savour the animal noises and screeches of lust that the perch had wrung from her throat. But now it was replaced and the zipper firmly closed. She heard a male voice, close to her ear, but what it was saying she had no way of telling, though the sudden tug of the leash clipped to her collar was a clear enough signal that she was expected to start moving.

Now Alison discovered how that other poor girl must have felt, stumbling along in tapering heels, completely blind and deaf and bumping against walls and doorframes as she struggled to maintain the cruel pace her tormentors were setting. The ground beneath her feet suddenly changed and the surface became much less even. At the same time, the blast of cool air around her all but naked body suggested they were now outside.

She was seized by the shoulders and dragged down, the feel of the soft grass against her skin confirming what the cool air had indicated. But she had little time to consider the implications of that, for her legs were hauled roughly apart and secured by their ankle straps to something that resisted her feeble attempts to test it. A moment later, she felt something thrusting against the lips of her sex, only this time it was warm flesh and blood and not the cool hardness of the rubber that had invaded her previously.

The man took her roughly, humping vigorously up and down before coming in a hot flood. His place was immediately taken by another, and then a third and a fourth. Alison was no longer responding to the couplings. Her bound arms, trapped beneath her, were causing her agony and it seemed as though something inside her had now switched off. She simply lay inert, gasping behind her gag, as her unseen tormentors used her as nothing more than something upon which to sate their lusts. To them, she understood, she was little more than a piece of meat, and tears stung her eyes and soaked their way into the tight leather that sheathed her head.

Marcia was faring a little better, but only relative to the treatment that had been handed out to Alison, and she had her own particular concerns to worry about.

A while after she had come round, a handler had appeared; a tall female with a strangely flat-featured face. Marcia guessed that her duties centred around the stable and its occupants, rather than anything in the house, for whilst she was not exactly ugly, she was very plain compared to Ralph's usual choice of handlers.

'Up,' she snapped, releasing the chain from Marcia's collar. Unsteadily, Marcia managed to regain an upright position, the two dildoes making their presence felt with every movement. She saw that the girl was holding a bit ready and, for a brief instant, considered trying to resist its being fitted, but the handler must have sensed the possibility of rebellion from the look in Marcia's eyes.

'You can be a good mare and we do this the easy way,' she warned. 'Otherwise, I'll summon help and shove a bar of carbolic into your mouth first. Your choice!'

The prospect did not appeal to Marcia and she opened her mouth obediently, giving the woman as big a look of disdain as she could muster. The handler simply laughed, thrust the tongue plate in firmly and connected both ends of the rubber bite rod to the waiting rings with practised efficiency. Reins followed and the woman quickly demonstrated their efficiency, for when they were tugged, the tongue plate shot upwards into the roof of Marcia's mouth, causing her to grunt and almost retch.

'There now, don't you make a magnificent animal?' the handler taunted. She turned Marcia and indicated for her to lead the way out of the stall, bells jingling and the heavy hoof boots making every step an effort. The building was laid out in simple efficient style, with a row of ten stalls down either side of its length, facing inwards to a central area which contained a number of ominous looking timber or metal structures and a small racing trap, to which the handler now guided Marcia.

She was forced between the shafts and turned to face forward, while harnesses and straps were buckled into place on either hip of the metal pants, to the ring at the end of the arm glove and to the back of her collar. After a final check, the woman seemed satisfied and climbed onto the padded driver's seat.

'Right, horsey,' she intoned. 'Forward, at a walk.'

The plate hit the roof of Marcia's mouth and at the same time the long leather whip slapped across her unprotected shoulders. With a sharp gasp she leaned her weight forward and began hauling the cart and its occupant towards the open door at the end of the barn. However, the outside was not their initial destination, for with a tug on the reins, the driver indicated that she wanted Marcia to head to where a large piece of sacking hung on the wall to one side of the doorway.

'Whoa,' she cried, leaping down to the ground again and walking around in front of Marcia. 'Right, I always like my ponies to see exactly how splendid they look when I've finished with them,' she said, and turned and tugged the sacking clear, revealing a large mirror. Marcia gasped and tried to turn away, but the woman simply slapped her face and ordered her to look at herself.

Indeed, Marcia thought, she did present the sort of

spectacle that would impress a lot of the people she knew, but never in her wildest dreams had she thought she would be the person to provide it. And how thoroughly the bitch had worked on her while she'd lain helpless. Her usually sleek black hair had been bleached pure white and starched in some way so that the high pony-tail rose up like a plume. For a moment she thought that the same treatment had been given to her eyebrows, until she realised they had been shaved off altogether and another pair, much higher, drawn in.

Around her eyes, in addition to the incredible false lashes, someone had added thick dark liner and dark blue shadow, over which had been added silver glitter that sparkled merrily at her every movement. She groaned, but not aloud, for she was determined not to give the bitch the satisfaction of seeing how the sight of herself really made her want to cringe. Instead, she kept her gaze resolutely ahead and stood absolutely motionless until the handler finally tired of the game.

'Okay, Dobbin,' she announced, slapping Marcia's hip with the back of her hand. 'Let's go for a little trot. I need a few things from the workshop, so you may as well take me. Hup there,' she cried, leaping easily back onto her seat, the sudden added weight making the shafts dip and almost unbalancing her poor pony. 'Let's move it my girl. Go right, and let's get some effort into this!'

Chapter Eleven

Stable Diets

Ralph Hancock tossed the miniaturised camera and the lock picks onto the table and glared at Melanie, who stood naked and chained between two female handlers, embarrassed and ashamed that his male member was in full view when she was not correctly attired for her role as shemale maid.

'I suppose you're going to tell me that this was for holiday snaps?' Hancock sneered. 'And these,' he added, flicking at the picks, 'are for cleaning your teeth.' He turned to the handlers. 'Take the little cunt away and string it up for a good whipping. I want to know the truth, but try not to damage the goods in getting it.' He waved them dismissively away.

'This was meant to be either sabotage, blackmail, or some sort of exposure operation, but this pathetic slut is only a pawn. The bloody queen is the one I'm going to make suffer and I intend to give her the sort of ride she never expected. Go on, get her out of my sight and she'd better be grateful that pitiful cock adds to her value, otherwise I'd have a certain friend of mine remove it and feed it to her on a plate!'

Alison was in some sort of open air compound, surrounded on four sides by a high mesh fence, though how high she could not tell, for the hood had been left in place since she had been ravished by the unseen handlers. They had, however, made certain alterations to the way in which she was dressed. She now had the use of her arms to assist her balance, though her hands had been rendered useless by lacing them into a leather mitten that was then doubled into a fist and locked immovably.

They had also exchanged her footwear for a pair of long leather boots with heels so high she was forced to walk on tiptoe, and only a trained ballerina could have stayed upright on them for long. Laced into the most severe corset yet, the heavy pendants still dangling from her sore nipples, she had then been dumped unceremoniously in her present confinement and left to make the most of her new environment.

How long she had been there she had no idea at all, for the enforced silence and blindness was as disorienting as it had been when she was strapped on the perch. But it was becoming a long ordeal and her throat was dry from lack of liquid. She wondered if this was how they meant to finish her off; left to die from dehydration like a neglected animal. She had to fight back the waves of panic that threatened to overtake her.

No, it was unlikely that was Hancock's plan, she kept repeating to herself. He had made reference to not damaging her, and the whippings she had received so far had not been anywhere near as severe as those she had seen inflicted on the girl on the frame. So, presumably, he had other uses for her, though it was not much better concentrating on that. Better to just wait, she reasoned, settling against the angle of the fences at one corner.

She tried to flex her fingers for the umpteenth time, but it was a pointless exercise. As in everything else she had witnessed at Dennison Hall, the hand restraints were professionally designed and made, and performed the task for which they were intended perfectly. If only something would happen. At least when they had been forcibly stimulating her there had been something to focus on and the dragging time had not seemed so bad. She opened her thighs a little and experimented with trying to put her hands down to her sex, but it was not very effective and there would be no relief gained that way.

Damn them and damn her, she thought fiercely. She'd become little more than a sex toy. There she was in mortal danger, quite probably, and all she could think of was that she was getting frustrated again!

She wondered how Marcia was faring, for it was now obvious that the dominatrix had slipped up and that had led them to suspect Alison herself. And then there was Melanie, also somewhere in the house. It was a real mess, and their only hope was Mike. Except the place was like a fortress and one of the handlers had let it slip, just before the isolation hood had been pulled into place, that there was a contingency plan for evacuation in the event of any police attempt to raid the estate.

Mike came out of the bathroom towelling his hair vigorously. Honey still lay languidly on the bed in another of her white latex catsuits, but for him, he had decided, enough was enough.

'Something's gone very wrong,' he said gravely. 'It's thirty-six hours since we heard from her. We ought to inform the police.'

'And tell them what?' Honey asked. 'With Hancock's contacts they'll block a search warrant attempt, and any routine visit will reveal nothing suspicious, you can bet. Besides, I know how the police work in these cases. Before they even go near Dennison Hall they'll want to start poking around here, and you know what that would mean. It would take days to dismantle and move everything from downstairs, by which time anything might have happened.'

'Well, we can't just lay around here screwing,' Mike protested. He studied Honey's delicious outline and his face softened. 'Much as I find it so delightful,' he added.

Honey sat up on the bed. 'I haven't just been laying around,' she said. 'The morning before she left to go up there, the Mistress gave me some names and telephone numbers, together with instructions of what to do in the event of an emergency. While you were in the bath I phoned the main number.'

'Whose number is it?' Mike asked, discarding the towel and reaching for the open packet of cigarettes.

'A certain lady who uses the name Miss Jezebel in our circles, though her real name is Hannah Levy.'

'And what does she do?' Mike asked. 'I mean, how does she fit into this?'

'I think it might be better if she told you herself,' Honey replied. 'Her talents cover a wide ranging field, as you'll discover.' She turned her head to glance at the bedside clock. 'In about another hour, as it happens,' she added.

Marcia felt more tired than she could remember in years, for the past twenty-four hours had been filled with constant activity, with no more than two separate hour long breaks in which she was permitted to get a little sleep. Throughout, she had been kept as a pony girl, the heavy hoof boots dragging at every step, as she was alternately forced to pull the little trap around the vast grounds and then "put to stud" as the stable handler, Rose, described it.

This entailed Marcia being forced to stand bent over in a timber pillory, still wearing her bridle, bit and blinkers, while the two dildoes were removed and a succession of strapping young pony boys, all similarly harnessed and booted, but with their faces masked, coupled with her forcefully. Afterwards Rose administered a heavy thrashing with a broad leather strap.

The worst part of her ordeal, though, was the humiliation she felt when Ralph simply stood and watched her being so cruelly used, not even deigning to avail himself of her defenceless situation.

'She always was a nag,' she heard him say to Rose, 'and nags should be used thoroughly. Strange, she doesn't look so bloody haughty now, does she?'

'Ponies quickly learn obedience here, Master Ralph,' Rose grinned at him, 'as you know. Each day can seem like a week, if I choose to make it so.'

Ralph laughed heartily. 'See if you can't make it more like a fortnight,' he said. He walked across to where one of the male handlers was re-harnessing Marcia to the shafts of the trap.

'Whatever your game is, bitch,' he sneered, 'it won't work. I've enough power in my pocket to make sure we get plenty of notice of any official activity, and you'll be in some nice little Arab stable long before then. I've already contacted potential buyers, and there's enough interest for me to hold a potentially very profitable auction.

'You and the bitch you passed on to me will be sold as a pair, once Rose has given her a bit of training too. She's only a little shorter than you, and you're both about the same build. Of course, she's a lot younger, so she'll help up your price quite a bit.' He reached out and flicked idly at Marcia's plume of blonde dyed hair.

'Interesting crowd, these Arab enthusiasts. Seems they don't like all this. They reckon that a big feathered plume is better, so we'll have to shave the pair of you completely before they get here. That'll be an interesting sight, won't it?'

Unable to reply, Marcia ground her teeth fiercely into the unyielding bit and fumed in silence.

The two women waiting in the room were dressed identically in tight leather trousers and leather bomber jackets, beneath which they wore what appeared to be some sort of leather vest. On their feet they wore leather ankle boots with spiked heels, though Mike noticed that the heels were no more than three inches high, which by the standards of what he was becoming accustomed to seeing in Marcia's establishment, was very modest.

The woman sitting nearer the door rose as he entered and extended her hand, the black nail polish glinting menacingly under the lights. She was perhaps five feet seven without her heels and had close-cropped black hair, dark eyes and very sharp, angular features. Mike guessed she had to be Jewish, even before she introduced herself.

'Hi, I'm Hannah Levy,' she said, flashing him a bright smile. 'And this,' she added, waving to her blonde companion, 'is Ruth.' The blonde girl stood up and likewise held out her hand.

'Ruth Goldman,' she said, gripping Mike's fingers even harder than Hannah had done. Mike tried not to wince and wondered how much training had gone into making her nearly six feet tall frame as athletic and powerful as it so clearly was. Extricating his hand, he eased himself into an empty chair and waited for someone else to take the lead. Opposite him, Honey coiled herself into a fourth chair and crossed her legs. Hannah broke the silence.

'As you may well know,' she began, 'Marcia had already spoken to me about this problem, although she didn't want us involved other than as a last resort.'

'Her "less than legal" resort?' Mike suggested.

Hannah nodded, her features suddenly grave. 'She was hoping that other more subtle methods might prevail, but it appears there's little chance of that now.'

'Not much chance,' Mike agreed. 'She's more than two

days overdue now, and Honey's tried Hancock's private line a couple of times. He's adamant that she left for Scotland, but we know she was headed straight back here, and that's only a few hours' drive.'

'So you think Hancock's holding her against her will?' Hannah asked.

'I don't think, I know,' Mike asserted. 'Plus he's got Alison and Melanie in there. If he's grabbed Marcia he must have rumbled our game, which means both the others are in deep trouble too. I don't know exactly how far he'd be prepared to go, but I know Marcia said she wouldn't put anything past him, even murder.'

'I doubt it'd come to that,' Hannah assured him. 'I know a bit about Ralph Hancock. Anyone in our line of, shall we say business, knows about him. He might hurt them, but he wouldn't kill them.'

'How can you be so sure?' Mike demanded.

'Because they're a valuable asset,' Ruth interposed. 'All he has to do is parcel them up and find himself a willing pilot and a remote airfield and presto, three lovely European slaves turn up in the middle east, two of them already nicely trained and the other a former dominatrix. The Arabs would just love that and they'd pay a high price. Marcia would probably be the most valuable, if only because they wouldn't be able to resist the thought of having a slave who used to be a mistress.'

'And Melanie would fetch a good price because of her own peculiar assets and attributes,' Hannah added.

'And Alison?'

'From what I've heard,' Hannah replied, 'she's an exceptionally beautiful girl, and seems to have taken to her role with a certain amount of relish. They'd pay well for her, believe me.' Her lip curled in distaste, and Mike was reminded that the Jews had only fought a bitter war with the Arabs the year before.

'It may already be too late then,' Mike said, his heart sinking.

Hannah shook her head. 'I doubt it,' she said. 'These things take a bit of arranging. Hancock will want the best price, even if he is just trying to get rid of them. He'll arrange some sort of auction, highest bidder taking the pot. He may not even sell them as a bulk lot. They may go to three different buyers.'

'So what are you suggesting?' Mike asked, his eyes moving from one girl to the other.

'A commando raid,' Hannah replied, evenly. Even though he'd suspected it might be something along those lines, Mike had to stifle a gasp, especially at the way the girl could suggest it so calmly.

'On the house?' he said. 'I've heard it's guarded like a fortress, with half wild guard dogs and suchlike.'

'Undoubtedly it is,' Hannah replied. She reached down behind the arm of her chair and, when her hand reappeared, it was holding a heavy and vicious looking handgun. 'These will take care of the dogs and their guards,' she said, with self-assurance.

This time Mike did gasp.

'You can't just go around shooting people in the dark,' he protested. 'Someone'll get killed and then the shit really will hit the fan!'

'Not with this,' Hannah grimaced. She pointed to the door, which was about thirty feet from where she sat. 'See the top right panel?' she asked. Mike followed her direction and nodded. 'Little knot, about four inches down and two in from the top right corner of it,' Hannah intoned, raising the gun. There was a dull crack and a whoosh of air, followed instantly by a much sharper crack as the long dart embedded itself right in the centre of the knot she had

210

indicated.

'Fuck me!' Mike breathed.

Hannah laughed harshly. 'Business before pleasure,' she quipped, lowering her weapon. Mike gaped at her in admiration.

'Where'd you learn to shoot like that?' he demanded. Hannah looked serious again.

'Three years with the Israeli Special Forces,' she said quietly. 'Major Levy at your service. Captain Goldman here had a year in the same unit and two years in the Israeli army before that. The rest of the girls have all done at least two years, so we're a pretty good team.'

'Girls?' Mike exclaimed, in open disbelief. 'You intend to raid that place with an army of girls?'

'Not if I can help it,' Hannah retorted. 'Oh, I dare say we could pull it off, but there's always the chance of one of our lot getting hurt and, in a place that size, they could form an inner perimeter and hold us off indefinitely, unless we got very lucky.'

'So what do you intend?'

Hannah tucked the gun out of sight again and sat back.

'Like I said,' she began, 'they'll probably hold an auction. Now, whether it's one buyer or three, they'll undoubtedly take them out of the country together. One clandestine flight carries less risk than several. That means they'll need a suitable airport, and there aren't as many of those around as you might think. In fact, looking at the map, there are only two they could possibly use, so we split our main assault group to cover them both.'

'And what if you're wrong?'

'It won't be the end of the world,' Hannah said. 'Well keep a reserve force of four of us and tail the vehicle they use. It'll be hard to miss it. To take three of them and a couple of handlers, probably a driver as well, they'll probably use a van. They may also send a car escort with a couple of heavies to watch their backs. I know I would.

'All three groups will be in radio contact, so we'll be able to redeploy at least one lot to reinforce us in time to take them at the airstrip.'

'How many girls have you got at your disposal, then?' Mike asked, bewildered.

'Right now, eighteen,' Hannah replied. 'If they don't make their move for another three days, I can have ten more. There's a group flying back home from Tel Aviv in the morning, but it'll take a little while to contact them all.'

'Back home?' Mike queried. 'So they're English?'

'Of course,' Hannah retorted. 'Jewish, yes, but as English as I am. And Ruth. I was born in Golders Green, but Ruth is a posh cow. She's from Canterbury.'

'But how come you served in the Israeli army?'

Hannah made a tutting sound. 'I thought you were supposed to be a journalist,' she sighed. 'There are thousands of Jews, from all over the world, who'd never seen Israel until four or five years ago. When it became clear there was going to be some sort of war, truckloads of us volunteered. After all, it's the land of our ancestors, and one Jew will always help another Jew.

'We were all involved in that madhouse last year and, though it's all simmered down a bit now, we'll all keep going back every few months for continued training. In the meantime, we've established our own little security firm here, and we're as good as any bunch of blokes.'

Mike's gaze travelled back to where the dart was still lodged firmly in the oak panelling. 'So I see,' he admitted. 'What's on the dart – a tranquilliser, I suppose?'

Hannah nodded. 'Very powerful and fast acting. We used to use it on night raids behind enemy lines. A couple of quick pops and you've got yourselves a couple of prisoners to take back for interrogation. It only lasts for about two hours, but if we can't get them out in that time, we deserve to have our arses kicked!'

The induction training of a pony girl was as arduous as the trainer was in a hurry, Alison quickly discovered, but it was such a relief to get out of the isolation hood that she hardly cared. And to her relief she saw that Marcia remained unharmed, even if that relief was seriously tempered by the sight of her initiating mistress in the same plight as herself.

After several hours drawing another of the single traps, the two women were brought together and a much more ornate looking cart produced. It was still designed to carry only one occupant, but the axle was much wider and the shafts further apart, so that the two "ponies" could be harnessed between them side by side. As the dour looking Rose and two male hands adjusted the various traces, Alison tried to sneak a sideways look at Marcia, but the older woman remained looking steadfastly ahead and the blinkers precluded any chance of either attracting the other's attention from the corner of an eye.

'This is a racing chariot,' Rose explained, moving around to take up a stance in front of them. 'The perimeter track of the estate is precisely four miles and one furlong, including its various bends and diversions. We have two days before you go up for auction, and during that time you will be trained to race over that course.

'You are both naturally fit, though not as fit as you would be if I had you here for a month, so four miles or so should not present too great a challenge to you. But I expect speed, precision, and good teamwork. If I do not get it, I'll put each of you in a team of four and let them run you half to death. Do I make myself clear?'

There was a jangling of harnesses and bells as two heads nodded in unison. Marcia, like Alison, had evidently decided that trying to resist or not cooperate was a pointless exercise.

'Good,' Rose continued. 'Now, I have set a time that I expect you to achieve by the time your potential new owners arrive. It is nothing compared to what a fully trained pair of pony girls can achieve, but they all understand that and all have excellent facilities to extend your training as far as necessary.' She made to turn away, but then hesitated, and a slow grin spread across her features.

'Oh yes,' she leered, 'and I nearly forgot. This evening we shave all your pretty blonde hair off for you. The Master thinks you may as well get used to it now as later, and I totally agree with him.'

Mike and Honey were having their first disagreement, and Honey was proving more forceful than he had anticipated. Out of her slave girl role, she was once again the independent minded young business executive, and she was not about to give way to him on any pretext.

'You just can't come along on this!' Mike protested. 'I know Hannah and Ruth and their little band are all females, but they've had proper training.'

'Okay then, so why are you going with them?' Honey demanded. 'You've not had training for this sort of thing, any more than I have.'

'It's different for me,' Mike argued. 'I'm a man.'

'Bullshit!' she snapped. 'Don't give me any of that male superior stuff now. Could you kill someone if you had to?'

'I don't know, I've never had to find out. But if I had to there'd be more chance of me doing it than there would with you. Listen, these bastards don't play games.'

'I told you that,' Honey said. 'But I'm not changing my mind. You want to go along because of Alison, which is fair enough, but I've got two friends up there. I happen to be very fond of Melanie as well as the Mistress.'

Mike sighed. 'But it's going to be climbing over fences, jumping walls, kicking down doors and all that sort of stuff,' he persisted. 'I just can't see you doing all that.'

'Listen, Mr Tough Guy,' Honey growled, pushing her face close to his, 'I've got three brothers who could tell you that I could climb trees faster and higher than them, run as fast as most boys my age, and punch just as hard. I've also got junior international medals for long jump, high hurdles and swimming, plus I played netball for my county and tennis for my university. Match that, if you can.'

Mike realised he had lost the argument. 'Okay, but promise me one thing,' he said. 'You and I – both of us – stay well back from the main action. I'm not such a male chauvinist as to think I can do what these hellions can either. Like you, I just want to be there to help a friend.'

'Agreed,' Honey said, smiling again. 'Meanwhile, we have six hours before we rendezvous with them, and just sitting here waiting will drive me bananas.'

Mike grinned at her. 'If you're suggesting what I think you're suggesting, I'm game,' he said.

Honey's smile became slightly lopsided. 'That's exactly what I am suggesting,' she said, 'but this time, if anyone's getting chained up, it ain't gonna be *moi*, okay? I wouldn't trust you not to leave me tied up in the cellar until it was all over.'

'Ah, but can I trust you?' Mike said.

Honey shrugged. '*Mais naturellement*,' she replied. 'After all, why would I try to stop a big strong man like you from sticking his fool head in a noose.' Suddenly, she became serious again. 'Listen,' she said earnestly. 'We *both*

215

go, okay?'

'Okay.'

'Then get shucked off, buster. I've got a few new tricks to show you!'

Chapter Twelve

A Day at the Races

Drawing the racing cart required a great deal of concentration from both human ponies. Not only did their blinkers cut out their peripheral vision, but the perfectionist Rose added another refinement, by strapping across their shoulders a lightweight metal frame, to which their head harnesses were anchored by short chains, adjusted so they were no longer able to turn their heads. Instead, they had to rely on their driver's skill and judgement, transferred to them by different pressures on their reins and spiteful urgings with the long driving whip.

They did two circuits of the perimeter fence, but there was no chance of their plight being spotted from beyond the double barrier of chain link and barbed wire. The estate seemed to be bordered on all sides by dense forest, with undergrowth so thick Alison doubted anyone could penetrate it.

After three hours, Rose called a halt and handed them over to one of the male stable hands to be watered.

He removed their bits in turn, but did not relax the tension on any of the harness straps, which meant that they were forced to suck in the cool liquid by means of a pliable nylon straw.

'Thanks,' Alison gasped, half under her breath, when he finally removed the tube from her mouth. The man, in reality a lad of no more than nineteen or twenty, with a shock of thick dark brown hair and a freckled, open face, regarded her sternly.

'No speaking,' he said, in a broad Scots accent. 'Ponies dinnae speak just because I take their bits oot tae feed 'em.' He grinned, quite maliciously. 'Nae that it matters mooch, hen,' he continued. 'I hear tell where you're bound they take away your speech cords by surgery.' He made a cutting motion with his free hand. 'Mistress Rose'll tell ye. All yon Arab pony girls can dae nae more than make a whinnying soond, jest like a real pony.'

Alison stared at him aghast, and next to her she sensed rather than felt Marcia stiffen in shared horror. She tried to see if the stable lad was joking, but his expression remained unchanged, and he added to their catalogue of horrors immediately.

'Mistress Rose reckons yons such a grand idee, she's gonnae get Master Ralph tae let her hae same of oor lassies done likewise. How'd ye fancy that then, pony girlie, gettin' put tae stud and made tae whinnie wi' pleasure?' He chuckled mirthlessly and began refitting Alison's bit, and despite herself, Alison felt the warm tears begin to trickle down her cheeks.

'Ruth's done a recce,' Hannah said, her eyes going from Mike to Honey and back again. 'There are three fences in all; a double inner fence and a single outer fence fitted with sensors, and in between is thick woodland for about five hundred yards.'

They were sitting in a blacked out van, parked off a B road, surrounded by woodland so dense that the late afternoon sun could not penetrate it and all around them was bathed in an eerie green glow. Hannah continued her report.

'Her party has been up here since last night and they've already effected a breach in the outer perimeter. Their alarm system is good, but Becky is better. She's our electronics expert, by the way. Nobody in the house knows we're about and so far the girls have managed to clear a path to within fifteen yards of the inner fence. We'll wait until it starts getting dark to do the rest, just in case.'

'I thought you said it would be better to try and ambush them when they tried to get the girls out of the country?' Honey reminded Hannah.

The dark-haired girl shrugged. 'In an ideal world, it would have been,' she admitted. 'However, this isn't an ideal world and my sources have tipped me off that there are several well known personages already on their way to this country. At least two of these men travel with a large entourage and you can bet they'll be armed, even if they don't collect their weapons until they're through customs.

'Now, we're talking serious people here, especially as the two men with the travelling armies are almost certain to be the two highest bidders. They'll take every precaution against being surprised out in the open, and I wouldn't put it past them to rig some sort of booby trap device to each of the girls. That would really put the cat among the pigeons.'

'Are you sure none of them have already arrived?' Mike asked.

Hannah shook her head. 'Both their flights arrive early in the morning, so they'll be expected here around mid to late afternoon. All we've got in there at the moment are Hancock's goons, and I'd back my girls against them in most circumstances. There's been some activity in the grounds for the past few hours, though Ruth didn't try to get close enough to see what it was, but nothing to indicate they're adding to their defences.

'Obviously they must know Marcia was up to something, or else they wouldn't have grabbed her, but my guess is that Hancock's informants have told him it's nothing to do with officialdom. Whether they've got it out of any of them about you and your newspaper, I don't know. Marcia's a tough nut, but I don't really know the other two.'

'Alison's tough,' Mike replied, 'but I don't know how tough.'

'Precisely,' Hannah agreed. 'Well, the plan, such as it is, is this. By the time we have full dark cover, we'll be at the fence. It'll be wired, naturally, so Becky will need ten minutes to sort something out for each one. That means we'll be inside the grounds around nine. After that, it'll probably be a case of making it up as we go.

'If Hancock's confident enough of his automatic defences, it shouldn't be too hard to get to the house undetected. There are probably cameras dotted about, but I doubt he's got anything that can pick up clearly in the dark. Even if he has, he won't be expecting us to come walking up as though we own the place.'

'What?' Mike exclaimed. 'You can't be serious?'

'Never more so.' Hannah indicated the form-fitting black leather outfit she was wearing. 'Even a night camera only picks up a vague greenish image,' she explained. 'In the dark we'll look like we're from their crew, as long as we keep our weapons shielded. And some of the girls will be dressed the way Hancock dresses his little slave maids, complete with collars, leads and cuffs; though the cuffs won't be locked, naturally.'

'Naturally,' Mike said. 'Tell me, how do you know so much about how he runs his show?'

'Marcia,' Hannah explained. 'We've spoken about it plenty in the past. I've got plenty enough props of my own for what we'll need.

'The idea is that the advance party comprises five handlers, in two groups, with a total of seven slaves between them. As soon as they reach the house and gain entrance we send in another group, only this time we'll be approaching from a different angle. From what I remember of what Marcia told me about the place, there's shrubbery and odd trees inside the actual grounds to give us plenty of cover back by the fence. Hancock should have cleared it completely if he wanted to be really certain.'

'And how long do you think the rest of the operation will take?' Mike asked.

Hannah held out her hands in a peculiarly Jewish gesture and grimaced. 'How long's a piece of string?' she countered. 'It depends on who and what we find inside the house itself. If we're lucky, it could be all over and done with in ten minutes. If not, well…' She shrugged again. 'And there's also a fair chance they might not be keeping them in the house itself. I remember Marcia saying something about a stable block, but I've no idea of its position in relation to the main house.

'Once we're inside the grounds, I thought we might have a quick scout around for it before we try the main building. We could get lucky, though it's unlikely they'll all be in the same place anyway. Just pray to whatever god it is you believe in,' she added. 'Now then, any questions?'

As the day wore on, Alison was not sure what she was most apprehensive about, the more immediate prospect of having her long blonde hair shaved off, or the slightly more distant threat of having her larynx doctored on the whim of some crazy foreigner. Hair, at least, could be allowed to grow back and there were always wigs in the meantime, but something as extreme as surgery was a different matter. Even if she ever did get back to civilisation, it was more than likely that the process would be irreversible and she would be forced to spend the rest of her life communicating by dumb show.

The tears had ceased soon after they began, but she still felt quite numb. Even Rose's whip hardly seemed to touch her, and the ground beneath her feet passed in a blur. Alison wondered if Marcia was suffering the same torment, and concluded it was most likely. In fact, it was probably even worse for her, if that were possible, for she had spent her life being the one in charge, commanding her own slaves in a world of make-believe that was far removed from the reality of what confronted them now.

The freckle-faced stable lad watered them twice more, but did not deign to speak to them again, although he did spend some time running his hands appreciatively over their sweating bodies. His fingers lingered especially as he caressed Alison's breasts, and he fondled her pierced nipples with slow deliberation. All Alison could do in return was stand there, forcibly erect, bitted and blinkered, and suffer the added humiliation in silence.

The sun was low in the west before Rose gave the order for them to be taken back to the stable building and washed and rubbed down. This time it was two female hands who unbuckled them from the shafts and led them to the standpipe alongside the timber building. Like the lad, they were barely out of their teens, but this pair spoke with accents that could have cut glass. Alison presumed they were rich paying guests, using daddy's money to exchange polo ponies for real girl-flesh ones.

'Mummy would love us to have a pair like this, Emma,' the slightly taller girl shrilled. She had almost white blonde hair that was very fine and wispy, which she wore pinned back into a sort of low bun. 'Daddy'd have a fit if he knew though, so we have to make do with spending the hols up here. Such a bore.'

'Our place is too public for anything like that, Daphers,' the second girl replied. She was as dark as her companion was fair. 'Besides, Mums and Pa would throw a blue funk if they ever knew what I really got up to. They think I'm hitching through the Himalayas this year.'

'Don't they ever think to check your passport for stamps and suchlike?' Emma asked, eyes wide with surprise. Daphers – Daphne, Alison supposed – trilled with laughter.

'Oh, old Ralphie's fixed that. He can fix anything. When I get back to the good old nearest and dearest, I'll have a passport full of little stamps. I'll have to pretend I lost my photographs, of course.'

'D'you know,' Emma said, her voice quite serious, 'I've often wondered what it must be like to be a pony girl here. I thought I might ask Ralph if I could try it out, y'know, just for a day or so.'

'You wouldn't!' Daphne sounded horrified at the prospect, but Emma persevered.

'I might just,' she said. 'After all, it might be quite exciting, especially the bit where they bring in all the studs. I quite enjoyed the other evening when that Texan chappie got me drunk and strapped me into that harness thingie. It was really quite exciting, lying there whilst he screwed me, and me not being able to resist. Not that I would have wanted to resist, of course. He was absolutely fabulous!'

'Well, these gels certainly seem to get a kick out of it,' Daphne agreed. 'Else they wouldn't be here. Though there's the money side, of course. Apparently they get paid a small fortune.'

'Me, I'd happily do it for a day for free,' Emma twittered. 'Yes, I think I'll definitely talk to Ralph this evening. Need to get a few Camparis down the old hatch first, though.' She tugged on Alison's lead rein, turning her in towards the tap stand. 'How about you, old horsey?' she grinned. 'Would you fancy doing it for nothing?'

If only she knew, Alison thought miserably. But then a

sudden thought struck her. These two inbred airheads might be as warped as a barn door in a flood, but they really did think this was all just part of a great big pantomime being staged for their benefit. If they discovered the truth, surely they might be persuaded to raise the alarm. It might mean things got a bit awkward for them, but surely they wouldn't just stand by and let two fellow humans be shipped off for the sort of fate that awaited Marcia and herself?

She turned her head towards Emma and made urgent grunting sounds through the bit, blinking her eyes furiously. The girl simply laughed.

'All this talk of studs is making horsey here all excited,' she giggled. 'Naughty horsey, and you've been all nicely plugged, too!' She patted Alison's tail over the base of the rear dildo. Alison let out a snort of frustration and tried again, but the tongue plate ensured she could utter nothing more intelligible than a gurgle.

'Never mind, horsey,' Emma chattered gaily on, 'I expect they'll get one of their nice stallions to give you a good seeing to before the day's out. What do you think, Daphers?'

Daphne grinned idiotically. 'I think I might get one of their nice stallions to give me a good seeing to,' she laughed. 'Mind you, not get up like these fillies. I think you're utterly bonkers even thinking about doing it that way.'

'That's me,' Emma agreed happily. 'Complete fruitcake, just so long as I get a good fuck!'

The pair were terminally stupid! Alison thought fiercely. They couldn't keep what passed for their brains off their clitorises for ten seconds. But then, had she acted any better? After all, it had not taken very long for the lure of the rubber, leather and chains to ensnare her lust and now it looked as though she were going to pay for that stupidity in spades!

When Emma and Daphne had finished washing down and drying their charges, they were returned to separate stables, but not once did they even mention removing their bits. As Marcia was led away, however, she managed to give Alison a big wink and walked with her head even more erect than the collar and harness necessitated. For a few minutes Alison felt heartened. If Marcia was not prepared to admit abject defeat yet, perhaps there was still some hope.

The trouble was, she knew, that their main hope lay with Mike Hallett, and it had been painfully obvious during the charade at Marcia's that he was even more out of his depth with all this scene than Alison was herself. Oh, why oh why hadn't she taken the chance to back out when it was offered to her?

'Not long now,' Hannah whispered, as she came loping back to where Mike and Honey crouched tightly together in the narrow pathway the girl commandos had cut through the undergrowth. 'We're through both fences now and there's a bit of cover. Ruth's taken two girls with her to scout ahead. There's a cluster of lower buildings about two hundred yards away from the main house, and there are floodlights on over the ground in front of the biggest one.

'That may well be our stable building and, if it is, it looks like they're preparing for something. There're a bunch of blokes in black leather bolting together some sort of low stage under the lights, and some more laying out seats, as though they're expecting an audience for whatever it is they're planning.' She held up the heavy binoculars that were slung about her neck.

'Luckily, several of the female handlers are wearing masks and the two maids I've seen are so heavily made up, even their own mothers wouldn't recognise them. Anna's back helping our "slave girls" get ready, and then I'm going to walk a pair of them as near to that stage as I dare.'

'If there's a stage and chairs for an audience it sounds like your auction might be going ahead tonight,' Mike said, his face creased with worry.

Hannah shook her head emphatically. 'No chance,' she said confidently. 'They may be intending to hold the auction there tomorrow, but this is something else. It's a warm night, so friend Ralph is probably putting on a little show for his guests out in the open. Which means, if I'm right, we've struck lucky.'

'How'd you mean?' Mike demanded.

In the darkness, Hannah's eyes gleamed. 'If this is our crowd's last night on the ranch,' she explained, 'then I reckon they're going to be top of the bill on tonight's entertainment. Knowing what I do of Ralph Hancock, he'll want to make sure he gives them something to remember him by.'

'Poor Alison,' Mike breathed, half to himself.

'Poor all of them,' Honey countered. 'Especially Marcia. He'll have something especially nasty lined up for her, you can bet on it.'

Chapter Thirteen

Showtime!

Honey's words were completely prophetic, although Alison had no way of knowing that at the time. All she knew was what she saw when the muscular Paula came to lead her from her stall.

Outside the stable building there had been erected a stage about two feet high and ten square, in the middle of which had been fixed a wooden pillory. As Alison came to a halt at Paula's tug on her bridle, she saw the ring of expectant faces beyond the floodlit area, and the knots of black garbed handlers on the far side of the stage. She also saw Marcia, still bridled as before, but now forced to walk in a stoop, back bent almost double by the chains that ran from her nipple rings to the ring that was now set in each of her outer labia. It was an arrangement which also ensured that her sex was kept gaping for all the eager eyes that watched from the darkness.

Alison peered into the gloom, trying to identify Ralph Hancock, certain that he would want to play master of ceremonies. But it was the thin figure of Kristin that stepped forward and mounted the stage.

'Ladies and gentlemen,' she began, as a hush settled over the crowd. Alison tried to estimate how many there were, but it was not easy with the blinkers hampering her vision. She guessed at least thirty, including handlers, but there may have been more for all she knew.

'Ladies and gentlemen,' Kristin repeated after a brief

pause, 'it is our pleasure to present for you a little added distraction. Tomorrow evening there will be a special auction of three slaves, two pony girls and a sluttish little male maid, who will be going on to new careers in pastures much further afield.

'All three slaves are guilty of treachery,' Kristin announced. 'The sort of treachery that could have been serious for all of us here, and so the Master has decreed that their punishment shall be most severe. First, the ringleader.' She clapped her hands and the young stable boy holding Marcia's reins urged her forward with a resounding slap across her buttocks. Awkwardly, Marcia tottered up the two steps to the dais and was led towards the pillory. With her arms still gloved together behind her back, only her neck needed to be secured, and this was quickly done.

'We shall save this slut until last,' Kristin announced, 'but before that we shall warm her up a little. Bring on her former maid slut.'

There was a slight stirring among the group of handlers on the far side, and they parted to allow the tall figure of Linda, the Australian trainer, to move through. In her hand she held the leather loop end of a short chain leash, the other end of which was attached to a ring through the foreskin of the hapless Melanie.

The poor male maid, tightly corseted, feet cramped into steepling boots, wrists chained up to a broad leather neck collar, gave Alison her first insight into what lay in store for herself and Marcia, for the poor creatures hair had already been shaved clean away, her pale cranium gleaming under the floodlights. Her face had been made up even more heavily than usual, but her tears had sent streaks of black coursing down each cheek. There was a ribald shout from among the guests, and a brief cackle of appreciative laughter as Melanie was led up onto the stage.

'This despicable little slut is now going to show us how she once serviced her former mistress,' Kristin declared. 'When she is suitably aroused, the Master will take her in front of you all. Later, after the third slut has been dealt with, she will be placed as she now is again and made available to any one of you who desires to fuck a humiliated whore.' Her words, Alison knew, were being carefully selected to cut right through Marcia, emphasising her complete change of role, and Alison could only imagine the effect such a public degradation was having.

Meanwhile, at Linda's prompting, the sad figure of Melanie dropped to her knees behind Marcia, shuffling forward until her face was buried between the tops of her mistress's thighs. Even from several feet away, Alison saw that Marcia immediately stiffened, responding to the intimate contact despite her situation. Close to Alison's right ear she heard Paula's harsh whisper.

'She can't help herself,' the trainer explained. 'Kristin's fed her a mixture of stimulants and aphrodisiac. She's running hot all the time this evening. Perhaps we should have done the same with you, but then you seem to be running hot all the time.' Alison closed her eyes, trying to blot out the scene before her, but Paula jabbed her heavily in the ribs.

'Watch!' she hissed. 'You'll be up there soon enough, and I wouldn't want you to miss a moment of what that bitch has got coming.'

The double trigger of chemical and physical stimulation was rapidly having the intended effect, and now Marcia was writhing and moaning from behind her bit. Gone was the coolly detached dominatrix, and in her place was a helplessly subjugated and aroused pony girl slave. Alison could imagine how Ralph Hancock, wherever he was, must be enjoying the spectacle his former wife was providing.

And then suddenly the man himself was on stage, resplendent in his gleaming leather chaps and spurred boots, his cock huge as it bulged against its harness, his head completely enclosed by a heavy leather mask, through which only his eyes and mouth were visible. He took up a stance behind Melanie, who was still working blindly at Marcia's vagina, and raised one arm aloft in triumph.

'Friends!' he bellowed, his voice ringing in the night air. 'Friends, you see before you what happens to anyone who dares try to cross the Master, and you are about to see the moment I have waited for these past ten years.' He reached down, seized poor Melanie by her collar and dragged her roughly aside. As he did so Kristin stepped forward, gathered up the reins that dangled from Marcia's bit, and passed them over the top of the pillory crossbeam.

Hancock seized them in his left hand, whilst, with his right, he guided his shaft unerringly into Marcia's soaking tunnel. As his leather harnessed testicles slapped against her flesh, he let out a cry of triumph and tugged viciously on the traces, causing Marcia to let out a strangled cry of anguish.

'Bitch!' he roared. 'Who'd never let me fuck her as my slave, hah? Well, what do you think of it now, my chastened little filly? And even better, you know you're going to come, whether you want to or not, don't you?' With that, he began to pump vigorously in and out of her and she instantly climaxed noisily. Still not satisfied, Hancock maintained his furious assault until she came a second and then a third time, but on the third time even he could not retain his usually masterful control.

With a scream of animal ecstasy he came himself, clutching at her hips and going into a violent spasm as his seed shot high into her womb. As the sound died away there was a silence of a few seconds and then, led by Kristin, the entire audience, apart from Melanie and Alison, broke into enthusiastic applause; whooping, whistling and cheering.

Withdrawing from his exhausted victim, Hancock stepped back, his still erect penis glistening with her juices, and bowed.

'Get her out of my sight!' he snapped at Kristin. 'But keep her handy for later. That cunt has a lot of work to do tonight.'

'Your turn, slut,' Paula said, nudging Alison forward. Heart beating, breath whistling in and out of her flared nostrils, Alison began the approach to the steps. This was it, she told herself. Above her head she could feel the high plume of her pony-tail bobbing with her movement, and wondered whether they would remove that immediately, or whether she would be made to suffer first, in order to draw out the suspense for her.

She quickly discovered which, for as Marcia was hustled from the stage, Paula quickly secured Alison into the pillory she had just vacated, stepped back and dealt her a stinging cut across the buttocks with her crop. Hancock, moving around in front of Alison's face, stooped down, and peered into her eyes.

'Well, little Mitzi,' he said, so quietly that only she could hear him, 'whatever you were and whatever you were doing, you're nothing but an animal now. Did you also know that, apart from taking your hair from you, these Arabs like to circumcise their ponies? You won't even be able to enjoy what they do to you. Isn't that a shame? So make the most of tonight, slut mare. It'll be your last fuck worthy of the name.'

He moved around behind her and Alison felt the rigid swelling of his cock head pressing against her labia, but fear had taken over from every other emotion and she was totally dry. This did not seem to deter Hancock, who thrust harder still until, thanks partly to the lubrication Marcia had left on his member, but mostly to his sheer brutal strength, he forced an entry, thrusting fully home in the same stroke. Alison gagged, screamed and tried to pull free, but he had a firm hold on her hips and there was nothing she could do but remain there, while he simply used her for his own benefit and the entertainment of the crowd.

It seemed to take forever before he came again, and Alison was vaguely surprised at how much he had left, considering his efforts with Marcia. The man was superhuman, she thought. No, sub-human was a more fitting description. He had called her an animal, but if there was an animal on that stage it was him. He pulled out of her, and she felt the stage vibrate as he stepped to the rear.

'Not very good, horsey,' he growled. 'Not worth the effort. We should have treated you the same as the other bitch first. Well, not worth it now. Shave her head, Mistress Kristin, and then give it a nice thorough polishing!'

Alison tried to close her eyes again, but found she could not, her gaze held by the approaching silver tray, with its burden of shears, clippers and something else in a large jar. Good God, she thought, they were going to use a cream to make sure there was nothing left!

Kristin placed the tray on the boards and reached forward to start removing those harness straps that would impede her progress. Alison could smell the woman's arousal and shuddered. She was almost as bad as Hancock, taking sexual delight from imposing the worst kinds of base humiliation on anyone unfortunate to fall into her clutches.

The straps fell away from her face and head, the bit falling from her lips to hang beneath her chin, but Alison was past the stage where she could take advantage of having

232

the power of speech restored. She simply stood there, stooped over, bound and pilloried, her eyes staring straight ahead as Kristin stooped to pick up the shears, straightened, and seized her pony-tail in her free hand.

'This'll make someone a nice wig, you treacherous little cunt!' the older woman spat. She clicked the shears in front of Alison's face, clearly savouring every moment, relishing her power. 'Or maybe they'll take it with you and use it to make your new tail,' she laughed. 'Yes, maybe I'll suggest—'

She stopped speaking in mid-sentence and her entire body went rigid. Her grip on Alison's hair relaxed and her other arm dropped heavily to her side, the shears falling from lifeless fingers to clatter onto the rough boards of the stage. Bemused, Alison peered upwards and cried out in alarm, for Kristin's eyes were just two slits of white, her pupils having rolled up under her upper eyelids, her mouth open, her jaw slack. As if in slow motion the tall blonde crumpled slowly to the floor. Looking down, Alison saw the long black dart jutting from the handler's neck, an inch or so beneath her left ear.

There was shouting among the onlookers now, cries of alarm and consternation. Alison craned her head to look sideways and saw the powerful figure of Paula go down, clutching at her throat. The Australian, Linda, was already on the ground. There was the sound of several muted explosions, and suddenly there seemed to be smoke everywhere.

And then the hairless figure of Melanie was standing next to Alison, fingers tearing at the catches that secured the pillory board about her neck.

'Wh-what's happening?' Alison shrieked. 'What's going on?'

Melanie was shaking and crying and laughing all at the

233

same time. 'W-w-w-we're being rescued,' she stammered. 'At least, I think we are. Quickly, let's get you out of this and find Mistress.'

The dark figure of one of the male handlers loomed out of the smoke, whip raised aloft. Alison, freed from the neck board, straightened up and made to back away, grabbing Melanie as she did so, and both girls toppled backwards from the stage. The handler rose above them, aiming his weapon, but then he too came crashing down, though not from the effect of any dart.

Instead, two black leather suited female figures, faces masked completely, tackled him with a ferocity that was unbelievable. Heavy boots rose and fell, there was a muffled grunt and the man twitched and lay still. The nearer of the two females reached out and grabbed Alison's hand.

'Alison?' Alison nodded. 'Thought so. And this must be Melanie. Fuck me, what a sight. Still, no time now. Come on, follow us. We've caught them by surprise, but there may be reinforcements in the house.'

'Where's Mistress Marcia?' Melanie wailed. The leather clad girl pointed into the thinning smoke.

'Safe,' she shouted over the noise of screaming and cursing. 'My instructions are to get you behind the lines, as it were, until we know whether we can take this place completely.'

Another dark leather clad figure sprung forward, but this time it was male. The girl raised her arm, there was a loud "plop" and he staggered backwards, clawing at the dart that was now embedded deeply in the folds of flesh beneath his chin. He was still trying to remove it when he hit the ground, totally unconscious...

The element of surprise, coupled with the ruthless efficiency of Hannah Levy's girl commandos, carried the day with surprising speed. With over half the handlers and half the guests down from either the effects of the tranquilliser darts, or the boots and batons of the dervish-like females, resistance at the stables crumbled quickly. Hands shot into the air as frightened faces backed together for protection, and those remaining on their feet were quickly rounded up.

Having checked the outbuildings and released the four pony girls they found inside, Hannah speedily reorganised to despatch a force for an assault on the house itself. They found all the doors bolted and barred, but within seconds a huge explosion blew the main front doors clean off their hinges and the Israeli valkyries surged forward again.

Alison stood amidst the chaos, clinging onto and comforting Melanie, who had dissolved into tears the moment she realised that they really had been saved. From the barn Marcia slowly emerged, bit and bridle gone, though with her newly bleached hair still in its bobbing plume. Around her knuckles she had wrapped the chains that had earlier been stretched between her nipples and labia, and the expression on her face was murderous.

'Where is that bastard?' she hissed, her voice surprisingly calm. 'I want him girls, and I want him badly. By the time I'm through with him, he'll need to use the ladies toilet.'

But Ralph Hancock was nowhere to be found.

They checked the fallen at the stables and paraded the captives under the lights, but he was not among them. When, in a surprisingly short time, the fighting inside the house had died down, there was still no sign of him. Nor, to everyone's astonishment, could they find any trace of Kristin, leading Marcia to suggest that he had managed to carry her clear in the smoke-filled confusion.

'He must have had a car nearby,' she said. But it was Ruth Goldman who discovered the subterranean viaduct leading out to the canal. There were four long barges moored and fuelled ready for immediate use, and a smaller more powerful launch at the head of them. There was also a loose painter dangling from the jetty into the water, and the smell of diesel fumes filled the damp air.

'Shit!' Marcia exclaimed, when Ruth reported back on her discovery. She pounded a fist into the palm of her other hand. 'It'll be far too late now. That waterway must join the river beyond the woods, and it comes out by a large car park that serves a golf club about six miles away. It'd take ages to get there by road, and they'll be long gone by the time we get there. I'd stake my life savings he'd have a car waiting there for emergencies.'

Hannah sauntered up and addressed Alison.

'We've found something quite interesting in one of the upstairs rooms,' she announced. 'I think you'd better come take a look. We've not disturbed anything until we get your opinion.'

Teddy was laying spreadeagled on his four-poster bed, his limbs chained to the corner posts, a look of anguish on his face that turned to relief as soon as Alison walked into the room.

'Mitzi!' he cried, with genuine pleasure. 'Thank God you're safe.' He rattled the chains that secured his wrists. 'The bastards turned on me when I tried to stop what they were going to do to you. I even told Ralph I'd top whatever the best auction price was, but he was completely out of his brain. He just kept going on about all the awful things that would be done to all of you, and then I tried to hit him. There was a bit of a struggle and then a crowd of his gorillas stormed in and that was it. I'm sorry, Mitzi, but I did my best. I'm just not very bright at times.'

Alison smiled down at him. 'Never mind, Teddy Edward,' she said soothingly. 'None of us are perfect.'

236

The little gathering at Marcia's the following afternoon was a curious one, if only because it was one of the rare occasions when any gathering at Marcia's did not comprise a crowd of people dressed in rubber, leather and various other fetishistic materials. Melanie was the odd man/woman out, but even she had abandoned her usual black rubber. Wearing a dark wig to cover her hairless pate, her maid's uniform was fashioned from elegant black velvet with satin trimmings, and her dark sheer stockings sported immaculately straight seams.

Of the others, Mike was dressed casually in denim jeans and a T-shirt. Marcia wore a smart two-piece business suit and cream silk blouse. Alison was bare-legged in bright red mini skirt and shirt, and Honey wore a flowing white cotton summer dress with her usual white high heeled sandals. Teddy wore a navy blue lounge suit with open necked shirt, though the cut of all his clothes, as with Marcia and Honey, betrayed the size of his tailor's bills.

The six of them had gathered to celebrate the freeing of the three captives, but their celebrations were tempered by a sombre note.

'He'll be back,' Marcia warned. 'You can all be sure of that.'

'But we've inflicted a lot of damage on his operation,' Mike said, with quiet satisfaction. 'Hannah's girls really worked Dennison Hall over, and that bonfire was going for hours.'

'And it won't matter a jot,' Marcia told him. 'He'll have duplicates of all the stuff they burned. And as for the costumes and equipment, as well as the camera systems, he'll simply replace them and start over again.' She looked across at Teddy, whose features were creased with concern. 'And that includes you,' she told him. 'Everything you saw with you in it will exist somewhere else. He's got pictures of all of us, though he won't dare try to use the ones of we three, for fear we'll just run to the police.

'With three witnesses all telling the same story, they'd have to do something. Knowing Ralph, he'd wriggle out of it somehow, but it wouldn't be worth the inconvenience to him, not when he's got so many other marks instead.'

'And we don't really have a story,' Alison put in. She reached out and took Teddy's hand in hers. 'I gathered up a lot of the photos that didn't show faces clearly, but that's all for the future. We could print something, but if Hancock's got the clout we think, especially now we've seen some of the other people involved up there, several other big papers would pour scorn on us and we'd end up looking stupid.' She felt Teddy squeeze her hand, and smiled.

'Still, there's always a next time,' she said, 'and I don't feel it's all been a complete waste of effort. I was scared shitless for a while, I admit, but at least no harm came to any of us. No permanent harm, anyway,' she added, looking across at Melanie and winking. The male maid pulled a face at her, but did wink back.

'All in all,' Alison continued, 'it's been the most... incredible few days of my life, and I've learned a lot in a short time, mostly about myself.'

'We've all been there, sweetie,' Honey drawled. Alison noticed the aristocratic girl had not taken her eyes off Mike since they'd arrived.

'Well, speaking personally,' Teddy said, 'I don't care what Ralph Hancock has on me. If the worst comes to the worst I've got more money than I could spend in a dozen lifetimes, so I'll just retreat to my little Caribbean island for a few years and let the world get on with it.'

'Carry your bags, sir?' Alison laughed, nudging him.

Teddy grinned sheepishly.

'I think I've let you sort out enough of my baggage these past couple of days,' he said. 'And now I think I ought to make a real effort to get my life straightened out. With your help, Mitzi – sorry, Alison – I hope.'

'Try stopping me,' Alison said. 'And it wouldn't worry me if you didn't have a penny in the world. I know I'd still feel the same.'

Honey giggled. 'Oh, how sweet,' she said, but her eyes betrayed her genuine pleasure. 'Now, if you don't mind, all this lovey-dovey stuff is making me feel a bit nauseous.' She uncrossed her long legs and stood up. 'If Mistress Marcia doesn't mind us borrowing one of the downstairs rooms, it's your turn to be slave, Michael.'

Mike looked up at her with a start. 'Hey, hang on a minute,' he protested. 'As I remember it, the last thing before Hannah—' Honey waved a hand airily.

'Oh, who cares?' she laughed. 'Just so long as I get a good time out of it. See you all at Blaine's for dinner at ten? I hate quickies, but needs must.'

'Quickies?' Mike echoed. 'Ten o'clock is another eight hours away!'

Honey looked at him and pouted. 'That's what I mean,' she said. 'I hate quickies. Still, I've phoned in for a week's sick leave, so we can make up for it after we've eaten!'